OUTLAW HEARTS

OUTLAW HEARTS

DIANE AMOS

FIVE STAR

An imprint of Thomson Gale, a part of The Thomson Corporation

THOMSON

GALE

Detroit • New York • San Francisco • New Haven, Conn. • Waterville, Maine • London

LIBRARY OF CONGRESS CATALOGING-IN-PUBLICATION DATA

Amos, Diane.
    Outlaw hearts / Diane Amos. — 1st ed.
      p. cm.
    ISBN-13: 978-1-59414-570-4 (alk. paper)
    ISBN-10: 1-59414-570-9 (alk. paper)
    1. Young women—Fiction. 2. Judicial error—Fiction. 3. Massachusetts—History—Colonial period, ca. 1600–1775—Fiction. I. Title.
PS3601.M67O88 2007
813'.6—dc22
                                    2007011876

First Edition. First Printing: August 2007.

Published in 2007 in conjunction with Tekno Books.

Printed in the United States of America on permanent paper
10 9 8 7 6 5 4 3 2 1

Dedicated to
Dave
After all these years,
you still make me smile!

ACKNOWLEDGMENTS

I want to thank the members of the Maine Chapter of the Romance Writers of America for their lively meetings, friendship, and inspiration, especially my travel companions, Bethany Oliver and Deb Noone.

Also, special thanks to Lisa Norato and Annette Blair for helping to brainstorm my book. You're the best!

ONE

Londonderry, New Hampshire—1868

"I say hang the son of a bitch!"

A gavel slammed on a hard surface. "Order, order in the court."

Rebekah Benson froze in front of the Londonderry Town Hall. She stretched on tiptoe and glanced through the open door.

Were her brothers here, they'd have whisked her away, determined to protect her from such unpleasant matters. Enjoying her freedom, she took a tentative step forward. A feeling of immense satisfaction washed over her. For the next three weeks she could listen to anything, go anywhere, and say whatever came to mind.

The air inside the hall reeked of cigar smoke and sweat.

"Hangin's too good for the bastard."

When the men at the rear of the room stirred, Rebekah spotted a judge sitting at a makeshift desk, pounding a wooden gavel. "Order, order in this courtroom. Zachariah Thompson, do you have anything to say for yourself before I pronounce sentence?"

Three guards tried to yank the prisoner to his feet. He shrugged off their hold and stood tall and proud. His gray shirt, rolled to the elbows and pulled tight across the shoulders, exposed thick and sinewy arms. His long stringy hair tied with a piece of rawhide hung over his collar.

"I've made my share of mistakes, Your Honor, but I've never killed a man."

The powerful, sandpaper voice peppered Bekah's arms with gooseflesh. Though he frightened her, she detected truth in his words.

The judge placed his elbow on the desk and leaned forward. "Your hands were covered with the dead man's blood."

"I already explained. I came to in the alley, saw him lying there, and checked to see if he was breathing."

"What were you doing behind the building?"

"I'd had a few drinks too many. I must have passed out."

"Some say you played cards with the victim and later had an argument."

"He cheated," Thompson said, his tone flat.

The judge tapped his fingers on the desktop. "His pockets were empty when we found him. Can you explain that?"

"I told you I passed out."

Rebekah sensed regret in his voice. She felt compassion for him.

"You were holding the weapon when they apprehended you."

"I picked it up to see if it had just been fired."

The crowd shifted.

Rebekah lost sight of Zachariah. Needing to know what would happen next, she crept along the back wall until she could see the man's profile. A thick, dark beard hid the lower half of his face. He was unkempt, uncouth, and probably uncivilized. She'd never seen such a man in her twenty-four-and-a-half years. A shiver raced down her spine.

When the judge spoke, no one stirred. "Zachariah Thompson, you are a disgrace to humanity. You are a drunk, a thief, and a murderer. At daybreak, in two days, you will hang by the neck until dead."

Bekah gasped.

Zachariah stared straight ahead, his face emotionless.

Bekah loosened the top button of her collar that had suddenly become too tight.

She wished she could help Zachariah Thompson.

The preposterous idea forced a smile.

Muttonhead, she called herself, because her brothers weren't there to voice the taunt she'd heard repeatedly over the years.

Help Zachariah Thompson!

She blamed the wayward thought on fatigue. She'd traveled until every bone in her body ached. Over the course of her journey from England, she'd been jostled, pushed, and bumped. She'd weathered rough seas and endless miles of rocky roads.

This criminal wasn't a helpless kitten. Or an injured puppy. This was a big, dangerous-looking man, most likely mean-spirited, too.

Fatigue had rendered her a simpleton.

Bekah studied Zachariah Thompson. His stance challenged authority. He was hard and uncompromising. He couldn't be trusted, but he wasn't a killer.

His looks alone shouted his guilt.

But Bekah didn't judge people on appearances. Deep in her heart, she was certain he had not murdered anyone.

The crowd jeered when Zachariah faced them. Bekah wanted him to react. As if following a beacon at sea, he stared straight ahead and locked his gaze on something outside the door. Bekah wondered if he was memorizing the colors of autumn, rapidly slipping away like his life.

Needing a breath of fresh air, Bekah hurried outdoors and stood beside her leather satchel. She needed to distance herself from the scene she'd just witnessed. She was becoming involved in something that was not her business.

Zachariah would hang, and she was powerless to prevent it.

What did she know about murderers?

Her theory that he was innocent was laughable. What proof did she have? Only a feeling.

Besides, her agenda didn't allow for dalliance. She had only three short weeks before meeting her brother Mark.

She rested her hand over the center of her chest and traced the half of a gold medallion she'd found hidden inside her precious doll, Annabelle. The medallion with the symbols that made no sense was a link to her past. She meant to do everything in her power to reveal its secrets.

The doors swung open, and the crowd spilled onto the wooden boardwalk. Before Rebekah could step back, she found herself standing toe to toe with Zachariah Thompson.

For a breathless moment, his onyx eyes held her captive. She stood unable to move, unable to breathe. She felt the heat of his body, his presence surrounding her.

As her heart pumped an unsteady beat, she saw anger in the pitch-black depths of his pupils and for a second, vulnerability. She wanted to reach out and touch him, would have if he hadn't blinked. The wounded look vanished, replaced with something else that rankled. He cocked a brow. One corner of his mouth lifted as his heated gaze undressed her.

The man had the manners of a swine!

The guard jammed a gun in Zachariah's back. "Get moving, or I'll save everyone a lot of trouble and shoot you now."

Zachariah's eyes went blank. As he stepped off the boardwalk, the rays of the sun flashed on something around his neck.

Rebekah's gaze lowered.

Her breath lodged in her throat.

In the deep V of Zachariah's shirt hung the missing half of her gold medallion.

Disbelief rooted Rebekah's feet where she stood.

She gulped for air, trying to steady her legs and clear her

mind. Finally, regaining her equilibrium, she forced her fingers around the handle of her leather bag. First, a room to spend the night. Then, somehow, she had to persuade Zachariah Thompson to sell his half of the medallion. She needed to speak with him and find out if he knew of its origin.

As she stepped around two children rolling a ball on the boardwalk, she clasped her fingers over the half-medallion beneath her camisole. Maybe, if she put the two pieces together, she'd be able to decipher its meaning.

Years earlier when she'd found the medallion, her brothers had shouted and pleaded to clutch her treasure, if only for a short while. She remembered holding the medallion in the sun, admiring the blinding light bouncing from its mirrored surface. The medallion was hers alone, probably a gift from her parents.

Had her parents buried gold, silver, or other riches? Would she find it? In her dreams, she'd traveled around the globe in search of the missing half.

As a child, she'd been certain the medallion stood for something wonderful.

As an adult, she believed the medallion would change her life.

She walked toward the town's only inn. Her excitement grew when she felt the cool metal pressed against her chest.

Lost in thought, Rebekah found herself in her room, satchel in hand with little memory of paying the innkeeper or climbing the two flights of stairs. She dropped her leather bag on the bed and strolled across the room where she glanced out the window at the street below.

She needed to pay Zachariah Thompson a visit but couldn't simply barge into the jail without giving the sheriff a valid reason. Telling the locals she might hold the key to a fortune seemed unwise.

As she gazed out the window, she spied a boy with a hat that looked familiar. It had the same sapphire color as the one in her satchel, only missing the veil and the cluster of velvet carnations that had adorned the hatband. The youngster had substituted an array of pigeon feathers, which gave the once beautiful headpiece a comical appearance. She laughed, certain the mischievous lad's mother would warm his bottom when she caught up with him.

Anxious to obtain the missing half of her medallion, she decided to freshen up, change into a clean dress, and go see Zachariah Thompson. When Rebekah opened her satchel, she nearly died from shock. Except for one nightgown, the bag was empty.

Without thought to propriety, Rebekah charged out of her bedroom door, down the stairway, and across the street, grabbing the boy by the collar before he could escape.

The shock turned to guilt as his blue eyes peered into hers.

She waved her hand before his face. "Where did you get that hat?"

He smiled innocently. "I found it. If you're interested, I could sell it to you for a good price."

She tried to calm down but failed when she glanced at the blasted pigeon feathers. "It's my hat, you little thief." The word *thief* caused her to remember three other children who'd stolen food to survive. Were it not for her adoptive parents, Ruth and Nicholas, she and her brothers might have starved.

"Are you hungry?" she asked, and saw the surprise on his dirty face.

"Is this a trick?" He tried to pull free, but she tightened her grip on his shirt.

"No, simply a question."

He had bright orange hair, freckles spattered over his nose and cheeks, eyes the color of the sunlit sea, and a look about him that tugged at Rebekah's heart.

"I might be hungry," he replied after a lengthy pause.

She eyed the pigeon feathers and almost changed her mind. But what kind of person would she be if she failed to show kindness to this poor waif?

Her voice softened. "I was hoping you could tell me something."

A skeptical look crossed his face. "What do you want to know?"

"Whether the sheriff will allow me to visit a prisoner."

"Who?"

"Never mind who."

He brought his grubby hand to his chin. "What are you gonna give me?"

"If you help me, I won't tell the sheriff you stole my things."

Again, he tried to wrench free. "You wouldn't do that."

"Are you willing to take that chance?"

"If I tell you, will you let me go?"

"Only if you help me find my belongings." He looked so small and so frightened that she added, "I'll give you a reward. If you know where the velvet carnations and netting are for my hat, I'll even throw in some peppermint candy." If her brothers could see her now, they'd laugh and call her a softy.

"All right," he said, drawing out the words. "Only relatives are allowed to visit the prisoners. Can I go now?"

"Not till you tell me where my clothes are."

Zachariah stretched out on the small cot with his feet hanging over the edge a good eight inches. His arm covered his face. He tried to quell the fear surging in his chest. He tried not to envision the rope taut around his neck or the crowd cheering as he drew his last breath.

But he could think of nothing else.

Would he disgrace himself and cry out at the last moment?

15

Would he beg for mercy?

He'd seen a hanging once.

He remembered the man's high-pitched wail, the way his arms and legs jerked, and the darkening spot on his trousers when he'd wet himself.

Every detail haunted him.

Zachariah heard the jangle of keys, the creak of hinges, and the approaching footsteps. He didn't budge, but instead, dwelt on his forthcoming execution.

Death by strangulation terrified him.

His windpipe contracted as he thought of it. Two more days and he'd be swinging from a rope.

"Your wife's here to see you."

All thoughts of his demise vanished.

Zachariah scrambled off the cot so fast he damn near fell on the floor. He'd done many things he couldn't remember, but one fact was certain—though he'd spent his last two years in a drunken stupor, there wasn't enough liquor in all of New Hampshire to make him get married. Hell, he'd even boasted to his companions he'd rather stick his neck in a noose than be saddled with a wife—though the humor of that comment now escaped him.

He couldn't believe his eyes.

Surely, this must be an angel. Had he already died and gone to heaven? Who was he kidding? Heaven wasn't on his itinerary. He uttered a low chuckle and saw fear streak across her face.

"Do you want me to stay, Madam?" the guard asked, clearly concerned for her safety.

Doubt registered in her blue eyes.

Zachariah expected her to bolt.

He wasn't prepared for the shy shake of her head directed at the guard as she stepped forward. She rested her hand on Zachariah's shoulder, encouraged him to bend, pressing a kiss on his cheek.

"I've missed you, Zachariah."

Her British accent reminded him of maple sugar candy. His favorite. He licked his lips and gave her a suggestive look. If the lady wanted to play this game, he was more than happy to oblige. "If that kiss was meant to cheer me, I'd say you've forgotten all I've taught you, dear wife."

She turned crimson.

Innocence was written all over her, from her trembling hands possibly clasped together in prayer, to her rigid spine. She was gussied up in satin and lace and wore a blue hat that had seen better days from the looks of the pigeon feathers poking up between fake carnations.

Before she could speak, Zachariah drew her to him, pressed his mouth over hers, and attempted to melt the starch from her spine. Between them, her hands exerted force, trying to shove him away. He pretended not to notice but instead moved his lips over hers. When he took the liberty of tracing the seam of her mouth with his tongue, she uttered a small gasp.

"I'll leave you two alone," the guard said as he slammed the iron bars and strolled away.

Zachariah had meant to intimidate her and he'd succeeded. Yet, he felt he'd been struck by lightning and had lived to tell of it. A simple kiss had never before affected him this way.

He guessed it might be his last.

He released her, felt an immediate loss, stepped back, walked to the narrow window in the cell, and glanced outside.

"I don't know what you're after, lady, but you're wasting your time." When he eyed the scaffolding going up in the town square, a shiver raced down his spine.

He turned, moved within inches of her where he could smell her flowery perfume.

Lust jolted him. And longing.

He hated her because she stood for life and his was ebbing away.

"Mr. Thompson." Her voice never wavered.

But how could he hate an angel with so much gumption?

"Mr. Thompson? Surely, that's no way to address your loving husband."

"I have some serious business to discuss with you."

"What would that be?"

Her gaze lowered, and she raised her dainty fingers to trace the gold charm he'd found near the dead man. The light touch intensified his fear because soon he'd feel nothing.

He raised his brow. "My time's at a premium right now. You'd better spit it out before it's too late."

She seemed embarrassed. "Yes, I'm sorry about that, which is why I figured you'd be willing to sell me your medallion."

He fingered the charm. "Why do you want it?"

She hesitated. Her face was easy to read. And beautiful. He knew she was going to lie before the words were out. "I saw it around your neck outside the courtroom. I was hoping to add it to my collection."

He stifled a grin. "And you collect charms that have been sawed in half. I imagine your collection must be substantial."

"Er . . . well, yes, I started collecting charm halves a short while back, so . . ." She bit her lower lip. "I don't have many . . . yet."

Her British voice made his mouth water. This time, he smiled. "How many do you have?"

Her forehead furrowed. "Not more than a few."

"How many's a few?"

Her chin jutted upward. "What difference does that make? Are you willing to sell it or not?"

"I don't need money where I'm going."

Her small hands fluttered nervously. "Are you willing to part with it?"

"Nope."

"Why not?"

"I've become attached to it."

"How about after . . . you know . . ."

"You want me to will this to you?"

Her cheeks colored. "Would you?"

"Nope."

"Would you be willing to lend it to me for one night?"

"How do I know you won't run off with it?"

She crossed her heart, a gesture he found endearing. "You have my word. Can you tell me where the medallion comes from?"

"That's a family secret."

"Has it been in your family long?"

The deputy approached the cell. "Is everything all right in there?"

Zachariah waved him away. "Can't you see we'd like a little privacy?"

He took her elbow and led her to his cot. "Seeing that you're my wife, shouldn't I at least know your name?"

"Rebekah Benson," she said, the British accent wringing another smile from his face.

"Sit down so we can talk without anyone hearing," he said, as he settled beside her on the narrow cot. He looped his arm around her shoulder, sensed her alarm, and whispered, "We have to look as though we're married." He didn't give a fig about anything but holding her close.

She looked him square in the eye, her bravado rivaled by the quaking beneath his palm.

"Bekah, are you afraid of me?"

"Maybe a little."

"You needn't be. I didn't kill that man."

"I know."

Her words comforted him. "You might as well come clean with me. You want my medal, and I'm not about to let you have it unless you tell me the truth."

"You won't tell anyone?"

"I'm a dead man, Bekah."

She flinched at his harsh words. "Years ago I found this hidden in my doll back home in England." She reached for the chain around her neck and pulled out a charm similar to his. "My parents were missionaries in America some twenty years ago. I think they found something of value, possibly buried it, and hid the directions on the halves of our medallions in hopes of returning later for the treasure. How long have you had your half?"

He scratched his chin. "I've had it for a spell."

Her eyes widened. "I don't understand why my parents would cut the medallion in two and not keep both pieces."

"Maybe they lost the other half."

"That's possible." She exhaled a short breath. "Now will you sell me your half of the medallion?"

He cupped her chin, ran his thumb over her smooth skin, and enjoyed seeing her pupils widen. "If you do me one small favor, I'll give you my half."

"Name it, Mr. Thompson," she replied, her voice ringing with excitement.

"Help me to break out of jail, and it's yours."

Two

Rebekah entered the taproom of the Londonderry Inn and chose a seat by the window. She ordered tea and stressed she wanted it strong. In her short time in this country, she'd come to realize Americans knew nothing about brewing a good cup of tea.

Two old gents, their voices echoing across the room, drank mugs of coffee and played checkers a few feet from the hearth of a stone fireplace where flickering flames kept the early morning October chill at bay. The innkeeper behind the bar handed a gentleman his polished boots while another couple signed the register. Posted on the wall to Rebekah's left were notices of upcoming events: a christening, a wedding and a hanging.

Bold print proclaimed Zachariah Thompson's forthcoming death.

Without regard to who might be watching, she snatched the paper from the wall and tearing it into shreds, shoved the tiny pieces into her reticule.

She glanced out the window where men and women mingled with the children, acting as if something wonderful were about to occur. She shuddered at the sight of the sturdy wooden scaffold being erected in the town square. Her heart pounded with the beat of the hammers. Tomorrow at dawn, Zachariah Thompson would hang.

Hell and Damnation!

She blushed at the silent curse, a part of Papa Nicholas's

vocabulary, certainly not hers, and wondered if she'd taken leave of her senses.

She turned away from the window, refusing to dwell on Zachariah Thompson and his stubborn hide. Thoughts of him had plagued her all night. She'd tossed and turned, aware of a yearning she didn't fully understand.

Margaret, the innkeeper's plump wife, arrived with her tea. "I hope this is strong enough for you, Miss Benson."

Rebekah sipped the hot beverage. "Yes, this is fine," she said, not wanting to hurt the dear woman's feelings.

"Can I get you something else?"

"Perhaps, in a little while."

Margaret scurried to the next table to take a young couple's order.

Rebekah's stomach turned over again. She attributed the fluttery feelings to her travels, yet admitted she'd had no such problems before seeing Zachariah.

She sipped the tea and again found her mind wandering. Zachariah's kiss, though shocking, had curled the toes within her tight-fitting leather shoes. She'd tried to push him away. But her efforts had been halfhearted, just enough to defend her virtue. Deep inside, her bones had liquefied. She'd wanted to run her fingers through his hair, but instead, had clung to his chest, fascinated by the strong heartbeat beneath her fingertips.

Rebekah set her cup down and sighed. She had to pay Zachariah another visit, certainly not because she wanted to. She was going to persuade him to tell her what he knew about the medallion.

Thoughts of seeing him quickened her pulse. She frowned. What was wrong with her? If she didn't know better, she'd think she was pining for Zachariah Thompson, a thief and a drunk, a man about to die.

Was he an innocent man?

Did she trust her intuition?

Confused and alarmed by her rambling thoughts, she glanced across the room and spied a familiar redheaded boy about to fill his pockets with fresh biscuits. His guilt-filled eyes met hers. She shook her head sternly and waved him over.

He hesitated and looked ready to bolt for the door, but instead hurried to her side with a mischievous grin. "I wasn't gonna take nothing, I was just checking to see if they was warm."

"I was hoping you'd join me for breakfast."

He shuffled his feet before looking her in the eye. "Really?"

She nodded toward the chair across from her. "I'd love some company."

When the boy began to sit down, Margaret rushed to Rebekah's table. "James, what have I told you about bothering the guests? You're to meet me at the back door of the kitchen. If you take out the slop bucket and help with the chores, I'll see that you're fed."

The freckled face registered embarrassment.

Rebekah raised her hand. "I've invited James to join me. I'm ready to eat now and so is he."

Margaret hid her surprise. "That's mighty nice of you, Miss. If James makes a pest of himself, let me know, and I'll take care of him." Though the comment was issued in a stern tone, Rebekah saw beyond the words. Margaret was a good-hearted woman who looked out for the boy.

Rebekah glanced across the table. "James, what would you like for breakfast?"

"Can I have one of them hot biscuits over there?"

"Margaret, along with biscuits, we'd like eggs, ham, a stack of griddlecakes, another cup of tea for me, and a large glass of milk for my new friend."

"Yes, Miss," Margaret said with a twinkle in her eye. "I'll get your order right away."

She whispered in the boy's ear, "You better mind your manners, or you'll be answering to me."

After bringing a plate of biscuits to their table, Margaret hurried from the room.

Rebekah took a biscuit and was delighted to see James's eyes light up when she offered him the plate.

"Can I have more than one?"

"Sure, help yourself."

He grabbed two biscuits, and when he thought she wasn't looking, he tucked another in the pocket of his loose-fitting coat.

She pretended not to notice. "May I call you Jimmy?"

"My name's James Tucker, but you can call me anything you want."

"How old are you?"

"Almost eight."

"My, you're tall for eight."

"Ma said I take after my pa."

Rebekah buttered her biscuit. "Are your parents around here?"

"My pa got hisself killed in the war, and my ma run off some time back."

Rebekah's heart went out to the boy. "I'm sorry to hear that."

He shrugged. "Nothin' to be sorry 'bout. I take care of myself, and I do a damn good job, too."

Instead of correcting his deplorable language, she watched another biscuit vanish, coated with a thick layer of butter. He grinned when he caught her looking at him, his teeth covered with crumbs. "I saw you go into the jailhouse yesterday. Why did you visit Zack?"

"How did you know I was there to visit Zachariah?"

"That's easy. When I stood on tiptoes on the porch across the street, I saw you in Zack's cell. Are you gonna go visit him again?"

"Maybe."

"Can you tell him his friend James says hi?"

"Yes, I can do that for you." The hammering outside reminded her of the inevitable. "You must feel really sad about . . . losing your friend."

"I wish Zack wasn't gonna die." He looked down and brushed his nose with a dirty hand. "But I'm gonna be there when they hang him."

Rebekah was shocked. "Why would you do that?"

He took another bite. "He needs to know someone who cares is there for him."

"You remind me of my brother William."

"Does he look like me?"

"No, but deep inside you two are alike. You stand by those you love no matter what."

Jimmy smiled timidly.

"What did Zack ever do to deserve a good friend like you?"

"Zack does lots of stuff. He gave me this coat."

"I thought he was a thief."

"Zack never stole nothin' from no one."

Rebekah considered Zachariah a poor model for the boy to emulate. "According to the judge, Zack took the dead man's money."

"He may drink too much, but he ain't no thief. Anyway, I love him just the same."

Rebekah blinked away the tears that sprang to her eyes. She ruffled Jimmy's hair. "You're a good boy."

"You can bet I don't hear that too often."

Jimmy looked as though he was about to say something and then changed his mind. Breakfast arrived, and he cleaned his plate along with half of hers.

The boy licked his fingers. "How come you talk so funny?"

"I come from England. Do you know where that is?"

He shrugged. "Ain't never heard of it. Do all the people in England talk like you?"

"I guess they do."

Jimmy reached into his pocket and pulled out the biscuit he'd hidden there earlier. "Give this to Zack for me. I hear the jail food is really bad."

Rebekah glanced at the thumbprint on the bun and got an idea. Men loved desserts with thick frosting. "Does your friend Zack like cake?"

"Yup. Me and Zack ate a whole cake once. We piled strawberries and whipped cream all over it. It took a long time for the red color to rub off my face and fingers."

Today when she visited Zachariah, she'd go bearing gifts. "Keep the biscuit for yourself. I'll see he has something really special to eat."

She and Jimmy left the taproom. About to return to her bedroom, Rebekah paused at the staircase.

Jimmy placed his hand on her elbow, his wide blue eyes filled with pain. "Zack didn't steal from the dead man."

She rested a reassuring hand on his thin shoulder. "I fear only Zachariah knows the truth about that."

Jimmy's chin quivered. "Zack doesn't know . . . 'cause I stole that money."

Rebekah grabbed his arm and led him outside where no one would hear them.

Jimmy wiped his nose. "Don't tell the sheriff, or he'll lock me up, too."

"But you should return the money."

"The dead man sure don't need it as much as me."

Rebekah sighed.

Guilt clouded Jimmy's eyes. "I saw who killed the man in the alley."

"You must tell the sheriff."

Jimmy hung his head.

"Zachariah's life depends on you coming forward."

"I can't. I'm afraid."

"Tell me what you saw."

"I was sleeping in a crate in the alley when loud voices woke me up. There was lots of cussing, the sound of a fistfight and a gunshot. When I snuck out of the box, I saw a big man running away, another man sprawled on his back with a bullet hole in his belly and Zack passed out cold. I tried to wake Zack up, but he was too drunk. I was ready to take off when I spotted a money clip near some boxes. I figured it had fallen out during the fight. I grabbed the money and ran."

As Rebekah hurried across the street to the jailhouse, she prepared what she was going to say. At the very least, she hoped to persuade the sheriff to postpone the hanging and allow more time for a proper investigation. In appreciation, Zachariah would press his half of the medallion into her palm and insist she keep it.

With a confident stride, she crossed the boardwalk, opened the door, and smiled at the guards. "Good day, it's imperative I speak to the person in charge."

"That would be me." A tall, barrel-chested man with a striped shirt, pipe hanging from the corner of his mouth, stood. "I'm Sheriff Walker." He motioned her to sit as he set his pipe on the corner of the desk.

Rebekah settled herself in the chair facing him. "You've made a terrible mistake. Zachariah did not kill anyone."

"Do you have proof?"

"Yes, as a matter of fact, I do. A friend saw what happened

that evening."

The sheriff tapped his fingers along the arms of his wooden chair. "Who's your friend?"

"I can't divulge his name, but I assure you he's a reputable citizen."

The sheriff quirked an eyebrow. "Tell me what you know about the guilty man."

Rebekah smiled confidently. "I don't know a lot of details because it was dark, but the man was a foul-mouthed brute, tall, wide shoulders, the type who uses his fists instead of his brains."

"That describes more than half the men in New Hampshire," the sheriff said, frowning. "You need to do better than that if you expect me to believe you. I can appreciate why you'd want to save your husband's life, but he needs to pay for his crime. I can't have every disgruntled cardplayer taking pot shots."

The sheriff picked up his pipe and blew out a ring of smoke. "The judge already pronounced the sentence. I can't change that without good cause."

Rebekah tried to think of another argument. Unfortunately, James had not seen the murderer up close so she didn't have a proper description. "Surely, there's something you can do."

The sheriff stood. "I'm sorry, but I can't stop the hanging."

As Rebekah rose to her feet, a heavy weight settled in her chest.

Later that afternoon Rebekah stared down at the cake she'd prepared with her own hands, thinking maybe she shouldn't have refused Margaret's expert help. Once she trimmed away the burnt corners, scraped the black crumbs from the bottom, and filled up the crater where the cake had stuck to the pan, it didn't look half as bad as when she'd first inverted it on the kitchen worktable. Besides, who'd notice these few imperfections once it was drenched with berries and slathered with whipped cream?

She quickly spooned the berries over the cake and heaped tablespoons of watery cream over the top because try as she might, the blasted stuff had refused to thicken.

A short while later Rebekah walked to the jailhouse. Some of the cream slid over the sides of the plate onto her hands and down the front of her skirt.

She opened the door and forced a smile. She'd decided to make this an enjoyable day for Zachariah. Since he didn't know about her efforts to postpone the hanging, she would not show her disappointment.

"Good day, I was hoping you'd allow me to visit my husband, Zachariah."

One guard was cleaning his rifle. Another guard near the door glanced suspiciously at her cake. "Madam, I hope you aren't trying to sneak in a weapon."

She had to cut the cake in quarters, exposing the oozy center that hadn't fully baked before they'd allow her to leave the room.

As she followed the guard down the narrow corridor leading to the back of the building, her heart thumped an unsteady beat. Her mind went blank when Zachariah's eyes locked with hers.

"Your missus is here again. Brought you a fine dessert, too."

Leaning against the cell wall with his arms folded over his muscular chest, Zachariah looked at her as if she were the dessert.

Unnerved by his steady gaze, she forced her wobbly legs forward. Had he not taken the plate from her hands, she might have dropped it. *Bloody hell,* she thought, noting that her common sense and her language had reached an all-time low.

"This looks great," Zachariah said, his smile deepening the

lines around his eyes and freeing butterflies in the pit of her stomach.

After setting the plate on a table beside his bed, he swiped at the cream with his forefinger, took a lick, and issued an appreciative groan. "Bekah, you are an angel for sure."

Steadying her hands, she spooned a large wedge of cake and slipped it onto a metal plate she found on the narrow wooden shelf along with the utensil. "Sit and enjoy."

"Aren't you going to have any?"

Her throat was so tight she doubted she could swallow even a drop of water. "No, I made this just for you."

He insisted she sit beside him on the cot. He spooned a large bite into his mouth, and chewed, and chewed, and chewed.

Were those tears in his eyes?

Were his lips puckering?

He swallowed, it seemed with effort. "Look I have another dish and spoon, I want you to join me." He slid a wedge of cake onto a plate and set it on her lap.

Rebekah glanced at his chest and was disappointed he wasn't wearing his half of the medallion. "All right, now that I think about it, I would like a piece. It took so long to make the cake that I forgot to eat dinner." She hoped to impress him with her efforts.

She swallowed a small bite. To say she was surprised by the tartness was an understatement. Because he was watching, she tried to act naturally, tried to pretend the cake was delicious, tried not to notice how the berries crunched between her teeth. "Do you think it might need a little more sugar?"

"You tell me, you're the cook. What kind of berries are these?"

"Cranberries, I was unable to find strawberries. Maybe I should have cooked them a little longer or added a bit more sugar." She figured she couldn't avoid the obvious. "It isn't very good, is it?"

He set his plate down and took hers. "Rebekah, it doesn't matter how the cake tastes. I appreciate the effort. It's been a hell of a long time since anyone's made me anything, though I suspect your motives."

She forced herself to face him.

His pupils narrowed. "Nobody ever gives me anything unless they expect something in return."

"That's awfully cynical."

"But true. Tell me you didn't come here to wangle my charm away from me."

"It might have crossed my mind, but . . ."

"Look," he said, taking her hand. "I'm glad you're here, regardless of the reason." He looked her over, head to toe. "Tell me you have a weapon hidden on you."

"I wouldn't do that. I don't even like guns."

He heaved a discouraged sigh. "I didn't think you would. But you can't blame a dying man for hoping."

She needed to change the subject, or she'd be crying. "By the way, James says hi."

Zachariah stood up and reached in his pants pocket. "Give him this. James has been after me to buy him a watch for a while. You tell him I said he better take good care of it."

With her heart in her throat, Rebekah took the pocket watch from his hand.

His fingers brushed hers; sparks nipped her fingertips.

She was so jittery she didn't trust herself to speak.

He rested his hand on her shoulder. "You feel it, too?"

"Feel what?"

"The attraction between us is a powerful thing. You can pretend you don't notice, but I know differently."

She pulled away. It was hopeless—tomorrow at dawn, he'd hang.

He stepped closer. "Will you do me a favor?"

"It depends."

A deep laugh rumbled past his throat. "That's good. You aren't as quick to answer as last time. This favor doesn't involve me as much as James." He turned, crossed the narrow room in three quick steps, leaned his forearm on the windowsill, and gazed outside. "I want you to get James out of town tomorrow. I don't want him to see me hang."

She heard the pain in his voice and watched his shoulders droop.

Rebekah stood, tears welling up in her eyes. "James wants to be there for you."

"That doesn't surprise me. He's a good kid, but I don't want him to see me like that. Understand?" He faced her, agony etching his features. He stepped forward and clasped her hands. "Say my name."

"Why?"

"Your accent flows over me like warm maple syrup. I want to experience that one more time."

Though she felt foolish, she couldn't deny his request. "Zachariah Thompson, Zach . . . ariah Thompson," she repeated, her voice breaking.

He uttered a long satisfied sigh. "I could close my eyes and listen to you talk all night. Would you spend the night with me, Bekah, if you could?"

"The guards would never permit that."

"I said if you could?"

Words failed her.

He traced the side of her face. "Never mind, my sweet Bekah, I see the answer in your eyes."

A tear trickled down her cheek. "I wish I could help you."

"I wish you could, too." He brushed the moisture from her cheek with his thumb.

His gentle touch amazed her, warmed her, and broke her

heart. "I know you didn't kill that man."

"Your confidence in my innocence isn't going to be worth a damn when that henchman loops the rope around my neck tomorrow morning."

"I know that." She hesitated, realizing this would be her last chance to broach the subject. "Can you tell me where you got your half of the medallion?"

He chuckled. "I was wondering when you'd get around to that."

"I thought you might let me put the two pieces together, right now, with you looking on. What harm could there be in that?"

"Bekah, you're my only hope. You want something I have, and I want you to help me escape. If I die, you'll never find my half."

"But . . ."

"No buts, Bekah. I'm running out of time. In case you change your mind, there's only one guard on duty tonight between nine and midnight. If James creates a diversion, and if I have a gun, I might stand a chance."

Her heart ached to think of him dying. "I can't do it. I'd like to help you, but I can't." She inhaled deeply, memorizing his spicy scent, the way he tipped his head to one side when he looked down at her, and the midnight shade of his pupils. She could have lost herself in those eyes.

And did.

His hands slipped around her waist as she watched his head lower and yearned for the feel of his lips. For a heartbeat, time stood still. He cradled her body against his. His mouth devoured hers in a way that was shameful.

And wonderful.

When he pulled away, she was breathless.

The guard arrived and unlocked the door. "Visiting time's over."

Rebekah stood on tiptoe, brushed her mouth against Zachariah's ear, handed him his watch, and whispered, "I'm coming back at ten. Make sure you have the medallion."

THREE

Later that night Rebekah followed Jimmy to an abandoned shed on the outskirts of town. He directed her to the rear of the building, where he lifted a board behind a barrel so they could climb inside. Frightened but unwilling to turn back, Rebekah crouched down and entered the dark shack.

Jimmy struck a match and lit the tallow candle on a sturdy wooden box. Long shadows danced along the rough plank walls. A musty smell filled the air. "Just wait till you see the fine horse I got you."

"Did I give you enough money?"

"Well." He waved his hand. "I had to throw in a little extra, or you'da had a broken-down mare. But don't worry none, we can square off some other time."

"Jimmy, I didn't want you to do that."

"If I'd used only your money, you'd be leaving town on a three-legged horse."

A nervous laugh escaped her lips. "Did you get the clothes?"

He flexed his hand by his side. "No problem, I got the quickest fingers in the East."

"I don't want you to go through life as a thief."

"Don't worry 'bout me. I can take care of myself."

She hugged him to her. "I wish I could be here to help you."

"I want to go with you and Zack tonight."

"You can't. It's too dangerous. I feel bad enough getting you mixed up in this. But if anything ever happened to you, I'd never forgive myself."

"If you let me go, I won't be any trouble. I'll cook and clean. I can do all sorts of things."

"Jimmy, it's not that I don't want to take you, it's that I can't. After tonight, I'll be an outlaw."

Lord, what was she doing?

"With my help no one will ever recognize you. No one will even know who broke Zack out of jail. Besides, I'll keep the guard busy so he won't even see you."

She heaved a nervous sigh. "I hope you're right, but it's still too dangerous. If you leave town tonight, the authorities might think you were involved. You can't come. You mustn't even think of it."

He pulled away from her and shrugged. "Yeah, well, that's all right 'cause I didn't want no woman bossing me around anyhow." He stalked off to the corner of the shed and shoved a wooden crate across the floor.

Rebekah knew she'd hurt Jimmy. If she tried to soothe him, he might decide to follow, so she said nothing and prayed God would forgive her for breaking the poor boy's heart.

He dug in the box and pulled out a pair of men's trousers. "These are the smallest I could find."

Rebekah caught the trousers and the man's shirts pelted at her head. She shook the clothes out and noticed both garments were huge. The smell of stale cigar smoke and sweat permeated the fabric.

As though he could read her mind, Jimmy nodded at the clothing. "I know they stink, but it's the best I could do in a hurry."

She motioned him to turn around. "Face the wall while I try these on." She unfastened her skirts, let them drop to the dirt floor, and slipped her legs into the large woolen trousers that felt stiff and scratchy.

Bunching the waistband in her hand, she looked at her feet hidden by the overlapping cloth. "Jimmy, do you have a pair of scissors?"

He turned and laughed, pointing at her as if he'd never seen such a funny sight. "Wait till Zack takes a look at you."

"Unless we hurry, he won't see us before morning."

Shoving his hand in his pocket, Jimmy rushed over. "Here, I got a knife. Hold still, and I'll cut the extra off."

Rebekah stood there, reeking of tobacco and mildew, holding the waistband of the ridiculous pants under her arms while Jimmy hacked a foot of cloth off the legs.

She wrapped a length of rope around her waist to hold up the trousers and watched her hands disappear inside the sleeves when she slipped on the shirt.

She rolled the sleeves to her elbows, but they still dropped over her hands. Cutting the ribbon she pulled from her hair into four lengths, she tied each piece around her elbows and her wrists. She then shadowed her face with a piece of charcoal and bunched her hair beneath a wide-brimmed felt hat. When she saw her reflection in the windowpane, she smiled despite the terror welling up in her chest. "Not even my brothers would recognize me dressed like this."

Jimmy nodded approvingly. "You're the scrawniest man I ever saw."

Rebekah squeezed both his hands and tried to pretend she wasn't afraid. "Don't take any chances. I know you love Zack, but it won't do him any good if you're killed. If there's any trouble, you forget all about our plan, and should anyone ask, you know nothing, understand?"

"Nothin's gonna go wrong. I got it all figured out."

When they stepped from the building, Rebekah spoke sternly. "Be careful, and you be a good boy."

"Oh, I almost forgot, take this." He tossed her a set of keys.

"They're the keys to the jail."

"How did you get these?"

He flexed his hand, wide grin on his face. "I already told you. I got the fastest fingers in the East."

A soft breeze brushed a wisp of hair from Rebekah's face as she hid in the doorway of the building next to the jail. Across town, a hound dog bayed at the quarter moon now hidden behind a bank of clouds where she hoped it would remain.

She was certain her pounding heart would leap from her chest. If they caught her, would they throw her in jail? Would she hang beside Zachariah?

The thought forced the air from her lungs.

How had Zachariah ever talked her into this? She admitted deep inside the decision had been hers.

She'd left England hoping to prove herself. And what had she done with her newfound freedom?

She was about to break a man out of jail!

Earlier that afternoon, she'd packed her bag, now fastened to the saddle of a horse tied to a hitching post alongside Zachariah's mount around the corner. Once they were a safe distance from town, and she was in possession of Zachariah's half of the medallion, she'd ditch these clothes. She and Zachariah then would go their own ways. The thought of never seeing him again saddened her, but she'd achieved what she'd set out to do. She'd have both halves of the medallion, and perhaps, answers to questions that had plagued her for years.

Her fascination with Zachariah would soon diminish, or so she'd told herself all afternoon.

The hairs on the back of her neck stirred when she spotted Jimmy running toward the jail. A million thoughts collided. What would her family think if she was caught? She imagined the disappointment on their faces when they had to visit her in jail. God, what was she doing? Panic gripped her. She took in large gulps of air until her head swam. Her hands trembled, and her legs felt unsteady. Could she go through with this?

She slumped against the brick exterior and closed her eyes, directing her thoughts toward Zachariah Thompson. She couldn't back out now.

She was his only hope.

Jimmy pounded on the wooden door of the jail. "Open up, quick. Someone's setting fire to the livery stable."

Dread tightened her throat. Rebekah had never felt such fear. She jammed her hand in the pocket of her trousers and wrapped her trembling fingers around the key ring. She watched Jimmy and the guard race toward the livery, where smoke poured from an open window.

With her heart racing, she hurried toward the jail, tripped over a pant leg, and scrambled to her feet. Since the door was ajar, she dashed into the office and down the corridor to Zachariah's cell.

"Bekah, is that you?" Zachariah wrapped his fingers over hers as she tried to unlock the door. Her hands trembled so much she couldn't insert the key in the lock. Finally, after three tries, the door clicked open.

"I knew I could count on you, Bekah." He took her hand and led the way down the corridor, pausing in the office. "Wait while I grab a weapon."

"Don't waste your time. I've already taken care of that."

"Where are the horses?"

"In the alley by the bank."

They were about to charge out the door when the burly guard burst through it. "You two going somewhere?"

Zachariah stared in disbelief as Rebekah shoved her hand in the pocket that drooped to her knees and glared at the guard. "Hold still, or I'll riddle you with holes."

Zachariah barely detected her accent in the gruff tone.

The guard gazed at the outline of a weapon beneath the thick woolen material. "How do I know that's a gun?"

Her upper lip curled. "You want me to prove it?"

Slowly, he raised his hands.

Zack then cuffed and gagged the guard and locked him in the cell. He raced back to the office where Bekah waited. "Let's get the hell out of here."

Beneath the black smudges, her face was deathly pale.

"Sweetheart, now's not the time to be passing out." He grabbed her hand and propelled her outside, then bolted around the corner with his arm securely wrapped around her waist. He'd planned to assist her onto her horse, but she swung into the saddle with an ease that rivaled his own. They took off at a gallop and never glanced back.

Zachariah's lungs filled with the sweet smell of freedom. He'd never expected to feel the air rushing against his face again, see the stars overhead, or race through the woods with a beautiful woman.

In spite of her blackened face and shoddy disguise, she was still beautiful to him, which worried the hell out of Zachariah. Though she'd smelled like an old geezer who hadn't bathed in a month, he'd still detected her flowery scent beneath the stench, a sure sign that he'd lost his mind.

But he wasn't that far gone. He knew instinctively the lady had class. She most likely believed in love, marriage, fairy tales, and living happily ever after. He believed only what he could see with his eyes.

Rebekah certainly didn't belong with the likes of him. Besides, he was a wanted man. The sooner they parted company, the safer she'd be.

As they fled from town, he admired her form. Beneath the thick woolen material, he could make out the outline of a nicely shaped behind.

He'd never thought she'd help him escape. When the hands of his watch had passed ten, he was certain she'd chickened out. And he wouldn't have blamed her.

She'd come through for him.

And he owed Bekah his life.

Unfortunately, he couldn't live up to his part of the bargain. He couldn't give her his half of the medallion.

It might be his only hope of proving his innocence.

FOUR

Rebekah's heart drowned out the pounding hooves of the animal beneath her. She feared someone might spot their silhouettes on the moonlit path between thick hemlocks. She couldn't believe she'd become involved in such a scheme, in fact, had masterminded it.

She could end up behind bars.

The wide saddle bruised muscles she hadn't known existed; thick woolen trousers chafed the insides of her thighs until her tender flesh felt as if it were on fire.

Zachariah remained behind her, the protector, looking out for signs of trouble. At least, she hoped he was a gentleman, a man of his word. The possibility that he might take off had crossed her mind, which was why she kept one eye on the path before her, the other on him.

The man cut a dashing figure. The outline of his massive form atop the horse stole her breath, a combination of awe and fear. Even in the dim light, she could make out his fierce expression, a look that made her doubt her actions. Few criminals ever admitted their guilt even when caught with the weapon in their hands. Yet, she'd freed Zachariah because she believed James when he told her he'd seen the real murderer that night in the alley.

Zachariah kneed his horse forward and motioned her to follow. She glanced behind them and saw a lone horseman fast approaching. She gulped, her throat clogging with dread.

While they waited behind a stand of poplars, Zachariah leaned toward her, the crackling of his leather saddle like thunder in the silence. "Stay here. Let me extend a proper welcome to our guest."

Stay here. She couldn't move if her life depended on it. And it might. When Zachariah vanished from sight, she thought he'd abandoned her. *Muttonhead. Nodcock.* The names did nothing to ease her mind, and right now, she wished her brothers were at her side, bossing her again.

The rider, a short man with a small build, was less than twenty feet away when her horse whinnied. He pulled back the reins and stared in her direction. Seemingly out of nowhere, Zachariah charged forward on his steed and knocked the intruder to the ground.

Rebekah leaped down from her horse and grabbed a branch in case Zachariah needed her help. As she raced to his side, he hauled the rider to his feet and knocked off his hat. "James, what in the hell are you doing here? Did anyone follow you?"

A wave of relief flooded through Rebekah.

The boy's shoulders stiffened. " 'Course no one followed. You think I'm dumb or somethin'?"

Zack grabbed James by the collar and the seat of his trousers and heaved him back onto his saddle. "Dumb? You sure aren't showing much sense by getting yourself tangled up in my mess. You go back, you hear, or I'll whip your bottom red, and then tie you to that tree trunk where the sheriff is bound to find you come morning."

Furious with his tone, Rebekah tried to elbow Zachariah aside. He didn't budge one iota. "You brute, how can you speak to an eight-year-old child like that?"

He glared at her. "This isn't just any child. This is James. He's old enough to know better."

Rebekah reached for Jimmy's hand. "Sweetie, you can't stay.

It's much too dangerous."

"I can't go back. The fire I set in the hay buckets spread. The livery stable burnt to the ground. The guard chased me, said when he got his hands around my neck, I'd be a goner for sure."

Zachariah cursed. "He's handing you a crock of bull. The kid's lying."

Jimmy turned away and brushed at his eyes.

Rebekah's fists clenched. "How can you send a poor defenseless boy away?"

"Because he's better off back in town than with us."

"That's what you say, but I don't think you want to be bothered. I'm surprised you even stayed with me this long."

He uttered a rude noise. "Now that's an idea worth considering. I should take off and leave the two of you to fend for yourselves."

Rebekah's chin rose in defiance. "Take off, you scoundrel. Jimmy and I will do fine without you."

He heaved a disgruntled sigh. "Mount up. I don't have time to bicker with you right now. Get your English behind back in that saddle, or I'll leave you both here."

Should she point out no gentleman would speak to a lady in such a despicable fashion? She caught a whiff of herself and decided to drop the subject when she nearly gagged on the stench of stale tobacco and sweat. "I'm not going without Jimmy." Her voice wavered despite her best efforts.

Zack stared down at her, anger twisting his features. She couldn't desert Jimmy, though it seemed clear Zachariah had no such problem. Anyone who'd abandon a child would think little of abandoning a woman. The thought frightened her. Without his help, she'd be lost. But she would not allow the rogue to see her concern. She forced her mouth into a nonchalant smile while her feet quivered in her shoes. "If you'll give me your half of the medallion, you need not concern yourself with either me or Jimmy."

She felt a moment's satisfaction as disbelief flashed in his black eyes. He raised his arms and dropped them back down with a clap. "Confounded, cussed female, I give up. Let's get out of here."

"I can come?" Jimmy asked, all traces of tears gone from his smiling face.

"Yes." Zachariah pushed the word through clenched teeth as he stomped toward the horses.

Rebekah caught up with him. She debated whether to broach the subject and decided she could not wait. Lowering her voice, she said, "You must never again call Jimmy a liar. He looks up to you. You're doing his young ego great harm by aiming such derogatory comments at him."

He wrapped his hands around her waist and assisted her onto her horse. "Even if it's true?"

After he'd released her, the warmth from his fingertips penetrated the thick woolen material and lingered on her bare skin, almost making her forget her throbbing limbs where the saddle pressed against inflamed flesh. She lifted her leg a little to lessen her discomfort. "I haven't known Jimmy a long time, but I trust him. Implicitly," she added to make her point.

He arched a brow. "That so?"

She nodded confidently.

"If you're such a great judge of character, how come you're running away from the law with a drunk and a thirteen-year-old boy?"

"Thirteen . . ." she muttered before she could stop herself.

He laughed and swung onto his mount. "Yes, the kid's thirteen, not eight. What do you have to say about that?"

The satisfied smirk on his face rendered her speechless.

Zachariah called himself a fool. He could make better time

without a woman and a child slowing him down. Especially a stubborn, mule-headed, British woman who had a way of looking at him with those blue eyes that made him feel emotions better left forgotten.

He'd rather feel nothing.

The sooner he got rid of her, the better off he'd be. What had possessed him to remain with them? When dawn arrived, he'd hightail it for his cabin and leave Bekah and James behind. He wasn't worried about James. The boy could take care of himself. Chances were the livery was still standing, and he could return to Londonderry without worry.

No one would recognize Bekah once she'd changed clothing. But when she looked like a woman again, Bekah wouldn't be safe with the likes of him. Thoughts of her had taunted him since the moment she'd entered his cell pretending to be his wife.

Zack's narrow escape from the gallows had intensified his yearning. He closed his eyes and imagined Bekah naked in a tub of hot water, soap bubbles clinging to her breasts. His mouth went dry when he pictured her standing. He'd towel her off, every rounded curve his to explore.

"I sure am glad you decided to take me along."

Grudgingly, Zack opened his eyes and speared James with a mean look. "Don't make any long-range plans. I don't want a snotty-nosed kid dragging after me."

Within hearing distance, Bekah scowled at Zack as if he'd crawled from under a rock. No doubt she'd be reminding him to watch his mouth around the kid. James was his friend, and the boy understood what he'd said was meant in jest.

"Just as well, 'cause I got my own plans, and they don't include following an old man around."

Zack felt much older than his thirty-two years. Lots of liquor and loose women had taken their toll. He didn't care. Yet when he caught sight of Bekah ahead of him, he wondered only for the briefest moment what his life might be like if he'd met her three years ago, before Elissa, back when he dared to believe in love, back when he still had something to offer a woman.

James spat on the ground. "I'm damn near grown. If it wasn't for me getting the horses and clothes, you'd be staring out the window of your cell counting the minutes till dawn."

"I appreciate what you did. But that doesn't mean I need to let you tag along. I'm a wanted man. I don't want you near in case someone takes a potshot at me. It's too dangerous."

"You're saying that 'cause you don't want to be bothered with me."

Zack said nothing. He spotted Bekah's cold blue eyes aimed at him, but pretended not to notice. He could barely take care of himself, much less a pain in the neck kid who stole and lied. If James hung out with Zack, he'd likely turn out a drinker, too. The boy had enough strikes against him without pairing off with a drunk.

As they wove their way deeper into the forest, Rebekah kept a close eye on Zachariah. Though she was fairly certain he hadn't murdered anyone, he was still a thief and a drinking man, and by the way he'd spoken to Jimmy, she'd assessed his scruples as lower than a snake's.

If her adoptive parents had displayed so little tolerance, she and her brothers would have ended up hooligans. Were it not for their stepfather's occasional drinking binge, theirs would have been a perfect childhood. She shook the unpleasant memories from her mind and focused on the present.

A niggling thought persisted. Since Jimmy had lied to her about his age, had he also lied about seeing another man in the alley the night of the murder? Of course, he hadn't lied, she told herself because she refused to consider the alternative.

Besides, when she'd first set eyes on Zack, she'd intuitively believed in his innocence. And her intuition was usually right.

Except for those few times when it had let her down.

She stole a glance at Zack. The moonlight carved deep shadows on his bearded face, accenting his scowling mouth. A shiver raced down her spine.

James led the way. Rebekah was next, and thirty feet behind Zachariah kept watch for signs of a posse.

Rebekah slowed her horse and allowed Zachariah to catch up.

"Something wrong?" he asked.

Every muscle, every cell in her body pulsated with pain. "No . . . well, yes. I lived up to my part of our bargain. I'd like your half of the medallion now."

He looked at her as if she'd lost her mind. "Now's not a good time."

"And what's that supposed to mean?"

"We need to put as much distance as possible between us and Londonderry. We have no time to waste."

She met his gaze. "A paltry few seconds isn't going to make a difference. Hand the medallion over now. You promised."

"And you fear I'm not the sort of man to honor a promise."

"Remember, I have the gun," she said, reaching into her pocket to make her point.

He tilted his head back and laughed. "Not for long, you don't. Hand it over."

"You're a criminal, a man of questionable character. I'm keeping the gun, and I'll use it if the need arises. You must think me a nodcock to even suggest such a thing."

His laugh deepened. "A nodcock?"

"A fool, Mr. Thompson. A fool," she repeated, hating it that she was losing control.

"Then why didn't you say that?"

"You're changing the subject. Hand over the medallion, or I'll riddle you with bullets."

"What kind of gun do you have?"

She refused to answer.

His eyes sparkled with humor. "You don't even know what kind of weapon you have, and you expect me to trust you with it. Chances are you've never even fired a gun."

"It doesn't take high intelligence to figure out the mechanics. All one has to do is aim and pull back on the finger thing. Hand over the medallion now."

"Finger thing." More laughter. He slapped his thigh.

To show she was serious, she made sure he could see the outline of the weapon inside the pocket of her woolen trousers. "Don't make me use this."

He undid the two top buttons of his shirt, revealing a thick throat and a hairy chest. For one insane moment, Rebekah wanted to feel the texture of that hair between her fingers.

"As you can see, I didn't wear the medallion. I hid it."

Again, she aimed the weapon at him. "Well, I'm waiting."

One corner of his mouth lifted. "Maybe you should turn around."

"Until I have your half of the medallion, I'm not taking my eyes off you."

He winked. "Suit yourself."

His suggestive look sent a shiver down her spine. She returned his intent gaze until he started to undo his belt buckle. "What are you doing?"

"Getting you the medallion."

She stared down at his fingers as he pulled the end of his leather belt loop out of the buckle. "But . . ."

"I pinned it to the inside of my trousers so the guard wouldn't take it from me."

"Oh." He undid one button on the front panel of his trousers.

Then another. Rebekah's heart fluttered. She turned her head around so fast, she felt dizzy.

Lord almighty, the man was about to strip in front of her.

He had the manners of a barnyard animal.

Before she could catch her breath, Rebekah found herself yanked from her saddle and sitting on Zachariah's lap.

"You're an uncouth barbarian. Return me to my horse this instant." He rudely stuck his hand into the deep pocket of her trousers and wrenched her jewel comb from her fingers.

"Tell me this is bloody English humor. Tell me you have a weapon hiding somewhere."

"I told you I didn't like guns. Someone could be killed."

"What am I supposed to do when the sheriff catches up with me? Comb his hair?"

"You needn't be so sarcastic. You have an attitude problem, Mr. Thompson."

"Yes, and it's rapidly deteriorating."

"I certainly wasn't about to put a gun in your hands. It's bad enough I helped break you out of jail. I wouldn't want another man's blood on my conscience."

"Trust me, the sheriff won't have any such qualm if he catches up with us."

"Then you'll have to see that he doesn't."

He lifted her up. Every muscle cried out in protest when he dropped her none too gently back on her own saddle.

She swallowed a painful moan.

"Here, you want this?"

Thinking he was going to give her his medallion, she turned and took her comb from his hand. "Thank you," she said because it was proper when all the time she wanted to wring his neck, maybe spit in his eye, and slap that damnable grin from his face.

Rebekah chose to ignore the man and the feelings running

rampant inside. Wring his neck! She didn't believe in violence, yet he brought out desires that alarmed her. If she attempted to wring his neck, she'd lose all sense of purpose when her fingers traced the corded muscles.

There'd be no telling what she'd do.

Or what he'd do.

Her thoughts lingered on those possibilities a moment, his large hands, his moist lips, his hard body pressed against hers. She'd better keep her distance because she did not trust herself around Zachariah Thompson.

They rode for hours, and Rebekah felt so tired she could barely keep her eyes open. She hadn't slept last night, her nerves too jittery with plans of breaking Zachariah out of jail. When she'd set out on her own, she'd never anticipated herself capable of such a foolhardy stunt. Yet, here she was running from the law with a thirteen-year-old boy and a convicted killer.

When they stopped to water the horses, her legs seemed molded to the saddle, and it took all her concentration to lift her behind from the leather and swing down without groaning. She managed the task with a smile and pretended she hadn't felt the effects of their long ride.

She'd intended to ask Zachariah for his medallion as he led his horse to the edge of the stream.

Jimmy came to her side. "Are you mad at me?"

She glanced at his serious expression. "Of course not. Though I don't know why you told me you were eight years old."

"I thought you'd like me more if I was a little kid."

James might be thirteen, but inside he was years younger. He craved the mothering he'd missed. Rebekah rested her hand on his thin shoulder. "You're still the same boy I met the first day. I like you no matter how old you are. But I want you to tell me the truth from now on."

He nodded enthusiastically, relief flooding his features. "You got my promise."

"I hope you haven't lied to me about anything else."

"No, I told you the truth, honest."

Was he telling the truth? "I want you to grow into a gentleman who stands by his word. I want you to be a man of character. I have great hopes for you, Jimmy."

"I want Zachariah to change his mind and let me stay with him."

That immediately dashed her hopes. Zachariah was a poor example for a boy to imitate.

Zachariah strolled toward them, extended his hand, and grabbed the reins. "Allow me. You go relax for a few minutes while I tend to the horses." As he strode away, Rebekah admired his wide shoulders. Though Zachariah Thompson had no manners, a bad attitude, wasn't fit to raise a child and couldn't be trusted, he appealed to her.

Cross with herself, she knelt and stretched out on the ground. She laid her head on her extended arm, covered her face with her wide hat, closed her eyes, and fell into a sound sleep.

When Zachariah found her lying there, he wanted to stretch out beside her, hold her tight, and kiss her senseless. He doubted Bekah had ever known a man, and he wanted to be her first.

The idea was laughable.

The thought of him with such a fine lady was ridiculous.

He realized this was his chance to escape. Besides, she'd be better off without him. If the law caught up with him, she'd be implicated in his escape.

He pulled James out of earshot. "If you do me a favor, I'll give you my watch."

"You mean it?"

"I said so, didn't I?" Even James questioned his integrity. Considering what Zachariah was about to do, he couldn't blame him. "I'm getting the hell out of here, and I need you to stay with Bekah until she's safe."

"You can't leave her here."

"That's why I want you to stay. Otherwise, she might get lost."

Zachariah handed the boy his watch, a gift from his mother. "Bekah's not from around these parts. She'll need help finding her way."

James's fingers curled around the pocket watch. "I want to go with you."

"Until I clear my name, I don't want anyone around."

"Afterwards, will you come for me and let me stay with you?"

He had no business raising a child. "No, I won't."

James's lip trembled as he shoved the watch in his pocket. "If that's the way you feel, then get outta here."

"Zachariah, are you leaving without giving me your medallion?"

Zack stared into Bekah's blue eyes, wishing he didn't have to see the disappointment in them. "Yes, I am."

"You never intended to give me your medallion."

"No, I didn't."

She placed her hat on her head. He was glad he could no longer see the condemnation in her eyes. "You're a big disappointment to me, Zachariah."

Her words wounded him, made him feel less than a man.

He wanted to explain that he needed the medallion to try to prove his innocence, but what did it matter? He was going back on his word, which he'd had no intention of keeping.

She moved closer. "You can't do this."

He swung onto his mount. "Just watch me." Years ago he'd learned to look out for himself first. If he didn't, no one else would. He leaned over, tipped her chin up until he could see her face. "Bekah, you trust too easily."

Anger blazed in her ice blue eyes. "And you don't trust at all."

He rested his hand on her shoulder. "I trust in myself, no one else."

As she stepped away, a shot rang out.

He watched her slip to the ground.

FIVE

When he thought of the noose awaiting him in Londonderry, Zachariah took off.

Filled with shame, he called himself a coward and a no-good bastard. He was no better than his old man. But he had no weapon and little time to escape.

Early on, he'd learned to take care of number one, but Bekah had shaken his selfish outlook on life.

She'd believed in him when no one else had.

Though she had her own agenda for helping him to escape, she'd saved him from hanging. Were it not for Bekah, about now he'd be climbing the steps of the scaffold. He shivered thinking of it. He'd rather take a bullet to the head than die of suffocation.

He wheeled his horse around, told himself he was crazy for sticking his neck out for another person. He wanted to run and never look back, yet he found himself staring down at her still form.

"Zachariah, give yourself up now before it's too late," came the deep voice from a distance.

Zachariah's instincts urged him to run.

But Bekah didn't deserve this. If he left her, she'd end up behind bars—if she survived.

Something inside him twisted at the sight of her lying there, a widening bloodstain on her oversized shirt. Amid flying bullets, he leaped from his horse and cradled her in his arms.

She moaned. Her eyelids fluttered.

His heart damn near burst from his chest. "Take it easy, Bekah. I'm getting you out of here." Had he imagined her slight smile as he lifted her limp body onto his horse? Ducking low, he kneed his horse forward. A few hundred feet ahead, he spotted James's coattails flapping in the breeze.

The sun rose in the sky like a golden orb, lighting every dark nook in the forest.

Zachariah cursed the daylight.

He cursed his stupidity for stopping longer than needed.

He cursed his raging emotions while he held the woman firmly to his chest. If he said he didn't care for Bekah, he'd be lying.

He cared. Too much.

"Is she gonna die?"

Zachariah regarded James's stricken face. Until now, he had refused to consider the possibility.

He couldn't lie to James. "I don't know. She's lost some blood. I need to clean her wound and try to staunch the bleeding. But if we stop, the sheriff will catch up with us."

"Her chest isn't moving. I think she's dead already." Tears rimmed James's blue eyes. Turning away, he sniffed and rubbed his face.

Zachariah's heart went out to the boy. "Her breathing is shallow, but she's alive." Long ago, he'd given up on prayer, figured God didn't have time for young boys who stole liquor and peeked at naked women through keyholes. He'd doubted God even existed, but this time, when he raised his eyes to the sky, he did so for Bekah. He silently whispered her name, just in case someone was listening.

"If you don't stop, she'll die," James said, his voice filled with alarm.

Zachariah made a split-second decision. "There's a cave not

far from here at the bottom of that hill. I figure I'll hide the horse there and take care of Bekah. No sense both of us taking a chance of being caught. I want you to get as far away from here as you can."

"I can't go without knowing she'll be all right."

"You need to go. Do it for her. She'd want you to be safe."

Again, James turned and brushed his hand over his eyes. "I wanna help."

"No, don't take crazy chances. You get the hell out of here."

As James rode away, Zachariah wished him well.

Zachariah followed the narrow trail that wound along the rippling brook and ended at an outcropping of rocks. He'd reached the bottom of the hill when he heard the thunder of hooves. Certain capture was imminent, he braced himself for the worst.

He heard a high-pitched whistle and recognized James's voice.

The posse never glanced in Zachariah's direction but took off at a gallop toward the sound.

As he slid off his mount, he tucked Bekah's head against his neck. She didn't stir or make a sound. His heart wrenched with fear. What if she died because of him? Carefully, he stepped forward, set her down at the mouth of the cave, and hurried back to his horse, tying it behind a large boulder where he hoped no one would spot it. He then removed the saddle and blanket from the animal and rushed back to the cave.

Wanting to make her comfortable, he slid his saddle beneath Bekah's head and shoulders. But did it matter? She seemed unaware of him or her surroundings.

He fumbled with the buttons on her shirt and winced when he saw blood gushing from the wound on her upper arm. If he didn't act fast, Bekah would die.

"Zachariah." She lifted her hand toward his face. "I knew you wouldn't abandon me."

Her faith amazed him. "I'm glad you knew because I sure didn't."

"You're too hard on yourself."

A feeling close to love surged to the surface. Since that emotion did not exist, he ignored the flutter in his chest. "You scared the hell out of me," he said, his voice deeper than normal. Without thought, he pressed his mouth to her forehead. "I want you to rest. Don't worry about a thing. I'm going to take care of you."

"You're a good man, Zachariah."

"Now you really have me worried. You're imagining things."

She closed her eyes, her faith in him evident by her peaceful expression.

He raced to the stream, yanked off his shirt, and ripped it in strips. It wasn't as clean as he'd have liked, but it was all he had. He dipped the material in the cold water and rushed back to Bekah.

He mopped up the blood with the moist cloth and was relieved to see the wound wasn't nearly as large as he'd first thought. He applied pressure to the bullet hole. "Bekah, open your eyes, let me know you're going to be all right."

He looked for signs she'd heard him but saw none. His neck muscles tightened, and he rolled his head from side to side. Once he'd curbed the bleeding, he fashioned a sling for her arm. Afraid that travel might reopen the wound, he decided to stay put for the rest of the day and travel after nightfall.

As he covered Bekah with the horse blanket, he glanced at her matted hair. He undid the pins securing the knot to the top of her head and felt the honey-gold locks between his thumb and forefinger.

If only she hadn't gotten herself tangled with him, she'd be resting in a real bed in some inn, her hair fanned out around her head on a soft pillow.

"Bekah, wake up." How he'd love to greet her this way each morning. But she didn't stir, and fear clogged his throat.

When she didn't answer, he closed his eyes, laid his head against hers and pretended she really was his wife and that all was right with the world.

Zachariah didn't know how long he'd slept when he awoke to the sound of an approaching rider. He reached for his Colt and remembered he didn't have one. A quick glance at Bekah showed she was sleeping fitfully.

He crouched by the cave opening, ready to spring on the intruder.

"Zachariah, it's me, James."

He stood and greeted James with a scowl. "I thought I told you to make yourself scarce. You're likely to get killed hanging around me."

"I figured you might need these." He motioned to the parcel in his hands and toward Bekah's horse. "I found him munching clover when I circled back. Bekah will need her things, and I got us some food, too, and a jug of corn juice for her pain."

Until now, Zachariah hadn't realized he was hungry. He took the worn feedbag from James and glanced inside at the hardtack, cups, and a tin of coffee grounds. "I could sure use a strong cup of coffee." Maybe laced with a little corn liquor, he thought, noting how his hands shook, certain a drink would cure what ailed him.

"I didn't get coffee. I got tea."

"What in hell did you do that for?"

"It's for Miss Benson. I figured it might help her feel better."

Shame nipped at Zachariah's conscience for once again thinking of himself first. "You're a smart kid."

James's face lit up at the compliment.

It saddened Zachariah to realize how little it took to please the boy.

The two entered the cave and while James held Bekah in a sitting position, Zachariah spooned corn liquor in her mouth. She swallowed and sputtered, made a gagging sound in the back of her throat.

Zachariah put his nose near the opening of the jug and inhaled deeply. His mouth watered. He considered taking a swig but decided against it. "This sure smells like potent stuff."

"I found it behind some hay in a barn where I hid until the sheriff and his posse were long gone. I bet some old man was hiding his stash from his old lady."

James wiped the dribble from her chin. "I bet Miss Benson doesn't usually drink whiskey."

Zachariah nodded. "That's why we aren't going to give her much, just enough to dull the pain. Or next thing we know, she'll be flying high and hitting her head on the ceiling of this cave."

James rested a comforting hand on Bekah's. "She's a nice lady. She even bought me breakfast."

"Be happy she didn't cook your breakfast." Thoughts of the cake she'd baked brought a smile to his face. "I have a feeling she hasn't been around a stove much."

As Zachariah pushed the cork back into the mouth of the jug, the urge to imbibe overwhelmed him. But he spotted the worried look on James's face, so he set the jug down and pretended taking a drink had not become such an important part of his life.

Rebekah awoke to the sounds of voices. At first, she was unable to comprehend what she was doing on a rock floor with a saddle beneath her head and a smelly blanket over her. She had a strange taste in her mouth. When she shifted, pain knifed through her shoulder.

She faintly remembered hearing gunshots, feeling a searing

pain, then swooning. Almost in a dream, she remembered Zachariah's reassuring words promising to take care of her. She remembered the concern on his face and his gentle touch.

She heaved a deep sigh and regretted her actions because the small movement ripped at her arm like a clawed creature. She shut her eyes and tried to unscramble her thoughts.

The next time she glanced up, she caught James staring down at her as if waiting for her demise. She guessed she looked no better than she felt. "Hello, Jimmy," she said, her voice barely a whisper.

He crouched down on his knees. "Does it hurt bad?"

"It stings a mite."

"You should have seen Zack. When you collapsed, he rode in after you, bullets whizzing by his ears. It's a wonder he wasn't killed. I never saw anyone as brave as Zack in all my life."

Everything was fuzzy in her mind. It was easier to accept whatever the child said as fact. She tried to smile to acknowledge his comments, but even that required too much energy.

Jimmy pointed over his shoulder. "Zack is heating up water. He's making you some tea. I told him it might help you feel better."

"Yes, tea will give me a lift." She gave his hand a light pat.

James seemed pleased with himself as he scrambled to his feet.

When he returned a moment later, Zachariah was behind him carrying a tin cup, worry creasing his face. "I heard you were awake. How are you doing?"

"Shaky but alive, thanks to you. According to James, you were a remarkable sight. I'm told, a gallant hero like no other."

Looking none too happy, Zachariah motioned Jimmy to be quiet. The boy left shortly afterwards.

"I sure don't deserve praise for what I did. The only hero around here is James."

She wanted to ask him what he meant, but the question drifted away.

Zachariah set the cup on the floor and supported her back so she could sit up. "I want you to drink this and eat a couple bites of hardtack. If you dip it in the steaming tea, it'll soften enough to be edible."

While she sat, her head spun. She leaned against Zachariah's arm, grateful for his support, feeling a moment of contentment.

Her vision steadied.

She lifted what looked like a flat cookie to her lips and bit down. Her teeth barely dented its rock-hard surface. "You Americans have a lot to learn about pastries."

He broke a piece off and dipped it in her tea, delivering the morsel to her mouth. "You really should try to eat something."

The touch of his fingers against her lips did strange things to her insides. She wanted to lick his fingers clean.

Unsettled by her thoughts, she looked down, took a sip of tea, and gagged. "Lordy, what's in this?"

"I doctored the tea with a little home remedy sure to dull your pain. Now drink up."

"You're as bossy as my brothers."

"Is that bad?"

"No, just annoying."

Once she drank half the tea, her annoyance vanished. Instead, she focused on Zachariah and how he smelled. It was a pleasant scent, totally his own, a combination of fresh air and spices.

"You smell soooo good," she said, shocked at her boldness and the silly giggle that followed.

"Oh, oh, I think you've drunk enough." He tried to take the tin cup from her, but she held on tight.

"No, you don't. I'm not finished yet." She tipped up the cup and gulped the rest.

He made a frustrated noise that she found amusing.

She couldn't remember tea tasting this good. She set the cup down and studied his damp hair, tied at his nape with a leather strip, leading her to believe he'd bathed. She could hear rippling outside the cave. The deep V of his unbuttoned coat revealed a thick neck and a naked chest ridged with muscles and sprinkled with dark hair that beckoned for her touch.

Those couldn't be her fingers toying with his beard!

Yet when she glanced down, she found they were. Even more shocking was the way she angled her head close, took a deep breath, and licked her lips. "You smell good enough to eat."

She loved the shocked look he shot her and lifted her brows to let him know she'd meant every word.

What had come over her?

Yet she liked the freedom, the courage, and the feeling of power running though her.

She watched in disbelief as her fingers wound into his beard, its texture soft as a kitten's fur. She pulled him closer.

His pupils dilated.

Thrilled with his reaction, she planted a wet kiss on his cheek. "I'd like another cup of tea, sir."

Though the words lacked humor, she laughed as if they were funny.

"You've already had too much tea."

She poked his chest. "You're . . . you're being bossy again." Her tongue tripped over itself before she could get the words out.

"Now that you're in the right frame of mind, I think I'll help you out of these smelly clothes."

"You, Zachariah Thompson, have the manners of a hog." If she found the idea so repulsive, why did she hiccup and laugh?

He helped her lie down. "Lift up so I can slide these trousers off."

My, she was tired.

"Lift up, Bekah," he repeated, louder this time, penetrating the haze surrounding her mind.

When she realized what he was trying to do, she gave him a haughty look. "You, Mr. Thompson, are a few tuppence short a quid."

"A what?"

Her laughter echoed along with his as he abandoned his quest and rocked her in his arms until she eventually fell into a drugged sleep.

Six

After Bekah fell asleep, Zachariah held her against his chest and called himself a fool for being attracted to the lady. This seemed all too familiar. A few years back he'd entrusted his heart to such a woman, only to discover that nothing he did was ever enough. When a better opportunity arose, Elissa had found someone richer, a fact Zachariah was unaware of until he caught her sleeping in another man's arms. That day, part of him died along with his belief in love and his trust in women.

He admitted Bekah had spunk and a certain drive that Elissa lacked, yet the similarities far outnumbered the differences. Common sense dictated he keep his distance—for his sake as much as hers.

Zachariah spotted the jug of corn liquor three feet away. More than anything he wanted to pull out the cork, lift the earthenware container to his mouth, and take a long swig. Saliva flowed freely in his mouth. His hands shook, the same tremor he'd noticed other times when he'd tried to stay sober. Certainly, a few swallows would do no harm. One drink would relax his muscles and reinforce his stamina for the long night ahead. But that one drink might lead to another and then another until he had no idea what was happening around him.

His last binge had led to his arrest for killing the man in the alley. His last drinking spree had almost gotten him hanged.

When would he learn his lesson?

He promised himself he'd take only one or two gulps and

then stop. Reaching out, he traced the contour of the jug, its texture rough and cool beneath his fingertip. The brew inside would blaze a fiery path down his throat, settle in his stomach, and steady him. He tapped the cork a few times, temptation urging him on.

Both Bekah and James relied on him, and though Zachariah didn't relish the responsibility, he figured he'd do what he could to get them safely out of here.

He did not trust himself to take one swallow.

The realization filled him with shame.

As he curled his forefinger around the jug's handle, he turned his thoughts to Bekah, her beauty taunting him, making him dare to believe she could be his. Common sense surfaced. Bekah sure as hell would never pair off with him, a drunk who could no more control his drinking than he could the setting sun.

He yanked his hand away from the jug as if burned by a flame. Forcing himself to let go of Bekah, he stood and looked down at her, her golden locks framing her perfect features.

Zachariah figured if the law caught up with them, he'd die before admitting she was responsible for helping him to escape from jail. He owed her that much.

But dressed the way she was, the sheriff would know she was the one who'd helped him. The sooner he destroyed her disguise, the safer she'd be.

He called to James, who hurried into the cave, looking as if he were about to bawl. "Is she—?"

"No. She's much better, but I need you to do me a couple favors."

"Anything you say, Zack."

Admiration shone in the kid's eyes. Another reason to send the boy packing first chance he had. James was too impressionable to be hanging around a man who swigged liquor, enjoyed loose women, and cheated at cards. "I want you to stop ranting about my being a hero."

"But I saw how you saved Miss Benson. When I'm grown, I want to be brave like you. Nothin' you say will ever change my mind."

Zachariah groaned. "Then keep your opinion to yourself."

James hesitated. "It's not like I'm saying mean things about you."

"I want the hero talk to end, you understand?"

"Sure thing."

"You wouldn't happen to have a shovel?"

"No."

"Then take one of the tin cups and dig a hole a few hundred yards from here. When you're done, come back, and I'll have some clothes for you to bury."

Once James left, Zachariah opened Bekah's satchel and searched for something appropriate for her to wear. He dug in the bag and yanked out several lacy undergarments, which he quickly threw aside and tried to ignore. The three dresses he pulled out were made of the finest silk edged with ruffles and lace and cut low around the neck. The thought of spending one minute with Bekah dressed this way was more than he could bear so he foraged for something less appealing. He settled on a simpler linen dress, though he doubted Bekah would look plain clothed in a burlap feedbag.

He dropped onto his haunches and peeled away the woolen trousers that hid drawers edged with ruffles and came below her knees. He tried not to notice the black ribbon lacing them shut or the embroidered daisies on her white silk stockings. He'd never again look at another blasted daisy without remembering Bekah.

When he slipped the trousers over her ankles, he wondered if his fingers shook for want of a drink or for need of a woman, this woman.

Dismissing the thought, he started to unbutton Bekah's shirt. He lifted her so he could free her arms from the long baggy sleeves, and he removed the crude bandage he'd fashioned from his gray shirt. When he lowered his head to inspect the wound, she wrapped her arms around his neck and urged him to move closer. He rested his face against her cheek and relished the soft feel of her skin. Her long eyelashes brushed his forehead like a butterfly wing, and he lingered a moment to kiss her eyelids. Beneath the heavy smell of cigar smoke on her flesh, he detected the hint of her flowery fragrance.

His breath quickened, and he tried to ignore the weight pooling in his groin.

Unable to stop, he pressed his mouth against hers. He called himself a bastard for taking advantage, yet his lips remained on hers. He memorized the feel of her mouth as she returned his kiss. He knew the kiss had to end but indulged another moment before pulling away.

Furious with himself, he looked down at her. Her lower lip bowed into a kissable pout, and her fingers threaded through his beard, encouraging him to kiss her again. He blamed her actions on the corn whiskey.

His behavior verified what he'd known for some time—he was a man with no scruples. As if to prove his point, his gaze settled on her small breasts barely hidden by the square neckline of her chemise. The chain holding her half of the medallion disappeared in the cleavage. He tugged gently, freed the charm, and looped the chain over her head.

For a moment he considered putting the charm back, but he quickly dismissed the notion as he laid her down and yanked his half from his pocket. Laying the two pieces beside each other, he tried to make sense of the markings but had little luck. He saw a symbol for water and another for land, but nothing that meant anything to him.

If Bekah was correct, this charm stood for buried treasure. Even if she was wrong, the charm might lead Zachariah to the person who'd murdered the man in the alley. That person might be on the lookout for its return. Zachariah figured he'd flash the charm around in a few saloons, making it known he had both halves and wanted to speak to the charm's owner. Once he cleared his name, maybe, he'd give Bekah back her half, but not until then.

He dropped both pieces of the charm in his pocket and stretched, noting how unsteady he felt.

He desperately needed a drink.

With trembling hands, he yanked out the cork and inhaled the sharp tang of the hard liquor. His mouth watering, he brought the jug to his lips and allowed the whiskey to touch the tip of his tongue. Closing his eyes, he tipped the jug back and filled his mouth with the corn whiskey. His parched throat relaxed. His jitters subsided. How easy it would be to swallow.

But he didn't dare take even one tiny sip.

Disgusted, he spat on the ground, recorked the jug, and licked the taste from his lips.

He shut his eyes and inhaled a shuddering breath. Whiskey would have to wait.

Zachariah left the cave, his fingers toying with both pieces of the charm hidden in his pocket. Guilt had long since vanished, replaced with the certainty he held the key to his freedom in his hands. Because he couldn't wait to get started, he summoned James to his side. "I want you to keep a close eye on Bekah. I need to go somewhere, and I should be back by evening."

"Where you going?"

"Never you mind. The less you know, the safer you'll be."

"Can I go, too?"

"Then who'd be here to take care of Bekah?"

Zack saw the disappointment on the boy's face. "I see what you mean . . . but I don't know nothin' 'bout doctoring. What if she wakes up and needs somethin'?"

"I've checked the bullet wound, and it seems fine. If she's in pain, brew her more tea, and add a generous dose of corn liquor."

Worry streaked across James's face. "What if you don't come back?"

Zack peered into the kid's eyes. "Are you asking if I'm abandoning you?"

"Never, Zack. You're my . . . hero."

Zack rolled his eyes, frustrated with the hero talk, but the child's dedication warmed his heart. If he had a son, he'd want him to be just like James. "If something should happen to me, you see to it that Bekah gets to a doctor. Say she accidentally shot herself while loading a gun."

"I don't think Miss Benson would want me to lie."

"Just don't say it in front of her. That way her stubborn chin won't rise in her defense."

Zachariah's concerns for Bekah and the boy faded as he neared the town of Litchfield, New Hampshire. He hitched his horse outside the Blooming Garden, a tavern run by a working gal dressed in bright pink. His hat low on his head, he studied each storefront, making sure no one was watching.

"Well, if this don't beat all. Look what the cat dragged in."

He touched his fingers to the brim of his hat. "Rose, you always did know how to boost a man's spirits."

She rested a hand on her shapely hip. Deep laughter jiggled the white flesh of her breasts spilling from the low, sequined neckline of her silk dress. "If you doubt that for a second, come upstairs, and I'll prove it to you."

He raised his hands in surrender. "I believe you."

"Once is enough for most men. You and me have had a few go rounds."

He sauntered inside the saloon and wrapped his arm around her waist. Rose slipped from his hold and winked at a customer. Zachariah looked around the room as he meandered toward the bar. He smiled at Daffodil and Violet. "How's business?"

Violet lowered her long, blackened eyelashes and flapped her fan in front of her face. Her blonde hair, piled high on her head, made a nice contrast to her lavender satin dress. She sashayed against him and lifted a leg onto the lower rung of the bar stool, exposing a lace garter and a shapely limb in the long slit of her skirt. "It's booming. Most men don't care whether it's night or day. How about you, Zack?"

The thick scent of her cloying perfume tickled the back of Zachariah's throat. Not so long ago he'd have taken her up on her offer, but he didn't have the time or the inclination. "Has anyone been bragging about killing a poor slob in Londonderry?"

She thought for a moment. "Not that I know of, but I can ask around. Give a guy a few drinks and a good time, and he's likely to tell me his life story along with every secret known to man."

"If you hear of anything, you know how to get hold of me."

"Sure do." She ran her finger along the buttons on his shirt. "I'd never expected to see you here. I heard you were on the run."

"You heard right."

"You look like you could use a drink." She waved at the bartender. "Joe, a double over here."

Zachariah hadn't intended to drink, but when the shot glass magically appeared, it was damn difficult not to notice how wonderful it smelled. He traced the rim until the glass hummed beneath his touch as he debated whether to take that first swallow. Lifting the glass, he swirled the liquor around. The deep amber color beckoned him like a long lost love.

When he remembered the noose awaiting him if he didn't clear his name, he set the glass down with a thud. He reached in his pocket, removed the two halves of the charm, and lifted them in plain sight. The glow from the overhead lantern lit the metal, flickering its golden light on the opposite wall. "Have you ever seen anything like this before?" He raised his voice enough to carry several feet.

The noise in the room dropped several decibels.

Violet fingered the charm. "What do the markings mean?"

"If I knew that or found its owner, I could probably clear my name."

Violet grabbed paper and a pencil from behind the bar. She slid both halves of the charm together and placing a piece of the paper on top, scribbled until the image appeared. "There," she said. "I'll flash this around to my customers."

Zachariah pressed his mouth to her cheek. "Be careful."

Her blonde hair brushed along his face as she whispered in his ear. "If the man you're looking for comes in here, I'll find him."

When Rebekah awoke, her head ached and her shoulder throbbed. She glanced around the cave and saw the embers of a dying fire and an earthenware jug several feet away. Bracing herself with one hand, she tried to sit but changed her mind because she was too lightheaded. Once the stone walls stopped spinning, she raised a tentative hand to explore her injury and was shocked when her fingers touched the soft fabric of her own dress instead of the stiff material of the shirt she'd had on when she'd fallen asleep.

Upon close inspection, she discovered the scratchy woolen trousers gone, too. Since she was in no shape to change her clothes that left only one person. Zachariah Thompson's heated gaze surfaced in her subconscious, stirring a temper she tried to control.

The man was a despicable hooligan!

The lout couldn't be trusted. Once more, she tried to sit and noted that after bracing herself on raised arms, her head steadied. Though her shoulder pounded like a bloody drum, she bit her lower lip and called out Zachariah's name.

When she glanced at the dress covering her person, she wanted to beat Zachariah over the head with a stick, though she doubted a paltry branch could damage the hard surface. The idea brought a smile to her face.

Because he didn't answer right away, she wondered if he'd abandoned her. When she felt for the chain around her neck and found it missing, she was certain he had.

"Blast the man," she said, her voice low because ladies shouldn't speak in boisterous tones, though Bekah never understood why her brothers could say whatever they wished and she could not.

She waited a few minutes and tried calling Zachariah again. When he didn't answer, her patience vanished, as did her good upbringing. "Damnation, where in the bloody hell are you?" she spouted in a tone fit for brawny men, noting the curse did nothing to rectify how she felt. Her curse echoed inside the cave until she wanted to cover her ears.

Relief flooded through her when Zachariah's form filled the cave opening. "Keep that up, and I'll have to clean out your mouth with soap."

"What happened to the clothes I was wearing, you loathsome creature?"

One corner of his mouth lifted. "Did you mean to wear them again?"

The mere idea of donning the filthy trousers and shirt made her gasp.

He stepped forward. "How's your arm feel?"

"You didn't answer my question."

"Maybe it's better that I don't."

"How dare you undress me while I was asleep."

"You should never drink."

Unwilling to let him see her rancor, she raised her chin. "Why?"

"Lady, as I remember, you were quite helpful." His mocking grin infuriated her.

She didn't like the way he said the word *lady,* even less the way he looked at her. In the back of her mind were memories of a bolder Rebekah, kisses, and saying things she couldn't believe. Surely, her disconnected thoughts were parts of a dream.

Or a nightmare.

His taunting laughter said more than words.

Goodness gracious, she'd thrown herself at him!

Bold as can be, he knelt beside her and reached for the bodice of her dress. She slapped his hands away. "Just what do you think you're doing?"

"I want to check the bullet wound."

"If you have a looking glass, I'll do it myself."

He tapped his temple with his forefinger. "I think I remember seeing one on the divan in our drawing room, my dear."

"I don't find your sarcasm amusing."

"Then stop being a pain in the behind and let me have a look at your shoulder."

Pain in the behind. The nerve of him speaking to her in such a manner. Her fingers itched to leave their imprint on his brazen face, but he caught her hand mid-flight.

"As I see this, you have two choices. Behave yourself and allow me to check your wound, or I'll do it with you hogtied."

She didn't doubt he meant what he said. His gravelly voice stirred the hairs on the back of her neck. "If my brothers were here right now, you'd be sorry."

He glanced behind him and had the audacity to grin. "Unless your brothers come to your rescue in the next few minutes, you're out of luck." One black brow rose. "So, lady, what's it going to be? Do I have to get a rope?"

With a grimace, Rebekah allowed him to slip the dress from her shoulder. When she glanced down, she saw the bloodstains on her chemise. The cap sleeve had been cut away and her upper arm was wrapped in gray material.

She watched him remove the bandage and felt her stomach roil at the sight of the ugly gash. She kept a close eye on Zachariah. Should his gaze stray to her bosom, she was ready to jab him with the sharp rock she'd found on the ground.

Disappointment took hold that he showed no interest.

He covered her quickly and stepped away. "The wound is looking much better. I bathed it." He paused. For the briefest moment their eyes connected. She felt naked under his scrutiny.

He cleared his throat and fastened his gaze at a spot above her head. "I cleaned it with water from the stream. Your arm will be swollen for several days, but I don't expect it to get infected. You're lucky the bullet just grazed you."

She realized he'd probably saved her life. She'd have thanked him if she hadn't pressed her hand to her chest and remembered what he'd done. "You scoundrel, you stole my medallion!"

"I wondered when you'd find out."

"I want you to return my medallion this instant."

"That won't be possible."

"But I helped you get out of jail," she said, hating the way her voice wavered.

"Yes, and I'm much obliged, my lady." He had the nerve to bow from the waist.

She wanted to hurl something at his head, but knew the effort would be fruitless. "And stop calling me lady."

A cocky grin surfaced. "Are you telling me you aren't a lady?"

As his gaze meandered over her features, her heart fluttered like a captured bird, awaking memories of hot kisses, his tongue dancing with hers. Her cheeks flamed, and she turned away. "You never intended to give me your half of the medallion, did you?"

"I'll be needing the charm for a while."

She jerked back around. Pain stabbed her shoulder. "At least, give me back mine." She'd have wrenched the chain from his throat, but his neck was bare as was his chest beneath his cowhide jacket.

He stepped away. "That won't be possible because I need both halves, yours and mine."

"Mr. Thompson, if I were a man, I'd spit in your eye."

He threw back his head and laughed. "Since being in my company, your fine British manners have taken a turn for the worse."

Once the sun set, Zachariah went into the cave to wake Bekah. He was surprised to find her crouched down, searching his saddlebags.

"Why you sneaky, conniving woman."

She gasped, landed on her fanny, and grabbed her shoulder. "How dare you creep up on me like that?"

"Sometimes that's the only way to find out what a woman is up to."

"I was merely trying to take back what's mine."

"I figured as much, but I'm not lamebrained enough to leave the charms where you'd find them."

When he saw her expression, he realized she was in pain so he hurried to her side. "Here, let me check that." Without a fuss, she allowed him to unbutton the bodice of her dress and to inspect the bandage that showed no signs of fresh blood. Pretending to secure the material around her arm, he took a gander at her tiny shell-shaped ear. It took all his willpower not to nibble a trail along the milky column of her neck. "Does it hurt much?"

She blinked away tears and raised her stubborn chin a notch. "Nothing I can't handle."

He grabbed the jug and a nearby tin cup. "I think you could use a drink." He certainly could, but for now, that wasn't possible.

She rested her hand over his about to uncork the jug. "You needn't bother. My drinking days are over."

"A few swallows will help you to relax."

"It might also put me in a situation I cannot control."

"If you're worried about me taking advantage of you, you needn't. You aren't my type."

For a moment she seemed at a loss for words but quickly recovered. "I certainly thank the dear Lord for that."

He bristled at the way she looked down her nose at him. His comment was meant to sting, but instead, it pained him to see her aloofness. "Bear in mind you need me to get you out of here safely."

"Bear in mind, I can no longer trust you. For all I know, you plan to leave me here." She waved a threatening finger in his face. "But I have two good feet. Even without your help, I'll find my way back to civilization."

He caught her finger, brought it to his mouth, and kissed it.

Looking flustered, she yanked her hand away. "Be warned, the next time you kiss me, I'm going to slap your face."

Her British accent made him grin. "The next time I kiss you, it'll be your idea."

SEVEN

"Bekah, we need to get going," Zachariah said, reaching down to assist her.

She spared him a glance filled with loathing and pushed his arm away. "I can manage on my own."

A gentleman would have insisted she needed his help, but he instantly shrugged a shoulder. "Suit yourself. If you aren't outside in two minutes, I'm leaving without you."

She watched his broad back disappear through the cave opening. "Bloody scoundrel," she mumbled beneath her breath. She lay stuck on her back like an overturned turtle, her arm on fire, blinking away tears. She bit her lower lip and somehow managed to sit. Standing was more difficult, but she fortified herself with thoughts of her stolen medallion and managed the feat in record time.

Bekah took a few shaky steps and exited the cave, where she leaned against a large boulder and forced a smile. "Good evening, Jimmy."

The boy grinned. "I'm sure glad you're feeling better."

If she was feeling better, then why did she fear she'd slip to the ground any moment? She spotted Zachariah eyeing her. "It takes more than a little bullet to staunch an Englishwoman's fortitude," she said, her strength ebbing away.

To gain a little time, she focused on the lovely stream gurgling over wet rocks turned silver by the light of a quarter moon. She inhaled several deep gulps of air, pushed herself away from the boulder, and stepped toward the horses. The landscape blurred before her eyes, and it became apparent she'd land on her backside if she didn't grab something for support. When the only available object came covered with a rawhide jacket and an I-told-you-so grin, she swallowed her pride and leaned against Zachariah's chest.

"Why the frown?" he asked.

Much as she hated to admit it, she needed him.

And he no longer needed her.

He'd made a fool of her—no she'd done that on her own by believing he'd give her his medallion. Not only had he gone back on his word, he'd stolen her medallion, too. She wanted to shove him away but couldn't. If she fell, he'd probably leave her there.

In the distance a wolf howled, reminding Bekah she had no choice but to control her temper. For now, she'd allow Zachariah to assist her. When the time came and she'd regained her strength, Mr. Zachariah Thompson would discover he'd picked on the wrong woman. She would not leave until she had both halves of the medallion. The thought eased her mind.

In the end, she'd win.

And Zachariah would be the one wearing the frown.

Bekah was the most stubborn woman Zachariah had ever met, and he prepared himself for the next confrontation. "Can you lift your foot into the stirrup?"

"Isn't this your horse?"

"I figured you'd ride with me."

She eyed him as if he were daft. "Well, you figured wrong, Mr. Thompson."

"You're too weak to ride alone."

Her pupils narrowed. "I'm feeling quite well."

"I can tell," he said, shaking his head as he took in her feeble attempt to stand without his help.

"There." She folded her arms over her chest. "I've regained my strength. I'm perfectly fine now."

He heaved an exasperated sigh. "You look about as steady as a leaf in a gale. Lady, if you think I'm going to argue with you every step of the way, you're sadly mistaken."

Before she could give him any more guff, he lifted her onto his saddle and swung up behind her, imprisoning her between his arms and his thighs. Too late, he realized she wasn't dressed to straddle a horse. He eyed the tiny embroidered daisies on her stockings pressed tight against his legs, and wished she could ride unassisted.

She blew a strand of hair from her forehead, the fire in her eyes directed at him. "You are a despicable crook, a man of no character, and when my brothers get hold of you, you'll wish you'd never met me."

"I already wish that. If it wasn't for you, I'd be long gone, a safe distance from the law."

"How quickly you forget, Mr. Thompson. Were it not for me, you'd be long gone all right, six feet under, and I wouldn't be an outlaw."

Guilt tightened his chest. If it weren't for him, she wouldn't have been wounded. Had he an ounce of decency, he'd drop her off in the nearest town and deposit both halves of the medallion in her palm. But no one had ever accused him of having a lot of decency.

The lady had gotten herself tangled up with the wrong man.

As they wended their way between thick hemlocks, Rebekah drifted in and out of sleep. Though it irked her, she felt safe within Zachariah's arms. The man was a dreadful scoundrel, but he exuded confidence. With him behind her, she could rest because deep in her heart, she was certain he would care for her until she was strong enough to do so herself.

She sighed and nestled deeper into his warmth, felt his fingers rest upon her face and toy with a strand of hair that had come loose. The thick pad of his thumb traced random circles on her neck. Her pulse jumped beneath his touch.

He'd saved her life. He was a hero according to Jimmy. And he'd probably prevented her from falling to the ground by insisting she ride with him. Bekah knew she could be stubborn because her brothers and her parents had reminded her of that fact hundreds of times. She decided to put her pride aside and to tell Zachariah she appreciated his efforts.

"I apologize for giving you grief about riding with you."

"It's nothing."

"And for saving my life with little concern for your own. I only wish I'd been awake to see you dashing in like a knight in shining armor on your steed while bullets flew overhead."

"I said it's nothing."

"Maybe so, but you saved my life, or at least saved me from certain imprisonment. That's something to me." She sighed.

"I'd like you to drop this subject."

"Though I've noticed your armor has several dents."

"It's kind of you to point that out."

"I haven't forgotten that you stole my medallion, but . . ."

She heard the sound of an owl, felt him stiffen. He clamped his hand over her nose and mouth. She struggled to free herself, her eyes widening in fear.

What was he doing?

Surely, he wasn't the sort of man to suffocate a woman.

Or was he?

She tried to pry his hand from her face, but he was too strong. He loosened his grip a little, lowered his head beside her ear, and pointed into the distance. "Shhhh."

She spotted a light and understood that he'd covered her

mouth to silence her. He removed his hand from her face and pulled his horse behind a thick stand of pines. She waited with bated breath as a lit torch approached.

"I can't believe they slipped by us," came a gruff voice.

"I'm certain I wounded one of them, which should slow them down."

"Maybe that one's already dead and buried."

Bekah shivered uncontrollably.

Zachariah tightened his arm around her waist.

"Sooner or later, I'll find Zachariah, the son of a bitch, and when I do, I won't waste time on a hanging. I'll put a bullet between his eyes, and that goes for his accomplice, too."

"Something about his accomplice bothers me. When I walked in on them about to make their getaway, the scrawny one reached into his pocket and held a gun on me. He looked damned familiar, but I don't remember ever seeing him around town."

"Maybe it'll come to you."

"Oh, it will, I never forget a face, and that's one face I ain't likely to forget. The clothes hung on the son of a gun, making me wonder if it might be a kid disguised as a man . . . or maybe a woman."

A shiver sluiced down Bekah's spine.

The two riders passed within thirty feet of their horses. Once they disappeared over the horizon, Zachariah kneed his mount forward and steered them deeper into the forest.

That's one face I ain't likely to forget. They suspected a woman had helped Zachariah break out of jail. Would she eventually end up behind bars, or . . . dead? Bekah had thought her disguise would protect her, but now, she wasn't sure. And if the sheriff caught up with them, he'd know she was involved because of the bullet wound.

Zachariah cupped his hand over his mouth and hooted several times.

Jimmy came out from behind a tree. He screeched like an owl. "Pretty convincing, huh, Miss Benson?"

"You had me fooled."

Pride on his face, he nodded. "Zachariah taught me bird calls some time back. He says it's a good way to warn your partner when someone is after you."

"You did good," Zachariah said. "I've decided to follow the stream. It'll take longer, but if the horses walk along the shallows, no one will be able to follow our tracks come morning. I want you to stay a few hundred feet ahead, Jim. If you see any signs of trouble, you know the signal."

The boy straightened his shoulders and kneed his horse forward.

Bekah aimed a dirty look at Zachariah, which he ignored. "What kind of thing is that to teach a boy?"

"What do you mean?"

"You taught him how to avoid the law."

"It was just a game."

"You expect me to believe that?"

"I guess that's up to you."

"I choose not to believe a word you say."

He touched an index finger to her chin and angled her head around until she was facing him. "Believe me when I say this. I'm no knight. I'm not a hero, and furthermore, I don't want to be one. All I want right now is to be rid of you and James and have myself a good stiff drink!"

Bekah again remembered her stepfather's drunken rages, his uncontrolled fits of anger, and his loud shouting. She'd never understood how a generous, soft-spoken man could turn into such a beast after drinking liquor. She turned and stared ahead into the darkness.

Zachariah's statement left her speechless. For once, she was certain he had spoken the truth. And his words hurt more than her injured shoulder.

Zachariah took the long way home to confuse anyone trying to follow their tracks. Fortunately, he'd kept to himself the last few years so the people in Londonderry didn't know he lived in Litchfield. As they meandered along the dirt path, he saw his log cabin and the Merrimack River in the distance. Dawn tinted the horizon a dull gray. The chill in the damp October air hinted at rain.

He pulled his collar against his neck and looked down at Bekah asleep within his arms. She was such a pretty thing. His heart went out to her. With her eyes shut, she looked so vulnerable and innocent, a fair maiden from England who'd turned his life upside down. He'd be damned if he knew what to do about it.

James rode to his side. "That your house?"

"Built it myself," Zachariah said, a measure of pride swelling inside.

"I bet you could teach me all sorts of things if you let me stay."

"And most of it not fit for a boy to learn."

"I could be a real help to you."

"James, we've been through this all before. It's too dangerous. I'm a wanted man. When Bekah is strong enough to travel, you'll be going with her. So don't be thinking otherwise." He speared James with a serious look. "Besides, I need to clear my name, which means I have to find the real murderer."

"I don't see why I can't help."

"You can't, so accept it."

"Since you were passed out in the alley, you don't even know what the man looks like."

"I think I have something that belongs to him. I'm hoping to flush him out."

"What if . . . ?" A guilty look crossed the boy's face.

"Is there something you aren't telling me?"

James glanced toward the horizon. His thin shoulders drooped. "No, I was just thinking about something."

When Rebekah opened her eyes, she was surprised to see a quaint log cabin surrounded by hemlock and white pines. A wide porch ran the length of the house. In a field about two hundred feet away stood a small barn and a shed.

James leaped from his horse. "This is great!" He ran onto the porch and swung the door open. "Mind if I go inside and have myself a look?"

Zachariah gave a nonchalant wave. "Go ahead."

"What a charming cabin," Rebekah said.

"I'm sure it's small compared to where you grew up."

"It is at that."

"You aren't the first to notice," he said, his tone cold.

Before she could say anything else, he swung down from the horse. His brooding expression warned her to drop the subject. When she glanced at his eyes, reddened from lack of sleep, she attributed his foul mood to exhaustion.

He offered her his arm. After riding most of the night, she was stiff, and her shoulder pulsed. She knew better than to refuse his help. Taking his hand, she slid off the horse, stood, and tried to steady herself.

"Lean against me," he said, wrapping a protective arm around her waist.

As weak as she felt, she glanced at his bare neck. Disappointment swirled inside. Somehow, she'd get her medallion back, and she'd take his half, too.

On wobbly legs, she stepped onto the porch. Nearby, a

donkey brayed. Chickens clucked. A chilling gust of wind swished her skirts around her ankles.

Zachariah kept her anchored by his side, and she was thankful for his assistance.

James shot past them. "I'm gonna go look at the animals in the barn," he shouted over his shoulder without waiting for a reply.

When they entered the house, Rebekah noticed a cluttered room set up as a living room, kitchen combination. Pieces of wood lay everywhere, some stacked along the walls; smaller chunks of wood lay on the table, the counters, and on the floor. She was surprised to see a pile of wood shavings beside a chair in the corner by a large window next to a rickety crate littered with empty whiskey bottles. It proved what she'd feared. Zachariah was a hopeless drunk.

"If I'd known I was having company, I might have picked up a little around here."

A little wouldn't have done the trick, she thought.

"My cabin isn't geared to a lady accustomed to fine things," he said, the sound of his voice unapologetic.

"I don't require much, and I won't be here long enough to miss life's comforts."

"Thank goodness for that."

His obvious relief pained her and made her wonder if he cared at all. Of course, he didn't. A caring man wouldn't steal from her. She appeased herself with the knowledge she'd even the score soon enough.

He swung a door open that led to a bedroom. "You should be comfortable here."

It was a well-lit room with a large bed adorned with an impressive mahogany headboard, a simple bureau, a wooden chair, and a chest, the wood's deep reddish tint accentuated by the light from the windows. A green coverlet with frayed edges was thrown over the bed, its rumpled shape giving the illusion someone was still sleeping beneath the covers.

Zachariah slapped his thigh. "Beauregard, you know better than to sleep on my bed."

Rebekah wondered to whom he was speaking. More importantly, she wondered where Zachariah was planning to sleep.

The misshapen bedspread stirred. Out popped the head of an ugly creature. Loose flesh hung from its bony skeleton like a stretched-out stocking. Its bloodshot eyes took her in before settling on Zachariah. When recognition struck, it emitted a mournful howl.

Rebekah jumped back in surprise.

The dog leaped off the bed and hobbled toward them, its short tail whipping the air. Zachariah's face lit at the sight of the mangy short-legged creature whose tongue lolled almost to the floorboards.

With a wide grin, Zachariah nodded. "Lady Bekah, I'd like you to meet my loyal companion, Beauregard."

"Is this a dog?"

"Yes, but don't let on because he thinks he's one of us."

"That's ridiculous."

Zachariah rubbed the top of the hound's head and winked at her as if they were sharing a deep secret. "Not to him, it isn't."

She'd grown accustomed to his scowl, but this side of Zachariah surprised her. She felt the effects of the teasing glint in his eyes clear to her toes.

Meanwhile, inside the Blooming Garden, Violet flashed the imprint of Zachariah's charm to every customer willing to look. As she sashayed by, a large bear of a man missing a front tooth pulled her onto his lap. "How 'bout letting me have a look-see at that there drawing."

Eight

Feeling incredibly tired, Rebekah rubbed her forehead and slouched against the doorframe. Before she could protest, Zachariah swung her into his arms, yanked the green coverlet from the bed, and set her down on the soft mattress. Her shoulder pulsed like a drum. If he hadn't picked her up, she might have slipped to the floor.

To hide her embarrassment she glanced at Beauregard. "What kind of dog is that?"

"A stubborn one. It wouldn't surprise me to find out he has English blood running through his veins." The hint of humor in his voice took her off guard.

He was comparing her to a dog! "You really know how to charm a lady."

"He's part hound, part only God knows what else," he said, avoiding her eyes. "He isn't perfect, and in case you haven't noticed, neither am I. I'll try to keep him from bothering you."

She liked animals, but she saw no reason to point that out. "How many rooms does this house have?"

"You've seen them all," he replied his tone dropping several degrees.

"Oh." She paused. "This is the only bedroom?"

"That would be my guess."

"Where will you sleep?"

"Is that an invitation?" The suggestive glint in his eyes brought a rush of color to her face.

"Where's my valise?"

He raised his eyebrows and glanced around the room. "I guess my servant hasn't brought it in yet. I assure you, I'm going to have a serious talk with him."

"I don't appreciate your sarcasm."

"Look, I didn't mean to sound off. But now that I have, let me make myself clear. I don't like having you here. As soon as you're well enough to travel, I'm throwing you out on your behind."

She did her best not to react. His lack of decorum astounded her. "I can almost feel my strength returning. I will not spend one minute more than is absolutely necessary under your roof, Mr. Thompson."

"That's a relief to me, Miss Benson. I'll get your valise and let you rest."

A few minutes later he brought in her bag and set it beside the bed. "I'm brewing some tea for you with a little corn juice to dull your pain and your tongue."

Since the throbbing in her shoulder radiated down her arm and into her hand, she nodded in agreement.

Zachariah slapped the side of his leg. "Let's go, Beauregard." The large dog stretched out and laid its head on its front paws. One drooping eyelid squinted open. Zachariah uttered a hopeless sigh and grabbed the animal by the scruff of the neck, yanking it out of the room.

When Zachariah and the dog had left, Rebekah dug in her valise and extracted a long hatpin, which she hid under the pillow.

If Zachariah tried anything, she was ready.

Zachariah poured water into the kettle and placed it on the cookstove. He glanced at his dog stretched out at his feet. "I know what you're thinking, and you can forget it. You have no more business sleeping in that room than I do. A woman like that isn't going to give either of us the time of day. So don't go getting any fool notions."

The door opened and bounced against the wall as James ran in. "Who you talking to?"

He nodded toward his companion. "Meet Beauregard."

"Wow, you have a dog, too."

"I'm afraid so."

"Who looks out for your animals when you're gone?"

"A neighbor keeps an eye on them."

"I never had a dog of my own. You sure are lucky. If I lived here, I'd take care of all the animals for you, but I'd take 'specially good care of Beauregard."

Zachariah ignored the pleading look in James's eyes and poured tea into a chipped mug. He took the jug of corn liquor he'd brought in earlier and topped off the cup. "Here," he said, "take this in to Miss Benson and make sure she drinks every last drop."

"How come you aren't calling her Bekah?"

Zachariah did his best to look mean. "If you want to stay with me awhile, you won't be asking a bunch of fool questions."

The boy clamped his mouth shut and nodded. A moment later Zachariah heard voices coming from his bedroom. Since the door was slightly ajar, Beauregard stuck his snout into the narrow opening.

"Get back here," Zachariah ordered.

The dog turned around, its drooping bloodshot eyes staring into his for a moment before ignoring the command.

Zachariah sat in his chair, picked up a knife on the table, and started to whittle. He'd been rude to Bekah and had acted like a real jackass. She brought out the worst in him. Maybe it was because she reminded him of someone else who'd trampled his heart and his soul until no life remained.

The blade of his sharp knife shaved off a thin sliver of wood along with a layer of skin. He swore and threw the knife on the crate. He was exhausted, hungry, and thirsty. He pressed his handkerchief to the cut on his thumb and closed his eyes. Whenever he tried to rest, he'd imagine Bekah's syrupy voice.

Damn that English accent.

He opened his eyes and shook his head. Was he losing his mind? He didn't stand a chance with Bekah, and even if he did, he'd turn it down.

Edgy, cross, and unable to think, he threw the piece of wood across the room and heard the ping of glass. He glanced at the chunk of wood, and behind it, the bottle of whiskey that seemed to be calling his name. He stared at the bottle, fighting a battle he knew he couldn't win.

Finally, feeling weak and defeated, he rose and hurried across the room. With trembling fingers, he pulled out the cork, lifted the bottle to his mouth, and drank.

He sauntered back to his chair, where he sat and let out a deep sigh. Every nerve in his body relaxed when he took another swig and felt the fiery liquid sliding down his throat.

Deep in his subconscious came the unwelcome thought; this wasn't right. Both Bekah and James depended on him to keep them safe.

He hesitated for only a moment.

Ignoring his responsibilities, he drank until all his troubles drifted away.

Rebekah awoke with a start. Damn that Zachariah, she thought, aware of the soft snoring coming from the pillow behind her and the weight of the body pressed against her back. At least he hadn't climbed under the covers.

He stretched, trying to claim what little remained of the bed, and took the liberty of curling his arm around her middle. His deep satisfied sigh stirred the hairs on the back of her head.

Lordy, his breath could stop a stampeding steed in its tracks.

And it wasn't simply his breath.

She wondered how she'd missed the pungent odor while riding with him. When had he last bathed?

The image of Zachariah Thompson wearing nothing but his skin was not one she wanted to entertain. But she did—for only the briefest moment—or possibly a tad longer.

He let out another heaving breath.

This time, she pinched her nose shut and counted her blessings—being a spinster had its advantages.

He edged closer, jarring her sense of propriety.

What if James walked into the room and found them lying in the same bed!

She reached beneath the pillow and wrapped her fingers around her long hatpin, ready to defend herself if need be. She turned and gasped when she spotted Beauregard's head on the pillow. The hatpin slipped from her fingers, landed on the floor, and rolled under the bed.

The startled animal let out a deep howl sure to wake the entire population of New Hampshire.

She prepared herself for the inevitable.

Any moment Zachariah would enter the bedroom with a sarcastic grin. When a few minutes went by without any sign of him, she assumed he hadn't heard.

The dog edged closer, took a sniff, and before she could stop it, ran its wet tongue along the side of her face. She shoved the creature away. "Behave yourself," she said. The beast was as ill-mannered as its owner.

Beauregard regarded her with watchful eyes.

Until now, she hadn't thought of her injury, but she felt remarkably better. Sleeping in a real bed had done wonders.

With great care, she stood and was pleased to discover she

wasn't dizzy. She slowly raised her left arm. Although it hurt, she could tolerate the discomfort. She was not yet as good as new, but she was definitely on the mend.

Her brothers liked to say she had the stamina of a racehorse, as Rebekah was always the first to bounce back from childhood illnesses.

But Zachariah didn't know that.

As she stood there, Beauregard eyeing her suspiciously, a plan materialized. Until both pieces of her medallion were safely tucked away in her valise, she'd make sure she recovered slowly. Until she was certain she could ride away with no one following her, she would pretend to be weak and helpless.

Otherwise, Zachariah would throw her out on her *behind,* not her choice of words, but his.

She smiled in satisfaction. Then she stepped across the room to test her strength. She wasn't ready to run a race, but she could walk unassisted.

She looked down at her nightgown and cringed. This wasn't appropriate attire for an unmarried lady to wear in front of a man.

Especially not Zachariah. His heated gaze seemed capable of melting away layers of clothing.

She dug in her bag for her wrap. Slipping on the outer garment, she secured the buttons clear to her neck and turned up the collar.

Once she was certain she was appropriately covered, she eased the door open and peeked into the living quarters. The sunlight coming through the window gave the wooden interior a buttery glow. Were it not for the clutter of bottles and wood littering the floor and shelves, it would be a pleasant dwelling.

The odor of alcohol permeated the air, reminding her that Zachariah's one true love came in a bottle or a jug. He was an impossible drunk. The thought wrenched her heart, and she tried to ignore the wave of sadness that followed.

She spotted him sprawled in an overstuffed chair, his head tipped to one side, the fingers of one hand curled around a chunk of wood, the other hand around the neck of a whiskey bottle.

According to her stepmother, little could wake an inebriated man.

Rebekah figured she'd use this opportunity to find her medallion. She wondered whether it might be on his person. Need be, she'd check his pockets, but not until she'd exhausted all other possibilities.

When she looked around, she spotted two wooden containers about ten inches in diameter on the shelf across the room. After casting a furtive glance at Zachariah, she took several careful steps and lifted the lid on the first container. Inside were strips of leather, assorted knives, and a wooden flute, its surface like satin beneath her fingertips.

She tossed Zachariah a sidelong glance before opening the next box. It contained carved birds: a robin, a blue jay, and a chickadee, each more beautiful than the next. She slid her fingers along the smooth surfaces and wondered whether Zachariah was responsible for the intricate detail.

This time when she glanced at him, she studied the piece of wood in his hands. Curious, she edged nearer. Even in its unfinished state, she recognized an eagle, its powerful wings in flight.

For the first time since meeting him, she saw a talented man capable of creating much beauty. Had she the power to do so, she'd wrap her arms around him and chase away his desire to drink.

But only he could control that demon.

Many men had tried and failed.

When she reached down to touch the carved feathers on the

eagle's chest, Zachariah stirred. She froze until she was certain he was still asleep.

Already growing weary but determined to find her medallion, she stared down at him and tried to fortify her courage. No proper lady dug into the pockets of a man's trousers—especially while he was wearing them! It seemed too intimate—and much too close to male body parts no real lady thought about.

She'd lost all sense of propriety!

Zachariah had driven her mind into the gutter.

She eyed him for a long moment, noting his thick dark lashes and steady breathing. She wondered how he'd look without a beard. Inhaling a deep breath for courage, she reached down and touched the edge of his pocket, willing her fingers to plunge inside.

Figuring she had no choice, she finally slipped her hand into the pocket and felt around. Once she was certain the medallion was not there, she pulled her hand out so quickly she knocked the bottle from his grasp.

It crashed to the floor.

And exploded.

To Rebekah it sounded like a bomb.

She leaped back, covered her mouth, and stared at Zachariah. The abrupt movement jarred her shoulder. Pain shot down her arm.

Still he slept.

She didn't know how long she stood there before daring to search the other pocket because it took considerable time to reinforce her courage. Once she made up her mind, she shoved her hand into the trouser pocket without hesitation. The sooner she completed the task, the sooner she could escape, and rest, and try to put this dastardly episode behind her.

A feeling of victory burst forth when she touched the medallion's jagged edge. She wrapped her fingers around both halves when a large hand gripped her wrist.

She lost her balance and landed over Zachariah's lap. She didn't want to meet his eyes, not while her hand was in his pocket, not while her backside was facing the ceiling. It was one thing to break the rules of decorum, quite another to be caught—red-handed—and in such an unladylike predicament.

Yet she couldn't stay like this forever.

It wasn't easy to banish the embarrassment from her face, replacing it with the haughty look of someone who'd done nothing wrong, but she did and lifted her head, taking in his steady gaze.

A cocky grin surfaced and widened. "Maybe you are my type of woman after all."

Zachariah squinted to clear his vision. His brain pounded against his forehead. His tongue, covered with a thick layer of moss, turned his stomach. Every hair follicle ached. He felt like hell. Yet his hangover almost vanished when he glanced down at Bekah dressed for a winter storm, lying over his knee with an innocent look in her eyes, her fingers in his pocket.

When he released her wrist, she pulled her hand out without claiming her prize.

"I see you're feeling much better."

She leaped to her feet and cradled her injured arm with her right hand. "I'm still a tad weak, and my head's a mite dizzy."

Her British accent soothed his roiling stomach. She brought her hand to her forehead and closed her eyes, but he caught her peeking between fluttering eyelids. "I'd appreciate it if you could help me back to bed."

"I bet if you try really hard, you can find your way by yourself." The flush of her cheeks added to her beauty. Her wide blue eyes reminded him of a summer sky right before a storm. Certain she was up to no good, he ignored her plea. He was shocked to see her take three small wobbly steps before slipping slowly to the floor.

"Bekah!" He hoped the fall hadn't reopened the bullet wound. He rushed to her side and hunched over her still form, lifting her into his lap. As he cradled her against him, he was relieved she hadn't bruised her face—what a shame it would be to see a blackened eye or a split lip. "Bekah, can you hear me?" As he peered into her face, he brushed a strand of hair from her cheek, noting its texture was as silky as freshly polished wood.

He cupped her chin in his hand and tilted her head up, checking for signs of injury. "Bekah, honey, open your eyes." He waited a few seconds for a response.

He let out an exasperated breath. "I'm a selfish good-for-nothing," he chided in a low tone and thought he detected the hint of a satisfied smile, which vanished the instant she opened her eyes.

"Zachariah, where am I?"

He feared the blow to her head might have done some damage. "You're at my cabin. You've taken a fall."

Looking disoriented, she glanced around the room. "Oh, I feel so weak and lightheaded."

"Do you think you can stand?"

"I can try."

"Here, let me help you to your feet. Maybe I should carry you."

"That won't be necessary. I don't want to be a hindrance."

Hindrance about summed up how he felt about her. She'd caused him a lot of trouble.

Though it pained him to admit it, he wanted his home ringing with the sound of children's voices. He wanted to share his thoughts and his life with a woman he loved.

She'd saved his life, but she'd reopened old wounds.

His past would never again allow him to trust another woman.

Clearly in worse shape than he'd originally thought, she stood on trembling legs and leaned into him, shaking like a newborn kitten. When she angled her head into the crook of his neck, he felt content for the first time in years. Holding her close seemed so right and at the same time so wrong. He could never have her, wouldn't chance that degree of pain again.

She smiled shakily. "I'm glad you don't think me burden-some."

He grinned. "Of course not. A nuisance maybe, but never a hindrance or a burden."

Her startled expression wrenched a laugh from deep in his chest. The twinkle in her eyes warmed him.

"You are not likely to ever sweep a lady off her feet with your charm."

Her words sobered him.

As he helped her to his bedroom, he had to step over Beaure-gard sprawled alongside the bed. "Would you like me to get him out of here?" he asked, inclining his head toward the dog.

"As long as he doesn't insist on kissing me again, I don't mind if he stays."

"Lucky dog," he said, the words out before he could stop them.

Her pupils widened before she glanced away.

Zachariah thought back to the first time he'd kissed her in his jail cell and the feel of his arms around her as she tried to push him away. How could he forget? He dreamed of Bekah every night.

He wondered how it would feel to have her kiss him back, urging him to love her.

If he hadn't had his arm around Bekah, he'd have slapped his head, hoping to jar some common sense into his dense skull. He wanted her, craved her with every cell of his being. What he wanted and what he could have were two different things. He didn't kid himself into believing he stood a chance with the lady.

He helped her to sit down on his bed and lifted her legs onto the mattress, his fingers lingering on her slim ankles. Her rosy complexion gave her cheeks a healthy glow. He adjusted the pillow behind her head.

Without realizing what he was doing, he bent, pressed his lips to her forehead, and hurried out of the room before he made a bigger fool of himself.

Zachariah figured he'd stay away from Bekah as much as possible. She had him hankering for things better left forgotten. He didn't need a woman in his life, or children, or love. For him, this didn't exist, never had, and never would.

As a kid, he'd crossed his fingers and wished for a brother and a sister and parents who cared.

As he grew older, he'd come to realize crossed fingers and wishes were a waste of time.

Behind him, the door to the cabin opened and slammed shut.

"You sure were a goner last time I come in here. Someone could have stolen the chair from under you, and you'd have been none the wiser."

Zack threw James a disgruntled look. "Can't a man have a drink without some wise-mouth kid giving him a load of guff?"

The boy shrugged. "I wasn't giving you a hard time, just looking out for you." A smile surfaced on his freckled face. "Besides, if you'd let me stay here, I could keep an eye on things when you can't."

Zachariah refused to broach the subject again. He handed James a plate of sandwiches. "Here, these are for you and Miss Benson. Take them into the bedroom, then come back for a cup of tea and a glass of milk."

"I'd rather have coffee, like you," James said.

"Growing boys need milk." He saw the admiration in the kid's eyes. "And the less you imitate me, the better off you'll be."

The boy took the plate and returned a moment later for the beverages. When he disappeared into the bedroom, Zachariah sat in his chair and peered out the window at the unfinished barn in the distance. What had happened to his ambition and his love of life? This train of thought led nowhere; he picked up the knife and the piece of wood from the table and whittled a few feathers on the chest of the eagle he'd begun weeks earlier.

His hands shook so much he could barely control the knife blade.

Only one thing could stop his tremors.

He glanced up, his gaze locking on the jug across the room. He set the carving and the knife aside and leaned his head against the chair. Earlier, his judgment had been clouded by his need for a drink. If the killer had come looking for the charm, Zachariah would have been in no shape to defend James or Bekah.

He was a sorry excuse for a man.

Disgusted with himself, he stared at the jug of corn liquor.

His mouth watered.

His heartbeat quickened.

The truth came to him like a drum roll.

By drinking, he'd failed James, who looked up to him as no other human being ever had.

By drinking, he'd failed Bekah, who deserved to be protected by him until she was well again. Were it not for her, he'd have rope burns around his sorry neck. He owed her his life, and yet he'd jeopardized hers by his callous actions.

As he licked his parched lips, the little voice inside his head whispered, *"One drink won't hurt."*

"Just one drink," the voice repeated, making him wonder if

he'd lost his mind.

He started to stand but slouched back down.

If he drank again, he'd fail James.

He'd fail Bekah.

Most of all, he'd fail himself.

He heaved a sigh, picked up the unfinished eagle and the knife and made a few cuts.

"*Just one drink,*" rang the incessant voice.

He concentrated on the feathers beneath the bird's neck.

Just one drink.

He swallowed hard.

The blade slipped, nipping off the tip of the beak, yet he continued to snip away slivers of wood.

He had to keep busy.

Just one drink.

The sharp blade gouged the top of the bird's head. Still he concentrated on the rapidly deteriorating wooden bird in his trembling hands.

He focused on the knife, trying to forget about the jug of corn liquor across the room.

Just one drink.

Somehow, he'd beat the devil in that bottle calling out to him.

Somehow, he'd find the strength to never drink again.

NINE

When Rebekah awoke, she heard Beauregard's soft snoring beside the bed. She sat and stretched. Her shoulder felt much better. Only a tiny twinge reminded her of the bullet grazing her arm. She'd be fit to travel in another couple of days. Meanwhile she had to find the medallion and hide her rapid recovery from Zachariah, which she assumed would be easy.

Though she'd faked her fall yesterday, the concern in his eyes had been real. She'd felt a moment's remorse but knew the deception was necessary. A surge of victory had rushed over her, as if she were sparring with a worthy opponent and had won. The feeling lingered even this morning. She looked forward to the next match. When she left with both halves of the medallion, Zachariah would know he'd toyed with the wrong woman.

From outside came the steady beat of a hammer, and she wondered whether James might be trying to prove his worth by doing repairs. He was willing to do anything so Zachariah would allow him to stay. Eventually, Zachariah would break his heart, and James would be homeless again. She wished she could help the boy, but she'd be staying at her brother's house, and in time, probably returning to England.

From the angle of the sunrays streaming through the window, she guessed it was slightly after dawn. She'd slept most of yesterday and all of last night.

She climbed out of bed and rummaged through her valise for something appropriate to wear. When she'd first arrived in

Boston, she'd left her trunks aboard the ship with instructions to deliver them along with her note to her brother Mark. She had little to wear, and one of her garments was bloodstained. Before donning a clean dress, she needed to bathe. How could she accomplish that in a two-room house? She'd rather smell like stale tobacco and sweat than chance baring it all to one Zachariah Thompson.

Leaving on her nightdress, she pulled her wrap over her arms and buttoned it to her chin, then inched the bedroom door open. She expected to see Zachariah passed out cold, but when she peeked though the small slit in the door, she noticed his chair was vacant.

She stepped into the living quarters and couldn't believe her eyes. Someone had swept the floor. The piles of sawdust were gone. Only a few pieces of wood remained next to his chair, but even they were neatly stacked. There were no bottles in sight. If one were to enter this house, he'd never suspect a drinking man inhabited the premises. The only liquor around was the jug of corn whiskey. When she pried the cork off and peered inside, she saw it was almost full—though probably not for long when Zachariah got his hands on it.

Behind her, she heard the click of Beauregard's claws on the plank flooring. She headed toward the water pitcher on the table, filled a glass from a nearby shelf, and drank. The dog's sad eyes followed her movement. She patted its head, and it lapped her hand. Figuring he might be thirsty, she found a large bowl, and after filling it with water, set it on the floor and watched him drink for a few seconds. Then she noticed the animal's deformed back leg, and she wondered how he'd been injured.

The relentless hammering again caught her attention. She peered out the window and was surprised to see Zachariah perched high on a ladder. Standing on the ground beneath him,

James was sawing a board in half. As she stood there admiring Zachariah's powerful build, she noticed someone had arranged the bird carvings on the windowsill. They were beautiful, each a work of art, except for the eagle. Words escaped her when she studied the beakless creature, its misshapen head, nicked wing, and uneven legs a sharp contrast to the exquisite detail of the wooden robin, the blue jay, and the chickadee. She reached the only logical conclusion: James must have whittled the poor specimen, and Zachariah was trying to encourage him, proving he wasn't a coldhearted man.

She picked up the eagle and ran her finger over its rough edges. Even a boy James's age should see the flaws in this carving. Were it not for the wide wingspan, she wouldn't have guessed its species. It was grotesque, yet warmth flooded her chest at the thought of Zachariah's kindness toward the boy.

"What are you doing with that?"

At the sound of Zachariah's booming voice, she swung around and dropped the eagle carving at her feet. She didn't have to fake her trembling limbs when she looked at him. His shirt was unbuttoned to the waist, exposing a wide expanse of his muscled chest.

"Doing?" she asked and realized her voice had sounded too strong. "Admiring the carvings," she continued, her tone wavering like an old woman about to draw her last breath. Much too quickly she bent to pick up the eagle, but she made up for her mistake when she straightened, screwing her features into a tortured look and pouting her lower lip, urging tears to spring to her eyes. Unfortunately, she'd never acquired the skill of crying on demand, and her efforts didn't produce one blasted tear.

He moved in front of her, overwhelming her with his size, his steady gaze hiking her temperature. He took the battered carving from her hand and examined it.

"I hope I didn't harm it when it fell," she said.

"I don't think you could hurt this if you tried."

She smiled and reached for his arm, a mistake because her fingers tingled from the contact. "I think it's wonderful what you're doing."

He raised a brow. "Since I don't usually see adoration on your face, you're either mistaken, or I did something I can't remember because I was drunk."

"The eagle in your hand. It's James's, isn't it?"

Without answering, he placed the malformed carving on the windowsill and regarded her for a long moment.

She brushed her hair from her forehead and tried to ignore his steady gaze.

"You seem stronger this morning."

His comment disturbed her. "Strong? Me? I'm feeling weak as a fledging struggling to leave its nest."

His grin turned cocky. "Are you up to something?"

She lifted a trembling hand to her brow, her lashes lowering. In her weakest voice, she mumbled, "Whatever do you mean? I found the journey from the bedroom to this window extremely taxing. I had to stop and rest at the table before continuing, and had I not taken a sip of water, I might have fainted dead away. And you dare to stand there asking whether I'm up to something." She flinched at the loud tone of her voice, but he mistook her action for pain.

"Does your arm hurt a lot today?" With infinite care, he reached for the collar of her wrap. "Maybe I should have a look."

She slapped his hand away. "Have you gone mad?" Fearing the indignation in her features might give her a healthy glow, she fanned her face with her hand. "It's awfully hot in here, don't you think?"

His arms wrapped around her waist, cradling her against him. "Here, let me steady you. I don't want you to collapse like you did yesterday."

Pushing him away would only discredit her. Though she liked being near him, she told herself she didn't. Unfortunately, she knew the truth. Smiling feebly, she clung to him, her trembling hands anchored to his arms. He smelled like pine trees and soap, an enticing scent. When she glanced up, his full beard brushed her forehead. To prevent her fingers from caressing his face, she clutched the front of his shirt. "I fear I may have already overdone this morning."

"Your eyes are beautiful."

Didn't he know what his heated gaze did to her? "I had to sit and rest in the chair by the table." This sounded familiar. Had she already had this discussion with him?

His voiced softened. "And when you blush, your eyes are even prettier."

She cleared her throat. "Were it not . . . for the drink of water, I . . . I might have fainted."

"When my mother was ill, I could see in her eyes when she was in pain."

She lifted her chin, daring him to say what was on his mind. "And what do you see in my eyes?" she asked, afraid he'd tell her she looked strong enough to leave.

"I see desire."

"What?" She wrung her hands.

"I can tell you want me."

"Your arrogance astounds me." Though she'd meant the statement to sound flippant, her tone betrayed her conviction.

As his face sobered, his gaze locked with hers. He rested his hand on her shoulder. One finger found its way to the sensitive flesh at the base of her neck. "Remember what I asked you in my jail cell?"

At the moment she couldn't remember her own name.

Running his fingers along the side of her face, he whispered, his tone deep and sensuous, "I asked you whether you'd spend the night with me if you could."

How could a woman forget a question like that?

"Do you know what you said?"

Her mind stopped functioning.

A corner of his mouth inched upward. "You said the guards would never allow that."

She pursed her mouth to say *oh,* but no sound escaped.

"I had some trouble sleeping last night, and do you know what thought struck me?"

She pried her tongue from the roof of her mouth. "What?"

"There are no guards here now. I wondered what you'd say if I asked you again."

He lowered his face to hers. She thought he was going to kiss her—prayed that he would.

"The last time I kissed you, I made a promise. For now, I'll have to content myself with this." He dampened his fingertip with his tongue and moistened her lower lip with his light touch. "If you want me to kiss you, you only have to say the word."

Want him to kiss her?

Did he even have to ask?

Was he having a jolly time intimidating the English spinster?

She started to glance away, but he rested a finger beneath her chin, urging her to face him.

"Well . . ."

She could either admit he was right or try to salvage her dignity. She pulled away from him, stiffening her spine. "Well nothing . . . this is preposterous. First, I break you out of jail, then you steal my medallion, and now you stand there suggesting I might want to throw myself at you." She took a breath, letting it out in short bursts. "You must be a muttonheaded nodcock to imply such a thing." Too late, she realized she was waving her hands around to make her point. Her feeble state had evaporated in the heat of anger.

"You still haven't answered my question."

"You're impossible."

He laughed. "If I'm wrong, then say you don't want me to kiss you."

His dark pupils mesmerized her, made her feel warm and woozy. She attempted a cool smile. "How will you know if I'm telling the truth?"

"Because I see the answer in your eyes."

"You're quite sure of yourself."

"Always."

The door creaked open, and James's voice rang out, "What's for breakfast?"

Rebekah leaped back. Though she'd turned from Zachariah, she felt his presence behind her. "Good morning, Jimmy," she said in a tone that belied her weak state. She lifted a trembling hand and turned so Zachariah wouldn't miss her fluttering lashes. "I'm a mite weary. I think I'd better sit."

Both James and Zachariah rushed to her side, assisting her into a chair by the table. Zachariah's hands lingered longer than necessary on her upper arm. "My neighbor made us a loaf of sourdough bread. I thought I'd cook eggs this morning along with ham."

"I'm not sure whether I have the strength to eat," she said, leaning her chin on her upturned hand and issuing a sigh.

He threw her a suspicious glance.

Could he read her thoughts? Would he force her to leave the instant he discovered she could ride again?

"Bekah, you have to eat to keep up your strength."

She inclined her head toward him, her smile tremulous.

He turned to James. "Don't you think Miss Benson looks stronger this morning?"

James stopped patting Beauregard and flashed Rebekah a

grin. "Yup, she looks fine to me." Then without fanfare he went back to patting the dog. "Beauregard stinks." The boy wrinkled his nose.

Zachariah eyed the pair. "Be careful, or you'll hurt his feelings. Besides, both of you would benefit from a good washing. After breakfast, I'll look around for some clean clothes for you to wear, and later when we're through working, you two can take a dip in the stream."

"Is the stream close by?" Rebekah asked, wondering if a weak woman would have the stamina to make the trip.

"Not too far, but if you want to bathe," Zachariah said, taking a cast-iron skillet off the peg, "James and I will lug in the tub and fill it with warm water after we eat."

"Yes, I'd appreciate that."

Zachariah spooned a wedge of lard into the skillet and cracked open several eggs. The smell of ham and eggs soon filled the room.

Fifteen minutes later Zachariah scooped a generous serving of eggs, ham, and fried potatoes into their plates before setting the fry pan in the center of the table. The mingled aromas of the cooked food, warm bread and coffee made Rebekah's mouth water. She was famished, but she couldn't dig in and ask for seconds with Zachariah watching. She couldn't even eat everything on her plate.

Weak people picked at their breakfast, leaving most of their food uneaten. She cut the crusts off a thick slice of bread, and after applying a thin layer of apple butter, took the tiniest bite. The flaky bread melted in her mouth, increasing her hunger.

She stole a glance at Zachariah and watched his hands shake when he lifted his cup of coffee to his mouth. Coffee sloshed over the rim. When he realized she was looking at him, shame streaked across his face.

Rebekah busied herself with the folds in her shirt, trying to erase the ache inside. Why should it matter to her that he was wasting his life? Once she had her medallion, she'd leave and never see him again. The hollow feeling intensified. Liquor was responsible for his deteriorating condition. It might eventually kill him. A rush of sadness swept through her.

"Zack says me and him are gonna fix up that old barn good as new, right Zack?"

Zachariah nodded and poured tea in Rebekah's cup. "You're a great help and a quick learner, too."

James beamed. "I sure like working with you. I figure if I spend enough time here, I'll be able to build just about anything."

Rebekah cut her toast into tiny squares and tried to ignore her hunger pangs. Wanting to encourage the boy, Rebekah nodded at the wooden birds. "I'm really impressed with the carvings on the windowsill. James, which is your favorite?"

He shrugged. "I don't really have a favorite."

"I especially like the eagle because it represents effort. Do you understand?" Rebekah squeezed his shoulder. The gesture, meant to encourage him, filled her with love for the boy.

James chuckled, clearly too humiliated to admit ownership of the nicked creation. "It looks like Beauregard carved the eagle with his teeth."

"It's not perfect, but I like it," she continued, hoping to ease the boy's discomfort. "You must never be embarrassed because your first attempt isn't perfect. Pity the man who goes through life never daring to take a chance."

Confusion clouded James's blue eyes.

Rebekah covered his hand with hers. "I love the eagle because the person who carved it has a special place in my heart."

James dropped his fork, looked at her as though she'd lost her mind. "Are you thinking I carved that?"

"Well, yes . . . I assumed . . ." If James was not responsible, then who?

Zachariah slammed his coffee mug down on the wooden table. "It's mine. Now if it's all the same with the two of you, I want this discussion dropped."

When she saw how he clenched his fingers to control the tremors, she understood. The embarrassment that streaked across his face was unmistakable. Wishing she had never brought up the subject, she trained her eyes on her uneaten meal.

Hoping to change the subject, she asked, "What happened to Beauregard's leg?"

"I don't know," he replied without a glance.

"When did it happen?"

"Beats me."

Finally, she understood. Zachariah had been too drunk at the time of the incident to remember. The thought saddened her.

Zachariah put his fork down beside his plate. "I was out hunting and along came a man, rifle raised ready to shoot his dog."

"How could anyone do such a thing?"

"Easy. At the time Beauregard could barely walk. His owner didn't want him. I thought the poor beast deserved another chance."

Face flaming with guilt because she'd jumped to the wrong conclusion, Rebekah kept her gaze riveted on her plate. Her opinion of Zachariah rose dramatically. He drank too much, was untrustworthy, but any man who'd rescue a deformed animal also deserved another chance.

For the next few minutes, the only sound in the room was the scraping of James's fork against his plate until he pointed toward Rebekah's breakfast. "If you don't want your bread, can I have it?"

Rebekah's survival instincts surfaced.

Her first impulse was to slap James's hands away. She stared down at the bread, the apple butter coating so inviting she dipped her finger into the sweet spread and licked.

Her stomach moaned, but she shoved her plate away and forced a weak smile, which was easy for someone on the verge of starvation. "I cannot eat another bite. Help yourself to anything you want."

Her mouth watered when James stuffed her bread into his mouth.

Zachariah pushed his plate away, too. She noticed he'd eaten very little, no doubt too hungover to enjoy this feast. Normally, Rebekah had a small appetite, but right now, she could have eaten the entire loaf of bread and asked for more.

She tapped her handkerchief on her lips. "Breakfast was wonderful."

Zachariah leaned back in his chair, his brow furrowing. "You ate very little."

Feigning exhaustion, she slouched forward, rested her elbows on the table, and supported her chin on her clasped hands. "I'm sure my appetite will return when I'm stronger."

"I'm beginning to wonder when that will be."

"Why is that?"

"One minute you seem fine, the next ready to kick the bucket."

She issued a long-suffering sigh. "If you are insinuating that I'm faking, you pay me a great disservice." The haughty tone of voice bolstered her case.

"Can you blame me for having some doubts? A short while ago, you looked as though you were on death's doorstep, and in the next breath, you're flapping your arms like an outraged mother hen. And yesterday, one minute you're a slick-fingered pickpocket, the next you're dropping to the floor like a rock."

She preferred the term feather to rock, but she kept her

opinion to herself. "Easy for you to sit there questioning my recovery. That bullet tore off a chunk of my shoulder."

"It was barely a scratch," he said, his taunting grin infuriating her.

"If you're so anxious to be rid of me, why don't you strap me to a saddle and send me on my way? I'll manage somehow. Though if I crumble to the forest floor and am attacked by bears, my demise will be on your conscience."

His smile broadened, his black eyes twinkling with amusement. "That's not such a bad idea. James, when you're through eating, check in the barn, see if we have a length of rope long enough to tie Bekah to a saddle."

While Zachariah and James hauled the tub inside and heated water for her bath, she gathered her soiled clothing from the bedroom. A few minutes later Rebekah discovered it took great effort to remember to take small steps. Her chemise hidden beneath her bloodstained dress, she managed to smile innocently at Zachariah as she crossed the room at a snail's pace and set the porcelain basin in the sink.

"I don't want you to overdo," he said, coming to her side and resting his hand on her elbow. "Why don't you sit down, and I'll wash that for you."

He started to take the garments from her.

"That's not necessary. If I'm to regain my stamina, I need to do things for myself." As she pulled the dress from his grasp, the bright pink chemise slid from her arm and landed at her feet.

The dastardly man scooped it up and ran his fingers over the delicate lace. "Very nice," he said, his heated gaze unsettling her.

Rebekah yanked the undergarment from his hands so fast the chemise blurred as she shoved it beneath her dress. "I'd appreciate a moment's privacy." What had ever possessed her to buy such a scandalous undergarment? She'd yearned for some excitement in her life. Besides, she'd assumed no one else would ever set eyes on it.

Once she'd washed her clothing, she needed to hang the garments out to dry. Earlier, while checking the view from each window, she'd noticed a rope strung between two trees behind the cabin. Grabbing the broom from the corner and using it like a cane, she started toward the door with her wet laundry.

Zachariah dumped a bucket of water into the tub, straightened, and folded his arms across his chest. "Are you sure you don't want me to do that for you?"

Remembering to take tiny steps, she shook her head. "The fresh air will do me good."

As she shut the door, he shouted, "Use the clothesline next to the house."

She continued across the veranda. Bracing herself on the broom handle, she carefully stepped down. She ignored Zachariah's instructions to use the clothesline beside the house where his shirts and trousers flapped in the breeze. Since she preferred to keep her unmentionables separate from his laundry, and since she planned to hide the damnable pink chemise, she chose the clothesline behind the house.

After what seemed like an eternity of little steps, she looped her dress and chemise over the rope suspended between two trees. When she glanced at the chemise swaying in the air, she slid it under her dress, hiding it from sight.

She took a deep breath and noticed the nip in the air, a sure sign of early autumn. The leaves on the old oak tree shadowing the cabin had begun to turn russet. A stand of evergreens bordered one side of the property, a stone wall another. She liked it here, and Zachariah's quaint dwelling had charm.

Without warning, the hairs on the back of her neck

prickled. Gooseflesh pebbled her arms. She had the strange feeling someone was watching her. When she looked around, she thought she saw a shadowed figure in the woods behind her, but the illusion disappeared before she could be certain. Her first instinct was to run. Fortunately, she didn't. How would it look to Zachariah were she to race into the cabin as though chased by the devil himself?

She threw another glance over her shoulder and assumed her overactive imagination was playing tricks. Leaning on the broom, she proceeded to drag her feet at a rate that taxed her patience. When she reached the veranda, she studied the dense tree line and this time saw a flash of white.

Had the sheriff or his posse caught up to them?

Her heart raced beneath her breast.

She didn't hear the door open or Zachariah step behind her. His hand on her shoulder startled her.

"I'm sorry, I didn't mean to spook you," he said, the warmth of his fingers penetrating the layers of her clothing. "You seem upset. Is something wrong?"

She eyed the trees and debated whether to tell him about her concerns. "I spotted something among the trees."

"Whitetail deer are attracted to my apple trees about three hundred feet from those hemlocks."

Bekah hoped he was right.

"Why, what did you think you saw?"

Common sense dictated the sheriff wouldn't hide behind a tree. He'd have ridden in here with his gun raised. "A deer . . . what else could it be?"

He took the broom from her. "Let me help you inside. Your bath is ready. Are you sure you'll be all right alone in here?"

"Certainly."

"I could help you into the tub . . . without looking, of course," he said, a twinkle in his eyes.

"Were you blindfolded with three feedbags over your head secured tight around your neck, I still would not trust you not to look."

A deep laugh rumbled from his throat.

After he and James left the cabin, she heard the rhythmic pounding of the hammer. She peeked out the window and unbuttoned her wrap when her stomach growled. She ignored the tub and headed full speed toward the half loaf of bread in the center of the table. Slicing a thick piece, she spooned apple butter over the bread, and with a deep sigh, bit down on a large chunk. Nothing had ever tasted as good.

In no time, that slice vanished. She cut two more pieces of bread, setting them on a plate along with a few scraps of leftover ham and potatoes. Rebekah didn't care much for coffee, but she emptied the pot into her cup because she'd need something to wash down the food. She slid a chair beside the tub and rested her plate and her cup on it. After glancing out the window one more time, she undressed and slipped into the tub of tepid water.

"Ahhhhh." She sighed. Never before had she considered a warm bath a luxury, yet she couldn't remember ever enjoying a moment more. She reached for the lilac-scented soap she'd taken out earlier, and sliding the soap up and down her limbs, worked away the built-up grime. When her fingers connected with her left shoulder, a sharp twinge reminded her of her injury.

Though the gash was still red, the swelling had decreased, and when she lifted her arm, she discovered she had complete mobility. Being careful of her wound, she ducked her head beneath the water, soaped up her hair, rinsed, and brushed out the tangles.

Still sitting in the tub, she wiggled her toes in the water and while watching the ripples, she polished off another slice of bread. Afterwards, she leaned against the back of the copper tub, and with her fingers brought each succulent morsel of potato and ham to her mouth.

She rinsed her hands and lips and climbed out of the water. Wrapping the towel around her, she grabbed the last piece of bread from the plate and strolled across the room to peek out the window at Zachariah and James busy rebuilding the barn.

She bit into the bread, took several steps, yanked off the towel, and started to pat herself dry. Out of the corner of her eye, she spotted something scurrying past the window at the rear of the house. The bread dropped to the floor. Clasping the towel in front of her, she inched along the inside wall until she came to the window and counted slowly to ten to bolster her courage.

Sucking in a deep breath, she stuck her head against the pane of glass and came face to face with a long-haired woman holding a rifle in one hand, Rebekah's dress in the other.

Startled, Rebekah screamed.

Ten

Zachariah leaped down from the ladder and was about to charge across the yard when the door to the cabin whipped open. Out shot Rebecca barefoot, clad in her crimson wrapper. Her easy stride and waving arms suggested she'd undergone a miraculous recovery.

"You thief, bring my dress back this instant," she shouted towards the poplars that lined his property. She ran about three hundred feet, stopped, and planted one hand on her hip; the other fisted hand punched the air.

Zachariah hurried to Bekah and cupped his fingers over her shoulder. "What's . . ."

She leaped back and twisted around, her fists raised in self-defense. "Are you a bloody dolt, sneaking up on a woman like that? You're lucky I didn't whack you a good one."

Her threat issued in her British accent forced a deep rumble from his throat.

"You needn't stand there howling, my brothers taught me how to defend myself."

"I'm sure they did. Sorry . . . I didn't mean to startle you."

With her standing this close, he saw the tears rimming her eyes. He lifted his hands, and much to his delight, she stepped forward, leaned into him, and wrapped trembling arms around his chest. It had been a damn long time since he'd held a damp woman in his arms. "What's wrong?"

She spoke into the cotton of his shirt. "I guess seeing a long-haired toothless thief peering at me in the window has thrown me off kilter."

"That was probably my neighbor, Mary."

Bekah pulled away enough to glance at him. "Your neighbor is a bandit, a crook, a brigand."

"Mary would never steal."

Righteous indignation skittered across her face as she stepped away and folded her arms across her chest. The motion tented the material of her wrapper, giving him a bird's-eye view of her cleavage. "She just stole my dress from the clothesline."

Breasts that would fill his palms. "You shouldn't have used Mary's clothesline," he finally said with much difficulty.

Bekah's forehead wrinkled in confusion. "But the clothesline is on your property."

Her damp satin wrapper molded her rounded hips and hugged shapely thighs. Zachariah tried not to focus on the lush breasts hidden beneath the shiny material. "Yes, but it's hers along with anything hanging on it."

"But . . ."

"I warned you to use the clothesline by the side of the house," he replied, making eye contact and trying his damnedest not to stare at her chest.

"You didn't exactly warn me. You casually mentioned it."

"You learn the hard way."

Her smile warmed him. "I've heard that before."

"It doesn't surprise me."

Bekah glanced down and then up again. She yanked the fabric of her wrap together and fastened her fingers around the material at her neck.

Zachariah grinned. "You didn't have to do that for me."

"Thank goodness James didn't happen along."

"He might think you were trying to lead me astray." Zachariah wiggled a raised eyebrow.

"I'd never do any such thing."

"You do in my dreams."

She didn't answer but instead glanced away.

He pulled her against his side, and starting toward the cabin, noticed how nicely her body fit against his. An underlying current zapped the air around them. Though Bekah would never admit it, he knew she was drawn to him.

He wanted her, needed her, and his obsession would not cease until they'd made love. Even then, he'd never be able to wipe her image from his mind.

But they would never make love.

Never, he repeated to himself as he inhaled a ragged breath.

His raging emotions frightened him.

He should keep his distance, which wasn't likely to happen while the scent of her lilac soap clouded his judgment.

When they entered the cabin, his gaze settled on the tub in the middle of the room, and he conjured up images of her naked body. "Next time allow me to scrub your back."

"You're impossible," she said again, her upturned face not looking shocked in the least.

Would she be a bold or tentative lover?

"Now tell me something I don't already know," he said, his voice an octave lower than normal. "Such as why is that plate on the chair beside the tub?"

Her blue eyes darkened several shades. "Oh, that . . ."

He grinned. "Yeah, that."

"It seems after you and James left, I felt a wee bit hungry."

"You know what I think?"

She shook her head.

He saw guilt behind her innocent smile. "I think you were hungry all along, but you didn't want me to know how much better you were feeling."

Her gaze darted side to side like a cornered animal. "Where's James?"

"At the stream, cleaning up, but you're avoiding the subject."

She planted her hands on her hips. "All right, Mr. Know-Everything, my shoulder is feeling much better. But I'm not leaving without my medallion. And yes, I was famished so when you went outside, I helped myself to the leftovers, a pitiful few crumbs I might add."

"Did anyone ever tell you your eyes light up when you're angry?" He strolled toward the counter. "If you'd like, there's more bread in the cupboard."

"No, I've had my fill. But I must say that's the best bread I've tasted in a long time."

"Thank Mary the next time you see her. She's the one who made it."

"But that doesn't give her the right to steal my clothes."

"She didn't steal a thing. She took her property off her clothesline out back."

Bekah sat down in the chair by the window and ran her forefinger over his carving of a blue jay. "None of this makes any sense."

He anchored his booted foot over the rung of a kitchen chair and rested his opened palm on his raised knee. "When I first built this cabin, I caught Mary watching me from behind that tree out yonder," he said, nodding toward the window and catching a glimpse of the whiskey jug on the floor. His mouth watered.

He tightened his trembling fingers over his knee. "Whenever I waved, she'd run away. Then one morning several weeks later, I spotted her hiding behind the same tree. After collecting half a dozen eggs from my chickens, I wrapped three in a white handkerchief and left them on the stump out back. She skedaddled, but when I checked a while later, the eggs were gone. The next morning I found a small bundle covered with a square of checked cloth on my porch. Inside was a loaf of molasses bread."

"Oh," Bekah said, her eyes misting.

Her adoring gaze unsettled him. "I knew I'd gotten the better deal, so I hung a clothesline near the old stump. Ever since then it's been an unspoken agreement between the two of us that whatever she finds on that line or on that stump is hers."

"Maybe you can persuade her to return my dress."

"It's her dress now."

"You infuriate me."

"I know."

She stood and started toward the bedroom.

"Bekah."

She glanced at him over her shoulder.

"In case you're interested, I'm a damn good back scrubber."

Later that afternoon Zachariah pulled James aside. "I need you to do me a favor."

"Sure, anything." Zachariah saw the admiration on the boy's face and knew he'd be disappointed when it came time to leave.

Zachariah gritted his teeth. "I need to go somewhere for a short while. I want you to keep an eye on things while I'm gone."

"Can't I come with you?"

"No, I want you to stay with Bekah."

"Ah, shucks."

Zachariah's heart went out to the child as he ruffled the boy's hair. "I thought you liked Bekah."

"Yes, but I'd rather be doing man stuff. Where are you going, anyway?"

"To Mary's place over yonder."

"Mad Mary is likely to shoot you, skin you, and feed your

carcass to her mangy cats."

"Mary may be strange . . ."

"She's crazy, and you know it."

"You have to learn not to believe every yarn you hear. I'd expect better from you. Besides, how do you know Mary?"

"Everyone in Londonderry knows about Mad Mary. She came to town once with a bunch of cats in a crate. You know what they say?"

"What?"

"They say when she's hungry, she eats cats raw!"

"James, that's ridiculous."

"Frank at the tavern said he was out at Mad Mary's once, and he saw her bite off a cat's head."

"You have to stop listening to these wild stories."

"I guess so," he replied with concern. "But what if you don't come back?"

"If I don't return by nightfall, you hightail it out of here with Bekah."

"I won't go without you."

Zachariah cupped the boy's chin and met his gaze. "Mary would never hurt me, but there are others who would. Give me your word that you and Bekah will leave if I'm not back by dark."

"I'll go looking for you."

"Promise that you'll do as I say."

"Oh . . . all right."

Zachariah watched the boy stroll across the yard with his shoulders hunched forward. Zachariah wished he could be the man that James needed.

A father figure, a role model, someone who'd teach him right from wrong.

He felt a close bond with the child, but he could barely manage his own life, much less take on the responsibility of a growing boy.

He'd already started down the path between the gray poplars when he heard branches crunching behind him. When he turned, he saw James running towards him with his arms pumping by his side.

"What in the hell are you doing here?"

"Something ain't right back there." James said, looking over his shoulder toward the cabin. "When Miss Benson heard you wouldn't be back for a while, she started yanking stuff off shelves. She's nosing into every corner of your house."

Zachariah bit back a curse.

"She says she's gonna find her blasted medallion even if it means tearing apart your cabin board by board."

"I'm sure she isn't going to do any real harm." But he wasn't sure.

"You didn't see the wild look in her eyes."

Zachariah heaved a deep sigh. "I'll be back soon. Meanwhile, do what you can to hamper her efforts. I'd like to have a roof over my head when I sleep tonight." Zachariah dug in his pocket and swung his half of the charm in front of James's face. "Tell her she's wasting her time. I have what she's after."

"What if she don't believe me?"

"It's up to you to see that she does."

"What good is half of a gold coin?"

"She has it in her head it'll lead to treasure or some such thing."

"Why don't you just give her the coin?"

Zachariah sighed impatiently. "I don't have all day. We'll continue this discussion when I return."

"You be careful around Mad Mary."

"Mary's my friend."

"Are you sure?" James asked before turning and disappearing

into the clearing that led to the cabin.

Zachariah had gone about three hundred yards when he heard twigs splintering. He glanced toward the sound and spotted a mare with a rider clad in a lavender cape, wending its way along the narrow path. He hid behind a tree trunk. When the horse neared, Zachariah leaped up and yanked the person off the saddle. Laughing, he threw the purple cape over the rider's head.

She squealed and batted her arms trying to free herself. "So help me, Zachariah, when I get loose, I'll throttle you."

"I don't think a woman in your position should be making threats. Besides, I thought you liked playing games."

Violet tried to kick him, but he foiled her attempt. "Only when I can win."

"You can't win now," he said, swatting her behind and yanking her cape from over her head.

"You darn, blasted, good-for-nothing," she said, catching her breath. "You scared me half to death."

"You still look plenty alive to me."

She waved away his comment. "What's a woman have to do to get an invitation to sit for a spell?"

"What brings you out this way?" he asked, craning his neck and looking around. "I hope no one followed you."

"Don't worry none. I meandered around so long, I almost got lost." Her pale blue eyes lit up. "I've got some good news, but first, I need a drink."

Zachariah reached for the horse's reins in one hand, wrapped his free arm around her shoulder, and led the way to his cabin.

After tying the horse to the hitching post, he swung the door open and stared in disbelief. Everything he owned was piled in the center of the room and on the table and chairs. Bekah was so busy emptying a bag of flour into a bowl she didn't notice him. "You sneaky, conniving woman. Are you looking for buried treasure?" he roared.

She leaped back. Flour poured down the front of her skirt. "Oh, I didn't expect you to return this soon."

"I can see that."

She glanced curiously at Violet.

"This is Miss Violet Champaign. She works at the Blooming Garden." With a nod, he continued, "Violet, meet Miss Benson."

Wiping her hands on her skirt, Bekah hurried in their direction. "Glad to meet you, Miss Champaign. If I'd known we were having company, I wouldn't have picked today to clean."

"You call this cleaning?" Zachariah asked with a frown. "Snooping is more like it."

She ignored him, and instead took Violet's arm and led her to his chair by the window. "I'll have this cleared in no time," she said, sending an apologetic look over her shoulder as she removed a stack of his shirts and set them on the floor. "Have a seat, and I'll brew us a pot of tea."

Violet laughed huskily. "Thanks just the same, but I'd like something stronger."

"Will whiskey do?" Zachariah asked.

"Yes, that would be great."

Without sparing Zachariah a glance, Bekah sashayed past him, yanked the jug from the floor and set it on the cluttered table. Zachariah located two glasses and poured a dollop of the amber liquor in each. He stared at the glasses in his hands. Out of habit, he'd filled one for himself. The sharp tang reached his nostrils as he inhaled deeply.

He craved this drink, felt the need clear to the marrow of his bones.

"Will I have that drink before nightfall?" Violet's voice jolted him from his pathetic musings.

Forcing a grin, he ambled across the room and handed Violet

the glass. "Bekah, would you like a little?" He assumed she'd refuse.

She snatched the glass from his hand. "Thank you," she said, sitting on a stool near Violet and directing her attention toward the other woman. "That's a lovely dress you have on. I especially like the sequins around the neck."

Violet looked pleased. "Thank you. This dress is my favorite."

Bekah glanced down. "You'll have to excuse my appearance. I've been cleaning, and unfortunately, my favorite dress was stolen by one of Zachariah's hooligan acquaintances."

Zachariah saw no reason in stating the obvious; Mary didn't steal.

"You work with flowers?" Bekah asked.

Violet's brow furrowed in confusion. "Where did you get that idea?"

"Well, when Zachariah mentioned you were employed at the Blooming Garden, I assumed . . ."

"The Garden is a tavern. I only wish my customers smelled like flowers," Violet said with a chuckle. "It would sure make my job a lot more pleasant."

Zachariah folded his arms and grinned at Bekah.

When she met his gaze, her face turned a delicate pink.

"Oh," she replied lifting the glass of whiskey to her mouth and swallowing. Tears sprang to her eyes. "Lordy, this is strong."

"It'll kill what ails you," Violet said, tapping her palm against Bekah's back to ease her coughing.

Bekah waved a hand in front of her mouth. With a timid smile she set her glass on the floor beside the stool. "I'm not much of a drinker."

Zachariah wished he could say the same. If Bekah hadn't taken the glass of whiskey, he'd be on his way to oblivion. He glanced at the chipped carving of the eagle on the sill, which served as a reminder that he must never again drink alcohol.

He stepped forward. "Violet, why don't you let me refill your glass, and then the two of us can go for a stroll."

Bekah's eyebrows arched, but she remained silent.

Violet set her empty glass down with a clunk. "I may take you up on that later, but right now, you and me need to go somewhere where we can talk without bothering Miss Benson."

Rebekah peeked out the window and spotted Zachariah with his arm around *that woman*. If she didn't know any better, she'd think the tight feeling in her chest was jealousy.

Her, jealous?

Never in a hundred years.

Besides, she didn't care a whit what Zachariah did. If he wanted to hug a woman, any woman, especially one with a bosom no man could ignore, that was his business.

Yet she rushed into the bedroom, withdrew her mirror and tried to arrange her disheveled hair as best she could. With a damp cloth she dabbed at the flour on her dress and told herself she was tidying up because of her good upbringing, and not because she cared a fig what Zachariah thought of her.

She glanced out the window and saw them vanish into the barn. A possibility tumbled through her mind. Maybe Miss Champaign had some information about the medallion. Otherwise, why did they need to discuss their business away from her?

Zachariah had called Rebekah a conniving woman.

Well, he hadn't seen anything yet!

She hurried to the back of the room, slid open the window sash, climbed out, and slowly made her way to the barn. Tiptoeing quietly, she climbed the ladder to the hayloft and crept on hands and knees until she was directly above Violet and Zachariah. When she dared, she brushed aside the hay and peeked between the slits in the boards. She could see the couple with their heads close together like conspirators up to no good. Or like long-lost lovers, she thought, a twinge of disappointment knotting her stomach.

Zachariah turned to Violet. "What did you want to tell me?"

"I flashed the picture of your medallion around to at least a dozen men. A big son of a gun nicknamed Grizzly says he has some information for you."

That bit of news angered Rebekah so much, she almost shouted, but with a force of will, she clamped her palm over her mouth. There'd be plenty of time later to tell Zachariah what she thought. The worthless hooligan had showed the medallion to Violet, yet he'd refused to let her see it.

"Did he say what he wanted?" Zachariah asked, resting a hand along the wall of a stall and widening his stance.

Violet pulled her lavender velvet cape around her shoulders. "I tried to wangle some details from him, but he refused to talk to me. He said I should get in touch with you and set up a meeting for seven o'clock next Wednesday at the Blooming Garden."

Zachariah sighed. Soon he'd be able to clear his name.

"Tell him I'll be there."

Rebekah resolved to be there, too.

"I don't want you to go alone. This man is dangerous."

Violet needn't worry. Zachariah wouldn't be alone, Rebekah thought with a wry smile. She'd be there as well.

"I'm not worried," Zachariah replied.

"I don't trust the man. He might try to ambush you on your way into town."

"What's he look like?"

Violet emitted a sultry laugh. "His nickname about says it all. He's big, hairy, has feral eyes. Oh, one other thing . . . the middle finger on his left hand is missing."

Hay shuffled. Someone gasped.

They both turned to see James in a horse stall with his hands cupped over his mouth, his face as pale as a freshly laundered sheet.

James bolted for the door and disappeared from sight.

"The lad looks as though he's seen a ghost." Violet batted thick black lashes at Zachariah.

"I was just thinking the same thing."

While Zachariah and Violet spoke in low tones, Rebekah crept to the ladder leaning against the outside of the barn and managed to climb down without breaking her neck. Lifting her skirt with her hand, she ran back to the cabin, where she spotted James sitting on the tree stump with shoulders hunched forward.

"James, what's wrong?" she asked, stepping toward him.

He dashed away the tears with the back of his hand. "Ain't nothin' wrong."

"When my brothers got into trouble, they often came to me just to talk."

"I ain't got no brothers."

"I know that, but maybe you could pretend I'm your sister."

"All the pretendin' in the world ain't gonna change the fact you ain't my sister."

"You're sitting in a dangerous place," she warned, hoping to change his mood.

He glanced at her, his pain-filled eyes confused. "How's that?"

"If Zachariah's friend, Mary, sees you there, she'll think you're hers for the taking."

A brief grin curled his lips.

"Jim, I thought you considered me your friend. Tell me what's bothering you."

He eyed her suspiciously. "I can't."

Rebekah sat next to him and rested her hand on his shoulder. "I'm a good listener. And I can't believe anything you tell me will be that bad."

"If I told you what I done . . . or didn't do, you'd hate me for it."

"I could never hate you."

He studied her a moment and shook his head. "That's what you say now, but how can I be sure you won't change your mind?"

"Jimmy," she said softly, "no matter what, you can count on me always to care about you."

Indecision played across his face a moment before he rested his hands over his knees and glanced away. "I recognized the killer in the alley the night Zack was arrested for murder."

It took a moment for Rebekah to understand what he'd said. "I thought it was too dark for you to see his face."

James sniffed and rubbed his hand along his nose. "I never got close enough to see his face, but while I was hiding in the crate, I caught a glimpse of his hands."

"What are you saying?"

"There's only one man I know who's missing a finger on his left hand."

"Why didn't you mention this earlier so I could tell the sheriff? That information might have created enough doubt to postpone Zachariah's execution."

"I couldn't tell you."

She wanted to erase the distress from his face. "Why not? I don't understand why you'd keep such an important fact from me."

"I couldn't tell you. You don't understand, but I couldn't tell anyone." Tears rolled down his face.

"Jimmy, you need to discuss this for your own good. If you can't speak to me, then talk to Zachariah. I can see that this is ripping you apart."

He sniffed. The lines around his mouth deepened.

Rebekah pondered the facts. Why would a boy who obviously loved Zachariah hide the one fact that might free his friend? "This man with the missing finger, what is he to you?"

A small sound started at the back of the boy's throat and came out as an anguished moan.

"Shhh," she whispered, rocking him against her. "I'm here for you. If you can't talk about it, that's all right."

Slowly, he lifted his chin and gazed at her with saddened eyes. For the longest time he sat without saying a word. "If I tell you, you mustn't say anything to Zachariah. He'd hate me till the day he dies if he found out I didn't 'fess up 'bout knowing who killed that man."

"I won't say a word to anyone," she said, taking his hand in hers.

"Do you swear?"

She crossed her heart. "Yes."

"The man they call Grizzly is my pa."

It took a moment for Rebekah to digest what he'd said.

James collapsed against her. "I know I should have told someone, but a boy should stick by his pa."

"I thought your father had died in the war."

"I pretended my father was a hero instead of someone who wanted nothin' to do with me."

ELEVEN

Zachariah assisted Violet onto her horse and watched her ride away. Once he cleared his name, he'd be free to go into town without fear of being thrown in prison. He'd then give Rebekah both pieces of the medallion. Until that time she and James would need to stay elsewhere, because his cabin was no longer safe.

Now that Rebekah was strong enough to ride, there was no reason for her to remain with him. Besides, he told himself he could hardly wait to be rid of her. Deep inside, he knew he'd miss her, but it was easier to pretend otherwise.

And he'd miss James, too, but the boy was becoming too attached to him. The sooner they parted company, the better it would be for both of them.

He finger-combed his beard and picked out pieces of sawdust in the tangled hair. Though he'd grown accustomed to having a beard, he'd decided to shave it off. Violet had warned him about the posters in town with his image and the offer of a reward for his capture. She'd said he looked no better than the man called Grizzly. He glanced at his reflection in the barn window and had to agree. For over a year, he hadn't given a damn whether he lived or died, and his appearance reflected his frame of mind. But since he'd stopped drinking, he felt hope where there'd been none before.

Once the real killer was behind bars, he'd be free to build a life for himself, a future with a good woman by his side. If he stayed sober, would a certain lady with a maple-sugar voice give him a second glance? Would she want anything to do with him once she had her precious medallion?

Could she love a man like him?

Would he want to take that kind of chance again?

He knew the answer, felt it clear to his soul, and the ache in his heart intensified. Someone like Bekah would no sooner get tangled with the likes of him than she would a killer. And in the eyes of the law, he was a killer on the run. If they caught up with him, he'd hang.

But the fear of hanging was almost as great as the fear of betrayal. He shut his eyes and remembered Elissa, beautiful and sincere, a lady to the core who'd professed her undying love for him. He had better focus on Elissa before he repeated his past mistakes.

Even with Elissa's memory raw in his mind, he kept picturing Bekah, her smile, her hair, and rounded breasts that would fit his palm.

And he wanted her in his life, wanted her with a certainty that frightened him.

He called himself a doggoned fool for allowing his mind to ramble on. Being sober had its disadvantages; he couldn't drown his thoughts as he once had.

He sharpened his straightedge razor on the leather strap hanging from a nail inside the barn. Looking at his reflection in a broken mirror, he shaved off his beard, leaving behind a thick mustache that hung over his upper lip.

Rebekah was about to put away the bag of flour when she heard the door open and shut. A gust of wind stirred the hem of her skirt. She recognized the clunk of Zachariah's boots against the pine floor and with a shake of her head, decided not to utter one word to the despicable man. Nor would she greet him with a smile. Now that she'd seen his choice of woman—not that she gave a fig about that anyway. He'd shown Violet both halves of the medallion, which wasn't fair since he'd not allowed her one blasted look. She was through conversing with the lout.

She vowed not to sleep a wink until she'd slid the two medallion halves together and solved its puzzle.

As Zachariah moved behind her, she felt his breath on the back of her head. The pleasant scent of pine, musk, and fresh air mingled and drifted toward her nostrils. She called herself a bloody fool for noticing, an even bigger fool for inhaling a deep satisfied breath.

A ripple of warmth surged through her chest as she tightened her resolve not to speak and replaced a box on a shelf. Ignoring him, she sashayed to the windowsill and dusted his carvings, including the beakless creature.

"Be careful with that." His deep voice rumbled behind her, a hint of humor in his tone.

She could not understand why he kept the mangled eagle. Setting down the carving, she hurried across the room.

He followed suit. "By your pained expression I'm guessing either your stockings are too tight or your chemise is bunched in a knot. Would you like me to have a look?"

"That does it," she said, swinging around and waving her finger at him, "you're a . . . a . . . ." Her mouth fell open where it hung like a broken hinge.

He rubbed his hand over his clean-shaven jaw. "Do I look that bad?"

She managed to close her mouth. Bad? No!

"I was hoping you'd trim my hair. Once I shaved, I realized how long it had grown."

"Yes, cut . . . your hair . . . I'll . . . do . . . that for you." She sounded like a ninny, all flustered like an infatuated schoolgirl. Pity she hadn't remembered her resolve not to speak. At least, she'd have retained an air of dignity instead of allowing her tongue to trip over itself.

"You look fine," she replied through clenched teeth, though the word didn't come close to doing him justice. "But your hair could use a trim." If she did him the favor of cutting his hair, then maybe she could persuade him to show her the medallion.

His grin drew her eyes to the thick mustache brushing his upper lip.

"Have you seen James?" he asked, turning away and glancing toward the window.

"Not for a while."

"I need to talk to him."

She stepped forward. "I hope you'll be gentle with the boy. He's had a bad day."

"I caught James listening to my conversation with Violet."

"Oh." Although she had no regrets about eavesdropping, she glanced away for fear he'd see the guilt on her face.

"I aim to find out what he's up to."

She picked up several cups from the table and returned them to the shelf. "Can't it wait until tomorrow morning? Jimmy needs a little time to think through his troubles. I had a talk with him this afternoon, and I expect he'll eventually come to his senses and tell you what's been bothering him."

"I don't like putting things off. James is a stubborn cuss. More than likely, he'll never come clean with me."

"What harm would there be in waiting half a day? Please."

He paused, his gaze setting her insides afire.

"I'll wait, but only because I suspect your maple-sugar voice has turned my brain to mush."

Zachariah yanked a chair away from the table and sat down. "I want you to take note, I have two ears on the sides of my head. I'd like to keep them, so be careful."

"Hummm, if I happen to nick one, not a soul will notice since your hair will cover the damage."

"Look," he said, expelling an exasperated breath, "maybe this isn't such a good idea. Especially in your current state of mind."

She snipped off a lock. "Precisely what do you mean by that?"

"Don't you think I know you're upset?"

She angled the scissors over his head. "You want me to tell you why?"

"Do I have a choice? Hey, be careful of the ear."

"Hold still, or I won't be responsible for what happens."

"Until now, have you ever cut anyone's hair?"

Rebekah laughed. She'd cut her oldest brother's hair once and her stepfather's, too. Both men had sworn never to allow her within thirty feet of them with a pair of scissors. "Don't you think it's kind of late to ask that question?" Another clump of hair fell to the floor. So far, her efforts had not yielded the results she'd envisioned.

She faced him, and bending at the knees, studied her handiwork. "The left is a tad longer than the right."

"Then I suggest you even it off."

"Precisely what I plan to do." She might have trimmed the hair on his crown a bit too short because it stood on end like porcupine quills. When she brushed her hand against the spiked strands, they sprang right back up. Maybe, if she cut a little more off, they'd go unnoticed. She soon realized that her attempts only worsened the situation.

Hiding her concerns, she adjusted the length of the hair on his right side to match the left, but even after three tries, it was obvious she'd failed.

Figuring she better broach the subject now instead of later, she smiled innocently. "I think it's only fair that you allow me to see both pieces of the medallion."

"How so?"

How dare he sit there, acting as though she didn't have a right? Anger coursed through her veins. "Because in case you've forgotten, I own the two pieces of that blasted medallion. And because . . ." The last of her reserve slipped away. "And because you showed my medallion to Violet."

His head shot up. His gaze pierced through her. "How do you know that?"

"Because I heard you talking to her, that's why. I hid in the loft," she told him, proud of her feat and no longer caring that he knew. "If you think you can fool me, you have another think coming. I will not leave this cabin without that bloody medallion even if it means cutting out your heart with these scissors."

He grabbed the scissors from her hands. "You've worked hard enough for one day," he said, with a wide grin, which dissolved the instant he stood and glanced at his reflection in the mirror on the wall. "Thunderation! What have you done to my hair?"

"It'll grow back," she pointed out, trying to encourage him.

His deep scowl convinced her she'd failed.

That night, as they ate supper in silence, Zachariah could almost hear the gears grinding in Rebekah's head. No doubt she was figuring ways to wangle the medallion from him.

James chewed quietly, his troubled gaze focused on his plate. If he didn't discuss his problems by nightfall, Zachariah would try to find out what was wrong.

Wearing a hat that now fit loosely, Zachariah decided after they ate he'd hand Rebekah the two pieces of the medallion so she could put them together and stop pestering him. He wasn't sure how he'd break the news that it wasn't a family heirloom, but he figured that information would probably go unnoticed once she had the medallion in her hands. He hadn't planned to withhold it from her this long. At first, she'd been too weak, and then he'd enjoyed the bantering between them so he'd put it off.

When he thought of her climbing the ladder to the hayloft, he smiled inwardly. He would have burst out laughing had he not remembered the scissors in her hands and his resulting haircut.

Bekah cast a tentative look at him. "I've been thinking about something."

"Yeah, about what, as if I don't already know?"

Her face flushed. "I think I have a solution to our problem."

"What problem?"

"Figuring which of us should keep the medallion."

Although he'd already decided to let her look at the medallion, he wanted to see what she had to say. "What exactly do you have in mind?"

"A battle of wits? A duel. Winner take all," she said, with a dramatic swing of her arm.

"With weapons?" he asked, remembering her dislike of guns. He figured he could beat her blindfolded with both arms tied behind his back.

"I thought we'd gamble."

"Play cards?"

"Yes, that's it, but I can't think of the name of the game I played with my brothers."

"You gambled with your brothers?" he asked unable to believe his ears.

"Yes, and I was quite good at it, too."

"How old were you the last time you played?"

"Old enough," she said, looking pleased. "And though I don't remember all the rules or the name of the game, I do remember collecting pairs."

"That sounds like poker."

"Yes, that's it," she said in an excited tone. "If you're willing, we'll play cards to decide who keeps the medallion."

"Of course, I'm willing, but . . ." He tapped his finger against the table. "I already have the medallion, so I've nothing to gain if I win."

She screwed her mouth thoughtfully. "Yes, I see what you mean. I hadn't thought of that."

James pushed back his chair. "Miss Benson, why do you want the medallion, anyway?"

"It means a lot to me because it's from my parents. While they were missionaries, they bought me a doll and hid the medallion inside."

"Why did they do that?" James asked, clearly interested.

"They might not have done it," Zachariah pointed out. "Someone else might have stuck it in the doll as a prank."

Bekah rested her palm over her heart. "I feel it in here. That medallion is much more than a gold object. It's my link to the past and to my parents. It might even be a link to my future."

"Gosh, what makes you think that?" James asked, his eyes wide.

"My parents wouldn't go to all the trouble of slicing a gold disc in two and engraving it with mysterious marks without a reason. I just know the medallion is important. I've dreamed of unlocking the puzzle ever since I was a child." A faraway look claimed her features. "I used to close my eyes and picture myself with a spade in my hands and an opened treasure chest filled with gold and dazzling jewels at my feet."

"You think the medallion will lead you to buried treasure? If so, you'll be needing a boy to help you dig when you find the right location, huh?" James asked, his face alight with excitement.

Bekah laughed. "There might not even be any treasure, but . . ."

Zachariah interrupted. "Finally you're talking sense. There's no treasure, and whoever marked the back was probably playing a trick, figuring someone would try to solve what never existed."

"You're quite skeptical," Bekah said.

"And a good thing, too. I know better than to go chasing rainbows and empty dreams."

"I'll chase rainbows and dreams if that's what it takes to solve the medallion's mystery."

"And you'll be disappointed if you come up empty-handed," Zachariah pointed out.

"Unless she finds a treasure," James added with the enthusiasm of a thirteen-year-old boy.

Zachariah looked at James. "First we've some serious card playing to do, and you have some chores to finish. When Bekah loses the card game, I'll go find you in the barn and show you the medallion."

"I've no intentions of losing the game," she said with a huff.

"Neither do I."

James left shortly afterwards and once the table was cleared, Zachariah slapped a deck of cards down. "Five card poker, deuces wild."

"That's fine with me."

Zachariah cupped his chin. "I think I've figured out what we can play for."

"We're playing for the medallion, of course."

"Yes, but as I pointed out earlier, I've nothing to gain."

She frowned. "What do you mean?"

"If you win, I'll let you have the medallion for a while."

"When I win, I'll keep the medallion forever."

"Yes, and you can, but first I need to borrow it." He raised his hand to silence her. "Only for a week, two at the most, then you can have both halves."

"How do I know you won't go back on your word? Lord knows you've lied to me before."

He grimaced.

"I'm merely stating facts," she said flatly.

He had that coming. "I figure we'll play strip poker, and if either of us backs down during the game, the opponent wins by default."

She paused for a moment and then slammed her palm on the table. "I accept your terms, and you'll back down long before I do."

He raked his heated gaze over her. "That won't happen. I've no reason to back down. I've never minded taking off my clothes for a woman."

Clad in everything she owned, Rebekah entered the kitchen a few minutes later prepared to win what had been hers from the start. Unfortunately, she hadn't played cards since she was ten so the fine points of the game were sketchy. The few times she'd won, she suspected her brothers had thrown the game because their stepparents had promised them an extra helping of pudding.

Still, a win was a win.

Besides, anyone could hold a few cards in her hands and arrange the matching pairs together. Though she'd been young, she still remembered the thrill of winning and collecting the buttons in the center of the table. Of course, this time the stakes were higher. She'd be playing for her medallion instead of buttons. But as Zachariah had pointed out, since she didn't have the medallion, it wasn't hers to lose. She felt quite smug that she'd figured that out, and he hadn't.

"What does 'deuces are wild' mean?" she asked, sitting in the chair opposite him.

"I can see I'm going to have to stay on my toes if I hope to win," he said in an arrogant tone. "It means the twos can be used to represent any number."

"Oh, I don't remember playing that way with my brothers."

"The twos don't have to be wild."

"No, that's all right. I kind of like the idea of playing with wild deuces."

"Why do I get the feeling you aren't playing fair?" he asked, eyeing her wardrobe.

She pushed up the veil of her sapphire hat so she could see the cards. "Whatever do you mean?"

"Your getup has me wondering whether you're going to bed or outside to confront a blizzard."

"It doesn't hurt to be prepared for any emergency."

He shrugged. "You're simply prolonging the inevitable."

"You needn't sit there looking smug, because I know a little something about playing cards, and in this case, you will bloody well lose the medallion along with your britches."

His grin widened. "Just so you'll know I'm not worried, I'll take off something." He undid his boots and threw them across the room. "I dare you to do the same," he said.

She smiled sweetly. "I'll not accept your challenge. But if you've a mind to continue, go right ahead."

He unfastened the buttons on his shirt, exposing a hairy chest. Rebekah had seen her brothers naked to the waist lots of times, but this was different. It seemed indecent. Sensual. Pleasing to the eyes. She had trouble keeping her gaze off the wide V of his shirt.

She needed to focus on the matter at hand instead of Zachariah's physical attributes.

Lordy, that would not be easy!

"Let's get this match going," she suggested with faked bravado. Inside her muscles clenched nervously. "Go ahead and mix up the cards."

"Of course." He lifted the deck with nimble fingers and

flicked the cards together at a speed she hadn't thought possible.

"Would you like to cut them?" he asked setting the deck in front of her.

She couldn't remember this part of the game and figured it must be an American tradition. It sounded like a lot of bother. Once the deck was cut, then what? Instead of asking what he meant, she waved a dismissive hand. "No, I'm keeping my stamina for the game."

She didn't approve of the foolish grin he flashed while dealing out five cards for each of them. His fingers moved so quickly she could barely see what he was doing. She wondered whether he might cheat and decided that a man who'd broken his word would be capable of anything. Clearly, she'd never be able to detect any impropriety in his lightning-quick movement.

Expecting to see cards on his lap, she peeked beneath the table and was disappointed to see none. He lifted up his left leg and rested his ankle over his right knee in a relaxed posture while every muscle from her aching neck to her small toe knotted with tension.

"Aren't you going to look at your cards?" he asked with that damnable grin stretched across his clean-shaven face.

She liked his strong jaw and might have admired his features a moment longer had she not an important card game to win. She picked up her cards, accidentally dropped one on the floor, picked it up, and tried to decide her next move. Since none matched, her options were limited.

"How many cards do you want?"

"Five," she replied, sounding confident and throwing her cards in the center of the table.

"You can't ask for more than three."

"You're starting to sound like my brothers by making up rules after the game's already started."

"Look," he said, sighing. "You can't ask for more than three cards. That is the rule."

She could have debated the issue but decided to save her arguments for more important matters. She picked her cards back up and kept a four of hearts and six of clubs. "I'll take three cards," she said through clenched teeth.

He discarded two of his cards, and his fingers blurred before her eyes as he flicked three cards toward her.

She just remembered that twos were wild and she'd thrown one out. "I've changed my mind," she said, trying to switch one of the cards he'd given her for her two.

His hand clamped over hers. "What do you think you're doing?"

"I'm taking back my two. I'd forgotten it was wild."

He laughed and released her fingers. "Sure, go ahead, but let me warn you not to try that with anyone else."

"Thank you," she said, slipping the two beside the queen of diamonds.

"Just so you'll know, that's the last time I'm allowing you to pick up cards you've already discarded."

Certain her pair of queens would win, she barely heard his voice over the drumming in her ears.

"Your call."

"Huh?"

"Put your cards down so I can see them."

Triumphantly, she dropped her cards face up.

"I win," he said, flashing three fours.

Not worried in the least, she removed her hat and set it on the chair beside her.

About forty-five minutes later trepidation seized her as she eyed the growing pile of clothing on the chair; her sapphire hat with velvet carnations had been joined by her dress, a nightcap that she rarely used, a bustle, two shoes, three pairs of stockings, two pairs of pantaloons, a corset, lace chemise, and a cambric linen petticoat. She was down to her nightgown.

Zachariah had shed his shirt when she'd collected three kings. He'd lost one sock in one match and the other shortly afterwards. Since she'd won only a few times, unless she resorted to drastic measures, she realized the odds of winning the next hand were slim. One by one, she'd removed her undergarments, hiding them beneath the billowing skirt of her dress. It was bad enough that he'd enjoyed himself immensely, but she'd die of embarrassment if she lost the next hand.

Since he'd already boasted he'd remove his hat last and that he wore nothing beneath his trousers, the next game would reveal more than she cared to show or see depending on its outcome.

Since it was her turn to deal, she tried to shuffle the cards, but a few slipped through her fingers and landed on the floor. Bending to pick them up, she was amazed to see two aces, a three, and an eight, at her feet.

Before she could change her mind, she dropped the aces on her lap and returned the other cards to the deck. Her heart pounded against her ribs. Had he seen what she'd done? Certain her misdeal showed in her eyes, she concentrated on the cards in her trembling hands.

Somehow she managed to deal five cards to both of them. "How many cards would you like," she asked a moment later, her voice higher than normal.

"I'll take two."

She ran her tongue over her lower lip. Chances were he had three of a kind. Since she had two aces, she needed either another ace or a wild card to win. Her stomach roiled with the fear of discovery when she switched two low cards in her hands for the ones on her lap.

She dealt him two cards and took three for herself. When she picked them up, it took an act of will not to toss her arms in the air and whoop victoriously as she stared with great relief at the pair of aces, a deuce, a ten, and a king. "Your call," she said, beaming a smile.

"Four threes."

Ever so slowly she set down her cards and stared blankly at his winning hand. She'd never see the medallion. She'd never solve its mystery.

In another few seconds she'd be stark naked!

His eyes twinkled with mischief. "Let's call the game a draw."

"What's that supposed to mean?"

"It means you can stay dressed. I've never forced a woman to remove her clothes, and I don't intend to start now."

The thought of him with other women rankled. "Does this mean neither one of us won or lost?"

"Yup."

She sucked in a calming breath, grabbed her wrapper from the chair, slid her arms inside, and fastened the belt around her waist.

Zachariah laughed. "Even before you suggested the card game, I'd already decided to let you see the medallion."

"You mean I went though all of this for nothing."

"That's right."

He reached for her hand and dropped the two halves of the medallion into her palm.

TWELVE

Rebekah squeezed her fingers around the medallion and felt the bite of the cool, sharp edges against her palm. For years she'd anticipated this moment, had dreamed about it, and had spoken at length to her brothers who laughed and patted her head the way one does a foolish child, calling her their muttonhead dolt of a little sister.

"You know," she said, because her heart was bursting, "as a small girl, I was certain this day would come. Regardless of the odds, I knew that somehow I'd find the matching half of my medallion. This is like a small miracle, my small miracle. Have you ever wished for something with all your heart, Zachariah, and then had it come true?"

She saw the indecision on his face and thought he might not answer. When he finally spoke, the tone of his voice chilled her.

"As a foolish kid, I wished for impossible things. I was stupid to think I might actually get them. I learned early on that if I wanted anything, I'd better figure out a way of getting it for myself or do without. Miracles don't happen to a little boy with a whoring mother and a drunken father," he said, clearing his throat and looking uncomfortable with his disclosure. "I'd better go find James. He'll want to see the medallion."

As he left the room, she fought the urge to go after him, knowing nothing she'd say could erase the pain in his eyes. A wave of compassion washed over her.

She couldn't shake the words from her mind.

A whoring mother and a drunken father.

She thought back to her own childhood and realized how fortunate she was to have had not one but two sets of parents who'd loved her. She didn't remember her birth parents, but her brothers had assured her of their undying devotion. Then Ruth and Nicholas had adopted them, and except for her stepfather's occasional drunken binge, she and her brothers had had a relatively happy childhood.

Zachariah had not been so fortunate. She wondered about his life. Had his mother loved him? What had become of his parents? She imagined Zachariah as a child, the same dark eyes and hair, embarrassed to be seen with his parents and taunted by the other children. No boy should have to endure such a sad upbringing.

The weight of the medallion in her hand roused her from her musings. She should not be sitting here heavyhearted. She should be jumping for joy because she'd finally claimed her prize.

Blinking away the tears that clouded her vision and opening her fingers, she admired the light from the oil lamp bouncing off her medallion. She slid the two halves on the table in front of her and because of her growing excitement could barely concentrate.

The cabin door swung open, and in rushed Jimmy on a gust of wind. "I can hardly wait to help you find where the treasure is hidden. Let me have a look." They butted heads as he leaned over her shoulder to study the gold disc.

Zachariah pulled a chair next to the table, turned up the wick on the lamp, and cast a casual glance at the medallion.

"What do you think, Zack?" Jimmy asked, his voice higher than usual.

"I've looked at the markings many times. None of them make any sense to me."

"No one would go to all this trouble without having a good reason." Rebekah ran a fingertip along the engravings.

Jimmy examined the medallion closely. "How did you happen to find this inside your doll?"

"Annabelle's head fell off when I was playing with her. Otherwise, I'd have never found the medallion. Just think of all the 'ifs.' "

Jimmy's forehead ridged. "Huh?"

She clicked off on her fingers. "If my doll's head hadn't fallen off, I never would have known this medallion existed. If I hadn't decided to go to Londonderry, I'd never have seen the matching half hanging on a chain around Zachariah's neck. Just think how many miles the medallion has journeyed. It originated here in America, traveled to England inside my doll, then returned with me. The chances of my finding the other half were so minute that I suspect there's more than just coincidence involved."

Jimmy's eyes widened. "You mean magic?"

She laughed. "Maybe. But I was thinking of fate. I'm certain destiny played a part in bringing the halves of the medallion together."

"What do you mean by destiny?" Jimmy asked, scratching his chin.

"A greater power intervened and made it possible for me to find both halves."

Zachariah's brow arched. "You're handing the kid a crock of bull. James, there is no higher power, no fate, no destiny. You want something? Then you make it happen. There's no magic involved here. Rebekah was lucky. It's that simple."

Jimmy turned to him. "But when I asked you about the card game, you said that Miss Benson was the unluckiest person you'd ever met."

"That's true. I'm guessing her winning streak has ended."

"How can you say that? I have the medallion," Rebekah pointed out with a smile.

Jimmy tapped the engraving. "Those curved lines could be a bridge."

"Or a rainbow," Rebekah added.

"Or the marks from a rake, or a dog's tail, or a cucumber, or just about anything," Zachariah said bluntly.

Beauregard hobbled into the room and reclined at Rebekah's feet. She reached down and scratched his ears. "This dog is another example of destiny," she said, ignoring the wrath on Zachariah's face. "If Zachariah hadn't shown up when he did, this animal would be dead. Too many occurrences in our lives defy explanation, and certainly, coincidence plays a part, but I'm convinced there's more involved. Whether you believe in destiny or in mystical powers or that it's simply coincidence is up to you, but I believe fate brought us together."

Jimmy glanced cautiously at Zachariah, who mumbled an expletive under his breath.

Thinking Zachariah narrow-minded, Rebekah continued, "Just think, years ago my parents probably sat at a table just as we are now, holding this medallion in their hands. Isn't that exciting?"

"Didn't you live with your parents?" Jimmy asked.

"No, they were missionaries to the Abenaki Indians in Maine, so they were gone most of the time. I was very little when they died, but my brothers told me a lot about my mother and father."

"Were your parents rich?" the boy asked.

"They were rich in the ways that matter most. They loved each other and their children. They barely could make ends meet, but they sacrificed everything they had in the name of God."

Zachariah pushed back his chair and stood. "I won't sit here and listen to you fill James's head with this bull."

Rebekah's chin shot up. "How can you be so cruel?"

"The sooner he learns not to believe such drivel, the sooner he'll be able to stand on his own two feet. All this talk about destiny and love and miracles is too much for me."

She leaped up and hurried toward him. "Every word I said was the truth."

"Your parents were no better than mine."

"What's that supposed to mean?"

He moved closer. "They were selfish."

"My parents were wonderful people. They loved each other. There was nothing they wouldn't do for their children."

His angry gaze bored into her. "If they loved their children so much, why didn't they stay home and take care of them!"

Zachariah stalked into the barn and sat on a bale of hay. Knees bent, head in his hands, he closed his eyes and damned his big mouth for spewing words better left unsaid. What had possessed him to say what he had? Years back he'd buried his past by building his cabin miles from his home, where he'd hoped to start a new life without degradation and shame. He'd vowed never to return to Maine, and to never again step foot in his mother's house, a brothel and very successful business, left to him after her death.

As a child, he'd detested the pity in people's eyes. With raised fists, he'd defended his name and his parents, but when he turned twelve, he finally accepted the obvious. His parents didn't care. He could have accepted almost anything else. Even hatred would have been easier to bear.

At least hatred took effort.

Even after all these years his gut clenched with disappointment. He shook his head in disgust. A grown man should be able to remember his past without dredging up the emptiness of his youth.

He stretched his legs in front of him and heaved a disgruntled sigh. He owed Bekah an apology. He hoped his cruel comment had not shattered her idyllic image of her parents. Who was he to judge? He knew nothing about love or how families interacted.

Keeping a low profile, Zachariah spent the night in the barn and awakened feeling stiff and ornery. He was too old to sleep on hay-strewn planks. Too old to be sleeping in a chair while Bekah slept in his bed. Without his daily dose of liquor to dull his senses, he was edgy, his temper erupting with little provocation. He blamed his sobriety for his recent outburst and promised to keep a firmer grip on his emotions.

He put his hat on his head and started outside. As he neared the cabin, he saw smoke pouring from the opened windows and Bekah standing in the doorway waving a towel.

Running, he leaped onto the porch. "What's happened?"

"Jimmy wanted to surprise you."

"He's succeeded."

"I cooked breakfast," came the boy's voice from inside. "The bacon is a little black, but I gave Beauregard a piece, and he gobbled it right up. I guess that means it can't be too bad."

Bekah's eyes implored him to be kind to the boy.

Did she think so little of him?

He suspected either this was another of James's attempts to let him stay or he was trying to atone for whatever he'd done. Sighing, Zachariah realized how much he'd miss the boy after he left.

He sauntered into the cabin, and grabbing a strip of bacon from the plate, bit down and grinned. "Beauregard was right. This isn't half bad," he said, taking two more pieces.

"I'm cooking eggs, too, and toasting some bread," James said with a wide grin. "Everything will be ready in a few minutes."

The smoke inside the cabin tickled Zachariah's throat. Trying not to cough, he went outside to find Bekah and to breathe some fresh air. "Here, I brought you something," he said, clearing his throat and handing her a black bacon strip.

Bekah took a bite. "I hope we don't have to eat much of this," she whispered with a smile that warmed him.

"I plan to slip a few pieces under the table to Beauregard. I knew some day that dog would come in handy."

"Jimmy's trying to please you."

"Don't you think I know that? I care for that boy, but I can't have him staying here with me. I'm hardly a shining example for him to imitate."

"He has no one."

"Why don't you take him in?"

Bekah slid her tongue over her lower lip.

The innocent gesture awakened lecherous thoughts in Zachariah's mind.

"I'd like to, but once I find out what the markings on the medallion mean, I'll be staying with my brother Mark and his wife. In time, I may go back to England. Were I to remain in America, I'd want Jimmy to come live with me."

Zachariah rested his hand on her arm. "I need to apologize for yesterday. I had no right to say what I did about your parents."

"You merely stated your opinion. I can't fault you for that."

"I had no business implying your parents didn't love you and your brothers. They had work to do. I'm sure they loved you. How could anyone not care for someone like you?" he asked, with a playful jab to her chin.

He cared for her.

"Nothing you said swayed my outlook anyway."

"Good, I'm glad to hear that."

Taking Bekah's arm, he escorted her inside, where the air had begun to clear. He closed the windows and door, and after throwing another log in the cookstove, sat at the table next to her.

James scooped a generous portion of runny eggs onto their plates. "Miss Benson and me were up late last night figuring out her medallion."

"I'm surprised you two weren't up early this morning digging up the countryside," Zachariah replied, instantly regretting his sarcastic comment, which went unnoticed by James.

"We don't know where to dig yet, or I'd have been out last night." The boy slid toast onto their dishes and then poured tea for Bekah and coffee for Zachariah. "Miss Benson said she'll share her treasure with me."

"Jimmy, I told you there might not be a treasure."

"Yea, I know, but I'm thinking there is. Just like you said yesterday. Your parents were sensible people. They wouldn't want to waste all that time scratching up a gold disc if it didn't mean nothing." James dropped himself down on a chair and scooped up a mouthful of eggs.

"I don't want you to be disappointed. My parents didn't value money and jewels. Besides, before the medallion can lead us to something wonderful, we have to translate its markings."

"Yea, but we figured out a lot last night."

"Our conclusions were only wild guesses." Bekah bit into her toast and chewed thoughtfully. "When I first looked at the medallion, I thought I'd solve the puzzle in minutes, but I was wrong. Jimmy, you shouldn't get your hopes up."

James waved his hand over the table. "I know that."

Bekah glanced toward Zachariah. "Once we find out where the other half of the medallion comes from, we might have a clue where to look for answers."

Zachariah smiled innocently and wondered how she'd react when she found out he'd lied about that, too.

"But it's nice to think about getting rich. I'd buy myself a real house. Just like this one," James said, turning toward Zachariah.

Zachariah spooned eggs into his mouth. "I'd think you could do much better than this cabin."

"This cabin is perfect, and I'll get myself a dog like Beauregard, along with horses, chickens, and a few cows. I might even put stuff on a stump for Mad Mary like you do."

"What would have happened to your animals if . . . well . . . you know?" Rebekah asked, blushing.

"You mean if I'd been hanged."

"Well, yes."

"Mary looks out for the animals when I'm away. I suspect in time, she'd have figured something had happened to me. Either she'd have slaughtered them for food or sold them."

"Beauregard wouldn't like living with her," James added. "I hear she has hundreds of cats living at her shack."

"I'm sure that's an exaggeration."

James finished his breakfast. "I thought I'd take Beauregard for a walk, and while I'm outside, I'll try to figure out the medallion's meaning. The sooner I solve it, the sooner everyone will be rich." He hurried across the room with a piece of toast in his hand for Beauregard. "Zack, I plan to share my half of the treasure with you."

Zachariah smiled at the boy. "If there is a treasure, I wouldn't feel right taking half of what rightfully belongs to you."

"You're my very best friend, and I'm giving you half no matter what."

"James," he said before the boy could shut the door. "Thanks for the breakfast." For a moment the words clogged his throat. "You're my best friend, too."

When the door shut, he turned to see Bekah smiling at him. "Zachariah Thompson, you're a very nice man."

"Where did you get that fool notion?"

"You help feed and clothe an old lady. You rescue a dog about to meet its demise. And I can tell by looking at you how much you care for James. I've decided you're probably one of the nicest men I know."

"Then you've led a sheltered life with a bunch of sons of bitches."

"The more I get to know you, the more you remind me of my brothers. On the surface you hide your feelings like they do, but inside you're no more than a big pussy cat."

"I've been called lots of things," he said, smiling at her choice of words, "but never a pussy cat. Though I suspect comparing me to the worthless creature does me justice."

"See what I mean?" she said, waving her hand. "You say one thing and mean another. You like animals, yet you won't admit that you do."

"I have no trouble admitting I like animals—dogs, cattle, and just about anything, but I don't like cats. The lazy creatures are worthless. All they do is lie around all day. They don't come when called. They're stupid."

Bekah sipped her tea. "Say what you want, but I know better."

"What's so appealing about cats?"

"They're cuddly and fun to play with. And they're smart, too. They come only when it's beneficial to them."

"I've never thought of it that way." He enjoyed being with Bekah and was relieved she didn't hold a grudge about what he'd said. "I imagine when you have your own house, you'll have at least one of the damnable, good-for-nothing, lazy creatures curled on your lap," he said with a playful roll of his eyes.

"I figure I'll have at least two cats so they can keep each other company when I'm not at home. And when you come to visit, I might even allow you to hold one," she said, in a teasing voice.

"That'll never happen."

"What won't happen? Visiting me or holding one of my cats?"

He couldn't fathom never seeing her again after she left, although he expected that to be the case. He almost pointed out his chances of visiting England were nil, but he caught himself in time. His blunt statement would ruin the closeness they shared. "When I do visit, I aim to take Beauregard along. He'll scare your mangy cats up a tree."

As they laughed together, he slid his chair closer to hers. He wanted to tell her where he'd gotten his half of the medallion, but he wasn't sure how to broach the subject. "I need to tell you something."

"If you're about to apologize again, I've already forgiven you. I've forgiven you for stealing my half of the medallion, too. I'm just happy to finally have it back."

"I explained that I'd need it for a week or two."

"If you expect me to simply hand over my medallion, you'll be disappointed because I'm never parting with it again."

"I thought you understood I'd be taking it back," he said and saw the anger flash in her eyes.

"You might have said something about it, but my mind was preoccupied. I was clad only in my nightgown and worried about losing it, too." Her pupils narrowed. "Besides, why do you need the medallion?"

He reached for her hand. "I swear to you, when I took your medallion, I never intended to keep it for myself. Once I was through with it, I had intended to give it back to you."

"I wish I could believe that," she said, hesitantly. "I want to believe you, but you've lied to me in the past. How can I be sure what you're saying now is the truth?"

"Because I mean every word I say."

She leaned closer. "Even if I believed you, I won't hand over the medallion. It's mine now, and I'm keeping it."

He figured he'd worry about that later. For now, he had more important matters to discuss.

James ran into the cabin with the dog at his heels. "I've been thinking about the medallion. I bet we'll find the treasure if we can figure a way of getting the person who owned the other half to tell us where it came from."

"I do, too," Bekah replied, looking at Zachariah and waiting for him to speak.

Zachariah cleared his throat. "I don't know where it comes from. I found it shortly before I met you. I know nothing about its origin," he said, reaching for her hand, and watching her pull away.

"But you said . . ."

"I may have implied . . ."

She shot to her feet. "Oh, you implied, all right. You downright led me to believe the medallion was a family heirloom. I'll never believe another word you say."

Zachariah had never visited Mary. She'd never spoken to him, and the few times he'd greeted her, she'd run off.

He'd heard she shot at trespassers. Though she'd never killed anyone he knew of, she'd maimed several drunks and intruders who hadn't had the good sense to leave an old lady alone. Most of her bullets missed their mark, and the only injuries he'd heard of had been flesh wounds, making him suspect she was either a damn bad shot or an expert markswoman.

If not friends, he and Mary were acquaintances. Though their relationship was not easy to define, he was certain she would not harm him.

Well, almost certain.

Against his better judgment and to make amends, Zachariah had decided to try to persuade Mary to give him back Bekah's garments. The old recluse had no need for such an elaborate dress. He'd simply explain the mistake and offer her something in trade.

Some twenty minutes later he spotted Mary's shack set in a grove of hemlocks about three hundred feet from the rippling water of the Merrimack River.

On the porch that swept the front of the cabin, he saw half a dozen cats decked out in colorful ruffled collars, basking in the rays of the afternoon sun. A dozen more felines slept on the porch's low roof. Other cats reclined on the woodpile outside the shack.

On the porch several lengths of lavender fabric flapped in the autumn breeze. He wondered why Mary would want such fancy material since he'd never seen her wearing anything but men's clothing. A fat tomcat missing half an ear and wearing a lace collar wound its way around Zachariah's ankles. Its loud purring grated on Zachariah's nerves. Shoving the animal aside only added to its determination. Finally, to shut it up Zachariah bent and scratched the gray cat's chin, a mistake that cranked up the blasted purring several decibels.

He straightened and continued forward, his furred companion almost tripping him. As he neared the shack, he called out, "Mary, it's Zachariah, your neighbor."

Every sense alert, he stepped forward. He hadn't brought along a weapon so she'd know he meant no harm. "Mary, I've come to pay a visit."

A bullet whizzed passed his head.

Zachariah jumped behind a tree and trained his eyes toward the shack, where he saw the end of a rifle poking from an opened window.

"Dammit, Mary, what kind of way is that for you to greet your neighbor?"

She fired again.

"I want to make a deal with you about the dress you took from my clothesline. I want to trade something for it."

Another bullet rushed by the trees.

Zachariah was about to leave when he noticed a cluster of embroidered violets on the scrap of lace around the cat's neck. The cat stretched his neck affectionately when Zachariah removed the collar and discovered it was a garter.

He eyed the porch where the lavender material shone like satin in the daylight. Could that be part of Violet's dress? He wasn't certain, but from this distance he thought he detected sequins along what might have one time been a neckline.

The hair on the back of his neck rose in alarm as he shoved the garter into his pocket.

"Mary, have you seen my friend, Violet? If she's in trouble, I want to help her."

After several seconds the cabin door creaked opened a few inches. With arms raised he started toward the shack. As he stepped onto the rickety porch, he saw a gun barrel aimed at him through the opened window. He ducked his head to clear the low doorway and stepped inside.

Once his eyes adjusted to the dark interior, he could see Mary waving a Kentucky rifle at him. Her steely eyes and her finger on the trigger of her firearm hinted their friendship was questionable.

"Mary, if you'll tell me where you found that material hanging on your porch, I'll mosey on back home and leave you to your business."

She darted a nervous glance out the window before shoving the door shut with her foot. She wore men's trousers with a navy-colored shirt that buttoned up the front. Her hair frizzed haphazardly around her head and added to her wild appearance. The lines on her face deepened as she contemplated her next move.

Uneasiness tightened the muscles in Zachariah's throat. He stared her down and forced his mouth into an easy smile. He could not afford to lose this battle of wills. "I originally came hoping you'd give me back the dress you found on my property, but that was before I saw this," he said, pulling the garter from his pocket. He rubbed his thumb over the embroidered violets. "I think this might belong to a friend of mine. I need to know where you found it."

Up close, Mary looked older and more threatening. It was easy to understand how she'd come by the name Mad Mary. The shack was sparsely furnished with a wooden crate serving as a table, two hardback chairs, and several barrels sawed in half and tipped onto their sides, most occupied by sleeping cats on tufted pillows. As he eyed the interior of the shack, it struck him that Mary took better care of her pets than herself. He spotted part of Bekah's dress already stuffed with feathers beneath an orange tabby.

When he noticed Mary following the direction of his gaze, he waved nonchalantly. "Don't worry about it, Bekah has plenty of other dresses." Unfortunately, her other dresses were miles away.

When the old tomcat butted its head against Zachariah's pant leg, he considered shoving it away. Instead, he bent and tucked the scruffy creature in the crook of his arm. With a sideways glance toward Mary, he scratched between the cat's ears and muttered in an affable tone, "What have you been up to, old buddy? I have something that belongs to you." He wrapped the garter around its neck.

The cat's deep purr broke the silence and the tension.

Mary's scowl softened.

Figuring he was making progress, he said, "I want to help

Violet. I'm her friend."

Without a word she lowered her weapon and waved for him to follow. They made their way up a narrow flight of stairs leading to a loft. Deep in the shadows under the eaves, he saw the outline of a person beneath animal pelts. Shoulders and head hunched forward, he carefully avoided the low rafters and hurried toward the makeshift bed.

Zachariah heard Mary going back down the stairs. He pulled the furs aside and from the light of one small window, caught a glimpse of Violet's hair.

"Honey," he said, resting his hand on her shoulder.

She came to with a start, scrambled away from him, and wrapped her arms around her bent knees. She whimpered, tears flowing down her face.

"Violet, don't be afraid, it's me, Zachariah," he said, removing his hat. "I shaved my beard and had my hair cut."

She squinted and directed frightened eyes at him. Her shoulders slouched when she recognized him. "If that old lady hadn't shown up when she did, I'd be dead."

Her voice was hoarse and barely audible. From the dark bruises around her neck, he assumed someone had tried to strangle her. "Who did this to you? Did you see his face?"

Tears filled her eyes. "Yes, when he tried to choke me, I saw who it was."

Zachariah moved closer and wrapped a comforting arm around Violet. He felt at ease with this woman, and no wonder since he'd spent most of his growing up years around whores. Someone like him had no business with a lady like Rebekah.

Violet nestled against him, her body shaking as she spoke. "It was Grizzly. He told me he killed the gambler in Londonderry and that if I didn't tell him where you lived, he'd kill me, too."

"What did you say to him?"

"Nothing. I knew he'd kill me no matter what I said."

Another shiver racked her body. "He wrapped his hands around my throat. I stared at his cold, unblinking eyes, certain I was about to die."

"How did you escape?"

"As I started to lose consciousness, I heard a shot. The next thing I knew Mary was helping me up the stairs and covering me with furs."

"Did she kill him?"

"I don't know. She doesn't speak to me. I don't know whether she can talk. I'm not sure how much she understands." Violet wrapped trembling fingers around bunches of material on his shirt. "I'm terrified he'll find me here. I want you to take me to your cabin."

"You're safer here than at my cabin." Tomorrow he'd send Bekah and James away. Finally, he'd be rid of the woman who'd raised havoc with his feelings. And he'd grown damn tired of seeing James's worship-filled eyes; no man could live up to such high regard. But deep inside, he knew his life would be meaningless without those two.

He pulled Violet's head against his chest. "Don't worry about a thing. I'm just glad you're all right. Once Grizzly's behind bars, I'll come get you."

"He'll find you," she said, echoing his thoughts.

"When he does, I'll be waiting."

THIRTEEN

Zachariah descended the stairs and found Mary sitting in a chair with a calico cat on her lap, another at her feet, her nimble fingers stitching a length of lavender fabric into a cushion. Leaning against the crate was a Kentucky rifle known for its accuracy. The cabin smelled of baked bread and not the stench of animal excrement that he'd envisioned.

"Mary, I'd like to ask you a few questions."

She ignored him and continued sewing.

He pulled closer the only other chair within sight and sat down. The lines on Mary's forehead deepened, but her gaze remained on her work.

"What happened to the man who attacked Violet?"

As she started to stuff feathers into the cushion, a yellow tiger kitten leaped across the room and caught a feather mid-flight. She shrugged and continued working.

"Did you shoot the man who tried to choke Violet?"

She brushed a gray strand of frizzy hair from her forehead.

"I need to know if he's dead."

Slowly she raised her head. Her steely eyes bore through him. "Ain't fittin' ta kill no one." Her voice shook with anger as she nodded toward the Bible angled against the wall beside a fat orange cat licking its tail.

Zachariah watched the animal for a few seconds and wondered whether Mary would change her mind about killing if he voiced his opinions about the worthless creatures.

A gray tiger kitten jumped onto his lap and kneaded Zachariah's legs before finally curling into a ball. When he looked down, he noticed the cat's ruffled collar was made from the material of Bekah's dress.

"I want to thank you for saving Violet. I'd take her home with me, but it isn't safe."

Mary tied a knot, brought the cushion to her mouth, and bit off the excess thread.

Figuring he'd exhausted the conversation, he set the kitten on the floor and stood. "I'll be leaving now."

He reached the door when a preposterous idea struck, and he called himself a doggoned fool for giving the notion a second thought.

But if he wanted to make amends with Bekah, he couldn't return empty-handed.

Zachariah gritted his teeth and hoped he wouldn't regret his fool-hearted gesture. "Mary, I have a really big favor to ask of you."

Rebekah placed her folded wrapper inside her valise with the rest of her belongings. She dreaded the thought of breaking the news that she was leaving to James. She didn't want to hurt his feelings, but had no choice. It was time for her to get on with her life. Now that she had the pieces of the medallion, there was no reason to remain at Zachariah's cabin.

First thing tomorrow, she'd saddle up the horse she'd ridden here and ask for directions to the nearest town. Once there, she'd send word to her brother and arrange transportation to his house.

Sitting on the edge of the bed, she glanced out the window at the bright red and gold leaves on the surrounding trees and thought how much she'd miss Zachariah. It was time to go before she completely lost her mind and her heart. He'd stolen from her, lied to her, and continued to lie to her. Although she'd forgiven him, she would never again trust him.

She was attracted to Zachariah, but she knew he'd be a poor choice for a husband. She remembered her stepmother's warning after one of her stepfather's bouts with the bottle. *Never get tangled up with a drinking man. Don't repeat my mistake, Beck.* Deep lines had bracketed her mouth. Memories of her stepmother's forlorn expression still saddened Rebekah.

She'd noticed Zachariah's attempt at abstinence, but she realized the fight to remain sober would never end. Her stepfather had fought the same battle many times and lost. His drinking had caused great pain for their family.

Don't repeat my mistake, Beck. The words ran through her mind as she slid her valise beneath the bed.

Knowing all this did not make leaving any easier. For reasons she couldn't understand, she cared for Zachariah and knew she'd always remember him. She prided herself for having the common sense to leave while she still could, for not falling victim to his mesmerizing dark eyes or his strong chin. Fortunately, she'd barely noticed his broad shoulders or the way one corner of his mouth crooked upward before he laughed. She wouldn't miss his taunting grin or his heated gaze that made her feel naked while fully clothed. She'd finally be able to walk across a room without blushing or thinking inappropriate thoughts.

She'd finally be free of him!

Then why did her heart feel as though it were caught in a vise?

She left the bedroom and spotted Jimmy with his head bent over the medallion. Seemingly lost in thought, he didn't hear her approaching, and he jumped when she laid her hand on his shoulder. "Have you been able to figure out anything else?"

"These squiggly lines could mean water."

"Yes, I do think you're right."

"And this square shape," he said excitedly. "Could be a building. I think these small marks are either people or animals."

She ruffled his hair. "When are you going to tell Zachariah what you told me?"

"Huh?"

His blank expression didn't fool her. "You know bloody well what I'm talking about. When are you going to tell Zachariah what you know about the murderer?"

"Soon, but first I gotta figure something out."

"You need to talk to Zachariah."

"I will," he said without conviction.

Rebekah knew he was nervous. "Good, I want you to do it this evening or first thing tomorrow morning."

"I'll tell him tomorrow when he wakes up."

"You promise?"

"Yup," he replied, lifting the medallion closer to his face. "Give me a couple more days and I'll figure out this puzzle. Then me and you can go dig up our treasure."

Zachariah arrived with a covered basket under his arm. He shoved the door open and upon entering his cabin, found James at the table with his nose six inches from the medallion. Beauregard, stretched along the stone hearth, greeted him with a yawn, while Bekah sitting nearby ignored him.

"I'm back," he said, expecting James to pump him with questions about Mary.

"Me and Miss Benson are convinced these lines mean water," the boy said, looking at Zachariah, then to Bekah for her approval.

"Yes, you have a sharp mind, Jimmy. If there is a treasure, I'm hoping you'll use some of your share to pay for schooling at a reputable institution. Even if there is no treasure, I plan to ask my brother to put up the funds for you to attend a school of your choice."

"I don't need no schooling, right, Zack?"

Zachariah lifted his free hand in surrender. "Don't put me in the middle of this. I'm in enough trouble already." He smiled at Bekah, hoping she'd return the gesture. Instead, she turned away and fingered one of the carvings on the sill.

"It never hurt a man to know how to read and write," he remarked, not wanting to cram the idea down James's throat for fear he'd do the opposite.

"I guess not," the boy replied, sounding doubtful, "but before I saddle myself with books, I aim to find the treasure. When I'm rich, I'll decide what to do about schooling."

"You don't have to decide tonight," Zachariah said, setting the basket on the floor beside Bekah's chair. "I'm sorry if I misled you about my half of the medallion. When you asked me about it, I had to lie. I was fighting for my life."

"And I think these marks here might be animals or people," came James's voice.

"I went to Mary's shack hoping to return with your dress, but since that wasn't possible, I brought you something else."

"I wonder what this mark means? Here's something I didn't notice before. There's a thin line that curves from one end of the medallion to the other. Since it's so long, I bet if we figured out what it means, we'd have our answer," James continued without glancing up.

"What's in the basket?" Bekah asked, looking curious.

"It's a peace offering." Zachariah grinned and hoped he hadn't compounded his earlier mistake by giving her something she didn't want. He certainly had no use for it.

"Don't think this will make up for all the lies," she said, swinging her hand and undoing the clasp on the basket. Out sprang two gray tiger kittens. One climbed up Zachariah's pant leg and held on to his thigh with sharp claws. The other made a beeline for the window, knocked over his carvings, climbed up the side of the wall, and then sat looking down from a rafter.

Jumping to her feet, Bekah covered her mouth with her hands. "Kittens," she said, her eyes filling with tears.

"I hope you want them, because I sure as hell don't have any use for two kittens."

"Of course I want them."

"Then you like them?"

"Oh Zachariah, they're perfect."

As he unfastened the kitten from his leg, he thought of several imperfections but kept his opinions to himself. Instead, he handed Bekah the tiny critter and allowed his hand to remain on her arm. "I'm glad you like them."

Her eyebrows arched. "I hope that other little fellow doesn't fall."

"You needn't worry. I've heard cats always land on their feet."

"But it's such a little thing. We can't leave him up there for long."

"I don't see why not. At least, that way we'll know where it is."

She tucked the other gray kitten in her arms and rubbed under its chin. She cooed at it and laughed when it meowed.

Personally, he saw nothing funny about a cat meowing, but he laughed right along with her because he felt so happy. Laughter came easily with her smiling at him as though he'd done something truly wonderful—like solve the medallion's mystery when all he'd done was arrive with two kittens.

He figured he'd enjoy himself while he could, and was surprised to hear himself say, "I'll go fetch the ladder and get that little guy down for you. He looks frightened up there all by himself."

Stranger still, Zachariah was whistling when he left to get the ladder, and he was still whistling when he returned a moment later, leaned the ladder against the rafter, and climbed up the rungs. As he neared the top, the kitten skittered to the far end of the rafter. Not to be outsmarted by a cat, he looped his leg over the beam and inched closer to the animal. It looked as if it were having a good laugh at the foolish human trying to rescue it.

"Be careful," Bekah warned from below.

"Are you concerned for my safety or the cat's?"

"Both."

Beauregard meandered across the room, eyed the kitten, and howled. He stopped baying only long enough to catch his breath.

Zachariah pushed himself along the narrow beam until he was within a few feet of his goal. "Here, kitty, kitty," he said, extending his hand. The kitten shifted its gaze from Beauregard to him, rounded its back, hissed, and swung sharp claws at his fingers, nicking two and drawing blood.

"Why you . . ." He almost said, good-for-nothing, his words going downhill from there, but he caught himself in time. Forcing a smile, he tried again. "Don't be frightened, here, kitty, kitty." As he tried to grab the cat by the scruff of the neck, it lashed out again, slicing his hand and wrenching a curse from him. Finally, on the third try, he managed to wrap his fingers around the small trembling animal and handed it to Bekah. She tucked the kitten beside the other one, and smiled adoringly at the creature.

Beauregard's incessant baying continued until James pushed the dog out the door, muting the blasted racket.

"Naughty, naughty," Bekah said to the kitten in a soft tone.

"That doesn't sound like a scolding to me," Zachariah said, hopping down from the ladder. "Will you be that softhearted when you have children?" The thought sobered him. Bekah would leave and marry another man, a man who would take her into his bed. Why was he torturing himself? He'd known from the start she'd never be his.

This would be their last night together.

A chill settled in the pit of his stomach.

He left to put away the ladder, sickened that their time together was about to end.

But he had no choice because it was no longer safe at his cabin. Eventually, Grizzly would arrive, and unlike Mary, he wouldn't have any qualms about killing anyone who stood in his way. If Grizzly didn't show up, then the law would, ready to loop a noose around Zachariah's neck. He couldn't chance having either Bekah or James implicated in his escape.

Once they were through with supper, he'd break the news that they'd be leaving first thing tomorrow morning.

Rebekah ate supper, her kittens tucked in their basket at her feet, the lining much like the silk of her chemise. Mary had made good use of the garments. Each kitten wore an adorable ruffled collar around its neck, the material like that of her missing dress. She would gladly have given Mary the dress in exchange for these two delightful kittens. Finding another dress would be easy, but finding such sweet kittens impossible. Every time Rebekah looked at her pets, she'd remember Zachariah's thoughtfulness.

Once she left, she might never see him again, but she was certain she'd never forget him. Even if she trusted Zachariah, and even if he wanted her to stay, she couldn't. They were too different. And his drinking. She would never put her future in the hands of a drinking man. The thought saddened her.

After receiving such a fine gift, it would be difficult to announce that she'd already packed her bags.

Convinced he was about to solve the markings on the medallion, Jimmy would be disappointed to hear she was leaving.

Maybe she could arrange to meet the boy in a few weeks so she could tell him whether she and her brother had figured out the puzzle. Meanwhile, she meant what she'd said. The boy was a smart lad who should attend a suitable institution of higher learning instead of refining his skills as a thief.

Maybe if she looked around, she'd find a person willing to take in the child. Someone kind and loving.

They cleaned up the supper dishes, and when she could no longer put off the inevitable, she hugged a kitten to her chest and glanced at Zachariah and then Jimmy. She'd grown used to living with the two of them. How could she tell them she was ready to leave?

"I have something to say," Zachariah said interrupting her announcement. He tried to shoo away the kitten that seemed intent on climbing up his leg.

Bekah watched him bend down, undo each tiny claw and then, looking as if he'd run out of options, he picked up the animal and set it in the crook of his arm. Zachariah blew out a slow breath. "The cussed creature thinks I'm a tree."

"He likes you." Rebekah wanted to add that she liked him, too. More than just a little. Since there was nothing to gain from this disclosure, she remained silent.

"I'm relieved to hear that," he said with a quirk of his brow. "He's already shredded my leg from ankle to knee; I'd hate to think what he'd do if he didn't like me."

"He's frisky."

"Is that what you call it?"

Reclining on the hearth, Beauregard opened one eye and growled.

Zachariah pointed at the dog. "Keep that up and you'll be sleeping in the barn tonight."

Heeding the warning, Beauregard rested his head on his paws and closed his eyes.

Scratching her kitten under the neck, Rebekah nodded toward the animal in Zachariah's arms. "I decided to name that one Spider because the marking on his forehead reminds me of a web and also because he's so good at climbing. This other I'll name Smokey because of its color."

"I've never heard tell of anyone naming a cat Spider until now." Holding the medallion, James came up beside them. "Zachariah, take a good look at this long line. I'm convinced it's important, but I can't think what it might mean. Do you have any ideas?"

"I told you the other day I wasn't able to figure out the engravings. And I still don't believe this medallion is a map to a hidden treasure. You'll be very disappointed if nothing comes of this."

"Well," James said, scowling, "You'll eat those words when I come knocking on your door with my treasure."

"I hope you're right, James. I wish you the best in your search. Let's sit down together. I have an important matter to discuss with both of you."

Zachariah's stomach clenched.

James's pupils narrowed. "Why do I get the feeling you're gonna say good-bye? 'Cause if that's it, I ain't leavin'."

"I have no choice. It's not safe for either of you to stay here." He looked at Bekah and wondered what she was thinking. He didn't have to wait long.

"I packed this afternoon. I'd planned to leave tomorrow morning. There's no reason for me to stay any longer."

The words knifed through Zachariah. For her own safety, he'd wanted her to go, but he hadn't expected she'd be this anxious to escape.

"Good," he replied for lack of anything better to say.

"What's gonna happen to the medallion?" Jimmy asked.

"Of course, I'll be taking both halves with me to my brother's house. I'll give you his address so we can keep in touch in case we figure out the medallion's meaning."

"You think I believe that? Once you leave, I ain't ever gonna hear from you again."

Zachariah tapped the boy's shoulder. "James, watch your language." Then, turning his attention to Bekah, he said, "For a while the medallion will be staying with me."

"Not on your life, Zachariah Thompson." Bekah snatched the medallion from Jimmy's hand and dropped it down the front of her dress.

"That's not going to stop me, so you better hand it over," Zachariah warned.

She moved forward, her eyes lit with fury. "Just try it, and I'll . . . I'll . . . well . . . just try it!"

"Look, I don't plan to keep the medallion, but I need it for a few days—a week or two at the most."

"Nothing you say will change my mind."

"You don't have a choice," he said calmly. "Your medallion is my only chance to clear my name. I found it in the dirt about ten feet from the dead man. I'm thinking it belonged to the killer. Violet showed the drawing of the medallion to some of her clients at the Blooming Garden. One, nicknamed Grizzly, showed a lot of interest in the medallion and my whereabouts. So much interest, in fact, that he tried to strangle the information out of her the other day."

Bekah gasped. "Is she all right?"

"Yes. When I went to Mary's today, I found her there recuperating. But if Mary hadn't shot at the man and frightened him away, Violet would be dead. Grizzly will be back, and the next time he might come here. I want to find him before he finds me. You both need to leave early tomorrow morning."

"Even if Miss Benson goes, I'm staying put," Jimmy broke in, his eyes wet with unshed tears.

Zachariah decided to drop the subject of the medallion until morning. Bekah wasn't leaving with it, but for tonight, he'd let her keep it.

She snatched the kitten from his arm. "The next thing I know, you'll be telling me you're keeping my pets. Well, you're wrong about that, too."

She stomped across the room. "And just in case either of you intend to sneak into the bedroom after I'm asleep, bear in mind, both halves of my medallion will be pinned to my nightgown. And I'm a light sleeper."

FOURTEEN

Rebekah ran into the bedroom and slammed the door. The nerve of that man, thinking she'd simply hand him her medallion! Her body shook with frustration and anger.

Zachariah had bluntly stated he wanted them to leave without as much as one word of regret. Not one sigh, not even a look that might indicate he'd miss her. She set both kittens on the floor and watched them chase each other around the room. How could he so easily talk of her leaving? Certainly, he must realize they'd never again set eyes on each other.

All day she'd pondered how to break the news that she'd packed her bags, several times rephrasing how she'd tell both Zachariah and Jimmy that she'd miss them, that she'd never forget either of them. She'd planned on saying she didn't want to leave, but an unmarried woman had no business living in the wilds of New Hampshire with a man and a boy. Especially with a sensual, good-looking man who drove her to distraction.

Then too, she'd discovered another of his many lies. She'd thought Zachariah's half of the medallion had been a family heirloom and had hoped to hear its extensive history. Now, she might never understand its markings.

Earlier, whenever she'd thought of Zachariah's stealing her medallion, her insides had clenched with disappointment. Now that she understood his reason for lying, that lie seemed almost necessary. Not that she condoned lying, but how could she hold a grudge against a man fighting for his life? Were she in the same predicament, she might do the same.

Sitting on the edge of the bed, Rebekah ran her fingers over the medallion's ridges and realized what she needed to do. She had to return Zachariah's half of the medallion so he could try to capture the man called Grizzly, a man capable of strangling a defenseless woman. A shiver skittered down her spine.

Since she'd arrived with only part of the medallion, she'd be in no worse shape. She decided to jot down its markings in her diary so she could later try to solve the puzzle.

After sketching the symbols in her book, she pinned both halves of the medallion to her nightgown, climbed into bed, curled up beside her kittens, and soon fell asleep.

She awoke as the sun crested the horizon. After swinging her feet over the edge of the bed and having her toes attacked by sharp claws, she scooted off the mattress and lifted her kittens in her lap. "How are my precious babies this morning?"

Smokey batted her finger, but Spider climbed up the sleeve of her white nightgown and swatted at the pin on her chest. She smiled at the mischievous animals, thinking how much she already loved the two when she noticed that the pin on her nightgown was empty. She pulled back the covers, certain the medallion had come loose and fallen in the bed, which didn't make an iota of sense because the pin was clasped shut.

She could not accept the obvious.

Zachariah had stolen her medallion. Again!

Barefoot and clad only in her nightgown, she ran into the living room, where she saw Zachariah slouched in his chair with his hat angled over his face and his legs supported on several crates. She wrenched the boxes out from under his feet and slammed her fists into his chest, shouting, "You no-good, thieving scoundrel!"

He jolted awake. His hat fell to the floor as he grabbed her hands. "I like a woman with fire in her eyes," he said, yanking her against him.

For a moment she expected him to kiss her. As she leaned against his chest and wrapped her arms around his neck, the empty pin jabbed into her chest, reminding her of her mission. She pushed free. "Wipe that damnable grin from your face, you despicable hooligan."

"What have I done now?"

"You know darn well what you've done."

"I do?"

"And to think I was going to give you back your half of the medallion this morning, but no . . . that's not good enough for you . . . you aren't happy with half, so you sneak into my bedroom in the middle of the night and take both pieces . . . I'll never, never forgive you for this." She sucked in a deep breath. "And furthermore, if you don't give me back my medallion, I swear I'll . . . I'll call the sheriff myself and tell him where you are."

His confused expression changed to disbelief. "You'd do that?"

Had she not spotted her empty pin on her nightgown, she might have retracted her ridiculous statement. "You bet I would. Now hand it over."

"I don't have your medallion." He jumped to his feet. "Have you checked the bed?"

"Of course I have. You needn't act as though you don't know where my medallion is, because I'm not falling for any more of your lies."

"Look," he said, his upper lip disappearing beneath his mustache. "You weren't leaving with the medallion this morning because I had intended to take it from you. But I did not sneak into your bedroom last night. If I had, you'd have known."

"Right," she said, waving away his preposterous comment. "I

can picture you tapping my shoulder before pilfering my medallion."

He moved close to her and lifted her chin with his forefinger, forcing her to look into his eyes. "You'd have known I was in your bedroom because it wouldn't have been the medallion I was after."

She saw the passion in his eyes along with the sincerity. She was convinced he was telling the truth. Knowing Zachariah was not responsible for the medallion's disappearance made the loss almost bearable.

The tightness in her chest eased. "I must be a muttonheaded numbskull because I believe you. If you didn't take the medallion, then who did?"

He wrapped his arm around her shoulder, and she sought the comfort of his warmth. "Maybe James borrowed it for the night. He knew his time to solve the puzzle was running out."

"But I had it pinned to my nightgown. How could he have taken it without waking me?"

"James's nimble fingers can pick the pockets of a man on a galloping horse."

"Where will you be going when you leave here?" Zachariah asked on their way to the barn.

"My brother, his wife Lorena, and their two sons live in Manchester. Mark is part owner of the Huntley Benson cotton mill."

"I've heard of the textile company. Your brother is doing all right for himself."

"Yes, he is."

"Will you return to England after your visit?"

"I may."

"I see," he said.

"What exactly do you see?"

"I see a woman who'd grow restless out here. I see someone who'll eventually go back where she belongs. Which is as it should be."

"Will you miss me after I've left?" She instantly regretted asking the question.

"I'll finally be able to rest," he said with a low chuckle. "How did you end up in Londonderry if you were heading to Manchester?"

"I disembarked from the ship in Boston and sent my brother a short note telling him not to worry, and that I'd contact him within three weeks."

"Mmmm, sounds mysterious."

"Yes, and I fear he'll want a detailed explanation when he sees me." She rested a hand on Zachariah's arm. "If I eliminate everything unfit to repeat, I've little left to say. I certainly can't tell him I was wounded while helping a convicted criminal to escape from jail. Or that I lived in your cabin with you and Jimmy without benefit of a chaperone." Or that since leaving England, she'd learned what it meant to be kissed and to lose herself in a man's embrace.

"If that's going to irk him, think what he'll say when you tell him you lost playing strip poker," Zachariah said with a hearty laugh.

"That match was a draw," she reminded him. "If I mentioned our card game, Mark would want to lock me up in a closet for the rest of my life."

"How many brothers do you have?"

Smiling, she replied, "I have two older brothers, Mark and William, each one bossy, always telling their little sister what to do or not to do. They won't acknowledge I'm an adult."

"Growing up in a family must be wonderful," he said, with a wistful look in his eyes.

"Though my brothers can be bothersome, they have their

good points, too. I complain about them, but even when they're ordering me around, I know they have my welfare in mind."

"That's strange," Zachariah said, his arm dropping away from her shoulder as they entered the barn.

"What's strange?" she asked, her stomach sinking at his tone.

"James is gone."

"Surely he'll be right back."

"He's taken off."

"How do you know?"

"His horse and saddle are missing along with his clothes. Chances are you've seen the last of your medallion."

"I don't believe that," she said, raising her voice. "Jimmy would never steal from me."

"If that's so, then where is he?" Seeing Bekah's disappointment, Zachariah gritted his teeth. "I should have never allowed that medallion out of my sight."

"Since James was able to sneak into my bedroom and take the medallion off my nightgown without waking me, he could have just as easily picked your pockets."

"Humph."

"I'll take that as a yes," she said smugly.

"James's running off poses a problem. You won't be able to leave today. I can't have you traipsing through the woods and getting lost. I'll escort you myself tomorrow."

She rolled her eyes. "I can tell by your tone what an imposition that will be. You needn't put yourself out. I've a fine sense of direction, and I can manage on my own. If you'll draw a map and write out the directions, I'll be on my way."

"Directions, now that's a splendid idea."

She smiled approvingly.

He pointed to his left. "You go that way for half a mile. When you get to the old oak with the busted limb, you bear right for about four hundred feet." He touched his temple. "Of course, if old man Whittier's already cut that oak tree for firewood, then turn at the stump."

"You needn't be so sarcastic. Even without the bloody tree, I'm sure I can find my way."

"To an outsider, every tree and rock looks the same. I'll take you into Litchfield tomorrow."

"But I'm all packed and I'd planned . . ."

"I'm responsible for your safety, so you aren't going anywhere today."

"You're just as bossy as my brothers."

"Smart men, your brothers," he replied, grinning. "If you hope to ever see your medallion again, I need to find James before he gets too far. I never thought I'd see the day when that kid stole from me."

"You want me to tell you why you infuriate me?"

"No."

"You don't trust anyone. You don't believe in anything."

"For good reasons, too," he said, not caring for her uppity tone. "You, on the other hand, believe everyone and everything."

"Thanks to you, my gullibility has diminished."

"I'm glad I could help," he replied, tipping his hat. "You can't go through life believing the stars are yours for the picking. It's better to be cautious."

"I don't believe in anything that ridiculous, but I happen to think there's more good than bad in people."

"A lot of people are rotten to the core, and most don't give a damn about anyone but themselves." The image of his parents sprang to mind.

"How sad it must be to live life with such a sour disposition."

"If there's more good than bad in people, answer me this."

She crossed her arms. "What?"

"List Grizzly's virtues."

Rebekah conceded the verbal match to Zachariah, but she

still believed most people were good. "Allow me to go with you. I'd like to speak to Jimmy and find out why he took the medallion."

"That won't be possible."

She blew out an exasperated sigh. "And why not?"

"It's too dangerous. Grizzly could confront me, and I don't want you there if he does."

"If he shows up here, should I invite him in for tea?"

Zachariah's stomach clenched. He didn't want to leave Bekah because he feared for her safety, but she was safer here than with him. "Mary wounded Grizzly. He's more likely to be in town licking his wounds than chasing through the woods." He paused and studied her stiff upper lip and the stubborn angle of her chin. "But just to be sure, I'm leaving you my gun."

"I told you before I don't like guns."

"I remember how we made our getaway. Trust me, your comb will not deter Grizzly."

"Leave your gun if you wish, but I won't use it. I don't believe in violence."

"Suit yourself." He dropped his weapon next to his chair. "It's already loaded."

Intending to follow Zachariah, Rebekah hurried to dress while he was outside saddling his horse.

He entered the cabin, crossed the room, and stood so close she could smell the autumn air on him. "I hope you aren't planning anything foolish while I'm away."

"You can be certain I won't be tearing apart this place looking for my medallion."

"At least that's a consolation." He hesitated a moment as if carefully choosing his next words. "I'd like you to go outside with me and practice shooting my gun."

The man didn't know when to quit. She rolled her eyes at him.

"All you have to do is squeeze the trigger."

"I'm sure I could manage that if I had to."

"You are the most stubborn woman I've ever met," he said with a resigned sigh. He stepped forward, wrapped his arms around her waist, and pulled her against him. His mouth captured hers in a kiss that was neither gentle nor harsh. She leaned into him and parted her lips because she wanted to taste him again, because this might be their last kiss.

"Bekah," he murmured. "You asked earlier whether I was going to miss you." He nibbled his way along her jaw and lingered behind her ear. Gently, he tugged on her earlobe. "You'll never know how much."

She stood on tiptoe, ran her tongue along his ear, and whispered, "You said you wouldn't kiss me again unless I asked you to."

He skimmed his fingers over her back, his hands teasing the sides of her breasts. "I thought you had. Next time, I'll ask you to repeat the request to be sure."

Pulling away, he tweaked her nose. "I'd better go." He strode toward the door and glanced over his shoulder. "With James gone, we'll be alone tonight."

"I know that."

"We've never been alone before."

"Well . . . no."

He uttered a dry chuckle. "Has anyone ever awakened you with a kiss?"

Not sure where the conversation was heading, she didn't answer.

"Then let me warn you. Tonight's the night."

"Don't tell me you're going back on your word again," she said, with a playful shake of her head.

"What do you mean?"

"You promised not to kiss me unless I asked you."

He threw back his head and laughed. "Before the night is over, you'll be asking me."

Warmth climbed up her neck and settled in her cheeks.

His smile widened. "Several times, in fact."

Lost in a warm haze, she watched him walk away and shut the door. With her mouth still warm from his kiss, she considered what he'd said in a teasing tone. Would he kiss her awake? A shiver of anticipation raced down her spine.

He'd also said he'd miss her. How could a simple statement fill her with such intense joy?

The sound of horse's hooves a moment later roused her. If she didn't want to lose sight of Zachariah, she had to work fast. She ran to the barn, slid a halter over a mare's head, and leaped onto the animal. Though she hadn't ridden bareback in years, she didn't have a choice. If she waited to saddle up, she'd never catch up to Zachariah.

In the distance she spotted his tan hat and his wide shoulders beneath the cowhide jacket. Being careful that he wouldn't spot her, she remained about four hundred feet behind him. Ducking her head to avoid tree limbs, she carefully maneuvered the mare along the narrow path. She watched a squirrel scampering from limb to limb and a rabbit hopping toward a large rock. This was pretty country, she thought, but too isolated.

At first, she feared she'd lost sight of Zachariah, but as she crested the next rise, she spotted him going over a knoll. He glanced around, and for a moment, she feared he'd seen her. When he continued, she knew that he hadn't so she kneed the mare forward. She didn't notice the low branch until it struck her forehead. The jolt knocked her off balance. With arms flapping, she slid off the horse and landed on the ground. The mare nickered and took off toward the cabin. Except for her pride, her injuries seemed minimal, so she stood and dusted off her skirts.

"Bloody worthless horse," she muttered under her breath.

Since there was no way she could follow Zack on foot, she decided to go back to the cabin. She rounded a stand of trees and heard a noise behind her. Thinking Zachariah had doubled back, she laughed, swung around, and came face to face with a grinning man missing several teeth. "Missy, if you ain't a sight for sore eyes."

"What can I do for you, sir?" she asked politely, trying to look calm.

He wrenched her arm. His foul breath gagged her. "Yer that gal from England, ain't ya?"

"Yes, I am."

"I been lookin' for ya."

Neither the man nor his clothing had touched a bar of soap in some time. Rebekah feared she'd lose her breakfast.

"I heared tell 'bout a gold piece with a treasure map. Some kid at the Garden been shooting off his mouth."

"Was that a tall boy with red hair and freckles?"

"Sure was."

"James was jesting. Besides, I no longer have the medallion, so you're wasting your time."

"Missy, I got plenty of time ta waste. That kid swore there was treasure, and he said he'd give me a share if I helped him find Grizzly, but I figured, ain't no sense sharing if I can git the whole of it fer myself."

"Where's James now?"

"Damned if I know. I roughed him up a little. When he ran off, he was spouting some nonsense 'bout Zachariah Thompson beating me up good."

Hoping to see Zachariah, she glanced around and was disappointed. "How did you know where Zachariah lived?"

"I heared his cabin was a distance from Mad Mary's shack. I've raised a ruckus at Mary's a time or two. So I took a chance and started combing the woods. I'd 'bout given up when I spotted you on a horse behind Zachariah. I guess it's just my lucky day." He shoved her ahead of him. "Now, git."

"I'm not going anywhere with you."

He pulled a large knife from his belt. "Don't give me no trouble. You and me are going to the cabin over yonder so I can have myself a look around."

"The medallion is not there," she repeated, her voice firm, although her legs shook so much she could barely walk.

"Ya think I'm dumb? Keep yer lyin' fer someone else." He pushed her hard.

She fell on her hands and knees, scrambled to her feet, and tried not to panic. When they entered the cabin, she lunged for the gun.

He knocked her to the floor. "Now, Missy, yer not thinking 'bout harming old Hank, are ya?" Laughing, he grabbed the weapon and hurled it out the door.

Given the chance, she doubted she'd be able to fire a gun at any man, but she'd feel safer with the weapon in her hands.

"Have a seat, Missy, 'cause old Hank's gonna have hisself a look 'round." He pushed her into Zachariah's chair beside the window.

Beauregard yawned and eyed the man. Rebekah had read of dogs accomplishing heroic feats, and this one was large enough to eat a person and still be famished. She waited for him to react. Beauregard sniffed the air several times.

"Be a good dog, and old Hank'll git ya somethin'." He hurried to the table and unwrapped the loaf of bread. After tearing off a piece for himself, Hank hurled what remained at Beauregard. The dog wagged its tail and looked adoringly at the man before tearing into the bread.

As Hank checked boxes and emptied shelves, Rebekah tried to figure out how to escape. She clasped her hands together to keep them steady. If she ran, could she open the door and grab the gun before Hank caught up with her?

The door was behind her and since the chair was deep, she'd need to first sit up and then stand. She eyed Hank's back, slid to the edge of the cushion, and sprang to her feet. She ran to the door and wrenched it open.

Rough hands wrapped around her neck. "Do that agin, Missy, and yer dead." Grabbing a handful of her hair, he yanked her back inside.

Trying not to cry out, Rebekah bit her lower lip. He threw her down hard on a wooden chair.

A low growl rushed past Beauregard's throat.

Hank reached in his pocket and threw the dog a strip of dried beef. "Be a good doggie."

Once the dog stretched out on the hearth and closed its eyes, Hank turned back to Rebekah. "You move from this here chair and I'll slit yer throat."

Rebekah knew he meant what he said. She couldn't count on Beauregard's help. Zachariah would not be back for hours. Her only hope of surviving was to cooperate with Hank.

Hank disappeared into the bedroom, returned a moment later with a bed sheet, and ripped the material into lengths.

She feared he was going to tie her up. "I was planning to make myself a pot of tea. Can I offer you anything?"

"Jest sit there and be quiet."

"On second thought, I'd prefer a little corn whiskey. Won't you join me?"

His black eyes lit. "Now yer talking."

She stood, and on wobbly legs, managed to walk across the room. She lifted the jug off the floor and started pouring the amber liquor into a glass when he came up behind her. "Yer sure pretty."

"Thank you," she said, smiling and trying to ignore the stench.

He took the jug from her hands and slid dirty fingers along the side of her face. "Ain't had myself a woman in a coon's age."

She decided he had weasel eyes, smelled like a skunk, and moved like a rat. "My, you're a handsome devil." She batted her eyelashes at him and glanced down demurely. As he reached for her breasts, she shoved the glass in his hands. "Drink up, there's plenty more where this came from."

"Missy, ain't ya gonna join me?"

"Sure." She splashed corn whiskey into another glass, then sat in the chair opposite him. Mimicking her brothers, she lifted her glass in the air. "Cheers," she said, trying to look as though she meant it.

He downed his drink. "Whooowee, this is potent stuff." Wiping his mouth with the back of his hand, he brought the jug to his lips. A bead of the dark liquor threaded down his neck.

She wondered how much corn whiskey it would take to render him unconscious. He was a stocky man with a large belly, a thick neck, and muscular arms. He had long graying hair and stained clothing. From his belt hung the long knife sheathed in leather. If Zachariah were to ask, she'd have to admit that Hank possessed no virtues, at least none she could see.

Her kittens scampered from the bedroom. Smokey batted around a wood shaving. Spider dashed across the floor and climbed up Hank's pant leg, settling itself on his lap. When Hank stared down at Spider, Rebekah feared he might hurt the kitten.

"Cute li'l cuss," he said, rubbing his hand along its neck.

A man who liked cats couldn't be all bad. That's what she'd tell Zachariah.

"Missy, drink up, 'cause I gotta git lookin' fer that gold piece the kid talked 'bout."

"James stole the medallion from me. I don't know what he did with it."

Hank stood, sidled up next to her, and brushed against her arm. When she glanced at his trousers, she saw the outline of a protruding shape.

She knew what he intended and damned the alcohol for not dulling his libido.

She remembered her brother advice, which at the time had turned her face crimson. If a man makes improper advances, hit him where it matters. As she stood and faced him, his grin widened. She slammed her knee into his privates.

He howled and grabbed himself.

She started to run.

He threw himself on her and tore at her hair. "Little bitch, yer gonna be sorry fer that!"

Kicking and screaming, she tried to defend herself. He was too strong, too heavy. She couldn't breathe, and as she gasped for air, certain she was dying, she heard Beauregard's deep growl.

"Git off, ya son of a bitch!"

Hank rolled off her, swatting at the animal. She sucked in a deep breath and tried to stand. Beauregard yelped. She turned and saw Hank swinging a chair at the dog. Looking dazed, Beauregard stepped forward and collapsed. Blood dripped from the wound on the side of his head.

Hank shoved her aside and cussed.

Tears rimmed Rebekah's eyes.

"This is yer fault," Hank said, slamming the door and bending to look at her. "I was gonna show ya a mighty fine time, but ya wrecked everythin'."

She spat in his face.

He wiped his cheek on his sleeve. "Yer sure a feisty gal, but I'm done with ya." He shoved her down in the chair and wrapped lengths of the ripped bed sheet around her arms and legs. He knotted the material several times and hurried into the bedroom, where she could hear him thrashing about.

Several minutes later Hank came out of the room, his eyes black with rage. "Mebbe you was right 'bout that gold piece not bein' here. When I git my hands on that kid, he'll 'fess up right quick."

"You leave James alone."

"You should be worryin' 'bout yerself."

"You better worry about what Zachariah will do to you when he sees his cabin."

"That drunken no-good won't find out nothin'."

She almost told Hank that Zachariah didn't drink anymore, but she wondered whether that was true. Besides, she was through conversing with the lout.

"Such a waste," he said, coming close and shaking his head.

She met his gaze.

"Ya jest don't know what ya missed." He bent down and kissed her cheek. "Too bad I gotta kill ya."

FIFTEEN

Horrified, Rebekah watched Hank pour lantern oil over the furniture and floor. He struck a match against the sole of his boot and set fire to Zachariah's chair. Flames leaped from the oil-soaked fabric. Gray smoke billowed, filling the room.

Rebekah knew Zachariah would not return in time to save her. She needed to stay calm if she hoped to save herself.

Hank tossed his head back and howled with laughter. "Ya don't seem so frisky no more, Missy." Grabbing the kittens at his feet by the scruff of the neck, he opened the back window and threw them outdoors. "If that gold piece is in the cabin, ya better tell old Hank right quick."

"If you'll untie me, I'll show you where I hid it."

"Missy, I ain't 'bout to fall for that. Tell me where ya hid the gold piece. When I find it, I'll set ya loose."

"You're a despicable, good-for-nothing excuse for a human being."

"Yer a disappointment ta me, Missy. I'd expected us ta git along real good."

Rebekah struggled to loosen her wrists and ankles, aware of the searing ache in her wounded shoulder.

Hank disappeared into the bedroom with the oil can. When he returned, he had her valise, and black smoke poured from the bedroom doorway. "Nothin' like a good fire ta light up the sky." His maniacal laughter filled the room.

"What are you doing with my bag?" she asked.

"I'm gonna cut the damn thing up ta make sure there ain't no secret compartment."

Gritting her teeth, Rebekah squirmed and tugged at her bonds. "If I had Zachariah's gun . . ."

"Yer really scarin' me, Missy." Hank poked his finger under Rebekah's chin and tipped her head up until she was staring at his wild eyes. "Damn shame. Me and you coulda had ourselves some fun."

Hank covered his face with a handkerchief, hurried across the room, and opened the door.

Rebekah coughed, trying to clear her throat. Her eyes felt gritty, and tears streamed down her face. Finally, she freed one hand. She struggled to untie the knots she could no longer see.

From a few feet away came Beauregard's deep growl.

"Git off me, ya son of a bitch . . . !"

"Get the beast," she shouted to the dog and realized those words might be her last.

The air grew hot and thick.

Sweat poured down her face.

Terrified, she stared at the flames crawling overhead. As she fought to undo the knotted fabric, she twisted and tugged at the material with her bound hand until pain shot up her arm. Finally, she freed herself and unwrapped the lengths of the sheet from her legs.

Trying to filter the acrid air, she covered her mouth with the hem of her skirt. Lightheaded, she crawled toward freedom and fresh air. She inched along the floor, but she lost her sense of direction. Her lungs burned. Her throat hurt. She gasped for air.

She could hear nothing but the roar of the flames.

She dragged herself another foot.

And then another six inches.

Soon she'd reach the door. The thought kept her going.

Another few feet and she could breathe again.

Surely, she was near the door. She'd crawl onto the porch and roll into the yard.

She'd be safe.

Alive.

She'd fill her lungs with fresh air.

She could do it. She was so close.

So very close.

Just a few more feet.

She reached her hand as far as she could. She moaned.

Weak and out of breath, she wrapped her fingers around the leg of the table.

Six hours later and half a mile from his cabin, Zachariah smelled smoke. He kneed his horse to a gallop. When he entered the clearing, he saw what remained of his home. Only the chimney stood, surrounded by a pile of smoldering rubble.

His insides clenched with fear.

Where was Bekah?

How had the fire started? He'd built the stone chimney, so he knew it was safely constructed.

Surely, Bekah wasn't . . .

Heart pounding, he jumped off the horse and hit the ground running. He dashed into the barn, ran its length, and checked every stall. Not seeing Bekah, he hurried toward the remains of the cabin, looking for clues.

The charred wood crunched under his boot heels as he strode over the burnt planks. Acrid smells gagged him. Surely, Bekah had escaped. If the fire had happened at night, he'd have cause to worry. But it was daylight, so she'd have been awake.

Unless Grizzly came looking for his medallion.

A feeling of dread crawled up his back.

He should never have left Bekah alone.

Guilt-ridden, he gazed at what remained of his possessions: a spoon sticking out from the ashes, the rung of a chair, part of a bowl, a metal pan. Kicking aside a burnt timber, he uncovered the knife he'd used to whittle.

His chair was flattened, his carvings destroyed. When he glanced at what had once been his porch, he saw the tip of a jagged wooden wing sticking from the debris. He dropped to his haunches and picked up the soot-covered eagle. The carving reminded him of his weakness. Bekah would say destiny had saved this carving from the fire. If she were here now, he'd tell her no such thing existed.

But she wasn't here, and he had to find her.

What if . . .

No, he wouldn't give credence to his nagging doubts.

Bekah had escaped.

He heard a sound and saw Beauregard hobbling toward him. "Hey boy, where have you been?" As he wrapped his arms around the dog's neck, he spotted the dried blood on its head. His stomach coiled in apprehension.

Setting the eagle carving down, he stood, looking for the gun he'd left beside the door. He sifted through the rubble, but didn't find it. Which, he figured, could be either good or bad news. If Bekah had encountered Grizzly, she might have taken the weapon and run. Or Grizzly had grabbed the gun after entering the cabin.

Of course, there was always the possibility the fire had nothing to do with Grizzly. In which case, what had happened to Bekah?

It struck him that Bekah might be at Mary's shack. If the older woman had spotted the smoke, she would have checked out his property. Finding his cabin destroyed, Mary might have invited Bekah to return with her. He decided to water his horse and then go see Mary.

When he entered the barn with Beauregard at his heels, he heard rustling overhead in the hayloft.

"Who's there?" he asked, his voice hoarse from the smoke.

When no one answered, he climbed the ladder to the loft and ducked a pitchfork hurled at him.

He jumped down and grabbed his rifle from the scabbard of his saddle. "You better come down before I start shooting."

Overhead, he heard tentative footsteps.

"Hurry up, I don't have all day."

When he spotted the trim ankle, covered with a sooty stocking dotted with daisies, he dropped his rifle and ran to the woman he loved.

"Bekah," he said, a wave of relief flowing over him. "Why were you in the loft?"

She eyed him for a moment. Tears slid down her blackened face, leaving behind white tracks. "I was hiding."

He wrapped his arms around her and pulled her to his chest. She smelled like smoke, but he barely noticed. As she clung to him, he remembered the joy that had consumed him when he'd first realized she was safe.

The woman he loved.

When had that happened?

He hadn't planned to love her, didn't want to love her, but he did.

He could no longer deny his feelings. He loved Bekah. His heart soared at the realization as he ran his fingers along the base of her neck. "What happened, Bekah?"

"Someone named Hank showed up looking for the medallion and its treasure map."

"Did he hurt you?"

"Not much."

"Are you all right?" He bent and studied her reddened eyes.

"I am now," she replied with a brave smile.

"Me too," he said, drawing her near and kissing the top of her head.

Though love frightened him, for a moment he basked in the warmth of his feelings. Love had crept up on him and stolen his heart. But this time, he wouldn't play the fool. Never again would he rely on a lifetime of empty promises.

For now, he'd take what little pleasure he could. For now, he'd allow himself to love Bekah with all his heart.

When she left, he'd try to forget her.

He led her to the water bucket in the corner. Taking his handkerchief from his pocket, he dabbed the smudges from her face and saw the scrape above her eyes. "What happened to your forehead?"

"I tried to follow you. But I didn't notice the low-lying branch, and I fell off my horse."

"Bekah, when are you going to listen to what you're told?"

She laughed. "Perhaps never."

Her upturned mouth looked kissable.

"I'm an adult," she said, her chin lifting stubbornly.

"So?"

"So, I don't have to take orders."

"I had your safety in mind."

She pointed her finger at him. "You sound just like my brothers."

"I'll take that as a compliment."

Looking worried, she said, "I haven't been able to find Beauregard, and I'm concerned about him."

"I saw him earlier. He has a gash on the side of his head, but he looks like he'll be all right."

"I'm relieved to hear that," she said. "Hank heard James talking about the medallion and its treasure. I wonder how many more men out there are looking for my medallion."

"I'm getting you out of here first thing tomorrow before

another fool comes looking for his fortune."

"You know," she said, sitting on a nearby barrel. "I think I know why James borrowed the medallion."

"James stole the medallion," he corrected.

"I won't listen to you talk that way about such a fine boy."

"Think what you want, but I'll draw my own conclusions."

"I'm afraid James will get himself in trouble."

"That's a sure thing. With him babbling about that damn medallion, he'll have half the derelicts and crooks in New Hampshire chasing after him."

"He's doing this for you," Bekah said, looking at him in a way that mellowed his anger.

"Doing what for me?"

"He's trying to prove he's worth your love."

"If you ask me, that sounds like a crock of bull."

She tugged on his hand so he'd sit beside her. "James swore me to secrecy, but now that he's gone, it's up to me to tell you."

Zachariah wrapped a comforting arm around her waist. With his free hand, he urged her to rest her head on his shoulder.

"I don't feel right divulging his secret, but I feel I must." She inhaled a ragged breath and brought her arm across his chest.

He could grow accustomed to this closeness, he thought, kissing the top of her head and closing his eyes.

"Jimmy saw the man who murdered the gambler," she said, changing the mood.

"He what?" Zachariah pulled away and stared down at her. "If that's so, why didn't he come forward at my trial?"

"He was torn between helping you and . . . turning in his own father."

Realization dawned in Zachariah's face. "Grizzly is James's father?"

"Yes, Jimmy felt a need to protect him."

"I thought his father was dead."

"He was ashamed to admit the man had abandoned him," Rebekah said.

Zack's heart went out to the boy. Everything was starting to make sense. The funny looks the boy gave him when Zack had discussed the murder. The sideward glances when James thought he wasn't looking. "I can't believe he didn't come to me with this."

"The sheriff wouldn't allow him to visit you in jail."

Zachariah removed his hat and ran his fingers through the spiky hair along the top of his head.

"James promised me he'd tell you."

"And when was that going to happen?"

"He said he'd tell you this morning, but that was before he found out we had to leave. I'm worried about him."

She searched his face, imploring him to understand. "He feels he let you down."

"I certainly understand the need to hide family secrets."

"He was afraid you'd hate him."

"I love that boy," he finally admitted.

Her eyes shimmered with tears. "Jimmy needs to hear you say that. He loves you too. He'd do anything for you. He thinks he's let you down, and now he's out there somewhere trying to find Grizzly so he can prove your innocence."

In the dim lantern light, Rebekah watched Zachariah carry a few blankets up the ladder to the loft. He fluffed up the hay and covered it with a horse blanket. "You deserve so much better," he said, stuffing hay into a folded blanket to make a pillow.

"I'm not complaining."

"Neither am I, because tonight I have you all to myself."

"Oh." The primitive setting, the hay, the dark barn, the earthy smells, the man—definitely the man—stirred the embers low in her belly, robbing her breath and quickening her heartbeat. She couldn't see his eyes beneath the rim of his hat, but she could feel his gaze and the heat pooling between her legs.

"We should be safe up here," he said with a nod when he spotted the kittens in her basket. "Can't they stay down below?"

Relieved that the mood had lightened, she breathed out slowly. "Smokey and Spider will get lonely."

"Beauregard will keep them company," he reasoned.

"But he's not downstairs right now, and besides, I'd miss my kittens if they were away from me all night."

"Keep the mangy things up here if you must," he said with a grin.

His tone convinced her that he loved her kittens almost as much as she did. She set the animals down and watched them chase a moth. "Aren't they the cutest little things?"

He dropped down on the blanket beside her. "What if I said your kittens are pesky creatures?"

"I'd know you were teasing me."

"That's what I thought," he said, thumbing his hat back. "What happened to Hank?"

"I think he ran away after Beauregard attacked him. I couldn't see because of the thick smoke, so I can't be certain."

He hugged her hard, as though he were afraid to let her go.

She twisted a piece of hay around her little finger. "Hank struck Beauregard over the head with a chair. I thought he'd killed the dog." She sighed and stared at the fire flickering in the oil lamp. "I tried to crawl to safety, but I couldn't see where I was going. I thought I was heading toward the door, but I ended up gasping for breath in the middle of the room. I think I passed out. The next thing I knew Beauregard was licking my face and grabbing my shirtsleeve with his teeth. He led me to the back window, and I climbed out. If Beauregard hadn't come in after me, I'd be dead."

She wondered whether the slight tremor that racked Zachariah's body was due to the chilly night air or her words.

He turned her to him. "I don't think I could have lived with myself if you hadn't survived. The guilt of leaving you alone at my cabin would have been too much to bear."

"You and James are a lot alike. You're quick to accept blame for matters out of your control."

"I'd like to wash up and change my clothing," Bekah said, climbing down the ladder.

"I thought everything you owned was destroyed by the blaze."

"Fortunately, Hank took my valise outside, intending to search for a secret compartment. When I was strong enough I brought my bag in the barn and hid it under the hay so Hank wouldn't spot it if he came back."

She'd just disappeared from sight when Zachariah heard her cry, "Come quickly!"

He hurried down the ladder and found Beauregard moaning, stretched out on the dirt floor. "We have to do something," she said, dropping to her knees. "He's in pain. I need to clean his wounds before they fester. Do you have a pair of shears so I can cut away the matted fur?"

"Bekah, let me to do that," he said, taking her elbow, but she wouldn't budge.

"Beauregard saved my life. This is the least I can do for him."

He found the scissors on the shelf with his tools. When he handed them to her, she looked as though he'd lost his mind. "You want me to use these filthy things?"

He wiped them on his shirt sleeve.

"I was hoping you'd start a fire so we can properly wash them and bathe the dog's wounds with warm water. The heat will draw out the infection." He'd started to go fetch water when she said, "Oh, and I need clean rags, too."

A few minutes later he entered the barn with an armload of

kindling and a bucket of water. "I couldn't find any clean rags. Whatever I have inside the barn was used to wipe down horses."

She dashed to the nearest stall. Brushing the hay aside, she pulled out her valise and extracted a pair of white pantaloons. She hurried toward him. "These should do."

"You surprise me," he said, eyeing the article of clothing in her hand.

"How so?"

"When we played strip poker, you took great effort to hide your undergarments beneath a growing pile of clothing."

"In cases of emergency, sometimes a woman must bend the rules of propriety."

The uppity British tone wrenched a laugh from his throat. "Lady, you're full of surprises."

"I'll take that as a compliment."

"And you should."

While he started the fire, she cut the pantaloons in lengths. She ripped off the lace trim and threw it aside. "What a shame," he said, his heart jumping in his throat.

"What's a shame?" she asked, glancing his way.

"I was thinking I'd have liked seeing those on you."

She ducked her head down and busied herself. Even in the dim light, he could see her rosy cheeks.

She scrubbed the shears until they shone, then with great care started to snip at the thick fur matted with blood. Beauregard lifted his head and licked her hand before closing his eyes and sighing.

"What can I do to help?" Zachariah knelt beside Bekah and stroked the dog's neck, fearing that Beauregard might bite if Bekah accidentally hurt him.

"Just keep patting Beauregard so he knows we have his best interests in mind."

For the next hour they worked elbow to elbow. Zachariah

took a moment to appreciate her tenacity. She wouldn't quit until she'd cut off all the long hair. Then she insisted he get his razor, and she carefully shaved the flesh around the wound.

She dabbed at the wound with wet rags until the inflammation ebbed and until Beauregard was sleeping peacefully.

"There, that should help," she said, wiping her forehead with the back of her hand.

Her arms were covered with dog fur, her dress spotted with the animal's blood. Zachariah could not think of one lady who'd willingly soil her clothing for a large slobbering dog.

And he loved her even more for it.

"Bring the lantern closer so we can examine his injury."

Down on all fours with her behind in the air, she eyed the wound up close.

Seeing her in such a position robbed the breath from Zachariah's lungs. He eyed her shapely posterior and jammed his fingers in his pockets or he'd have been tempted to mold the flesh with his hands.

"What do you think?" she asked.

"Think?" His mind cleared a little. "Oh, think . . . yes . . . I think what I see looks damn good."

"I think so, too," she replied, unaware that Zachariah was not referring to the dog.

Sixteen

Zachariah eyed Bekah with concern. "You look exhausted. You even have dark circles under your eyes."

"Perhaps I am a little tired, although I suspect the dark circles are due more to soot than to fatigue."

He dampened his finger and brushed it along her cheek, removing a dark smudge. The light touch sent a shiver of anticipation up his arm. How would he survive a night with her without . . .

He cleared his mind. "It'll be safer for us to spend the night in the loft in case anyone else comes hunting for treasure."

She glanced at the dog a long time. "He seems much better, but I hate to leave him."

"He'll be fine. Besides, I'll check on him during the night, and if he makes a sound, we'll be able to hear him."

While Bekah washed, Zachariah went outside and slid the barn door shut. He set his rifle down within reach. Removing his shirt, he sauntered to the rain barrel and grabbed a bar of soap, then splashed water over his head and chest and scrubbed the soot and grime from his limbs.

Knowing he'd be alone with Bekah, he inhaled a deep breath, fortifying himself for the night ahead. He fisted his hands and swore he would not take advantage of her. Loving her as he did, he wanted only the best. He would not steal her virtue. Only a despicable, worthless louse would do such a thing.

In the moonlight, he saw the silhouette of the chimney and

several burnt planks pointing toward the starry sky. Come morning he'd have another look around to see what he could salvage.

Despite its small size and somewhat rough appearance, the cabin had been his refuge for two years. He'd grown accustomed to his worn chair, his way of life, and his drunken existence. He'd never considered the cabin home because a home was more than four walls and a roof.

As his heart clenched, he admitted his need to be loved and to have a home with Bekah by his side. Being a practical man, he knew that was not possible.

Her brother was wealthy and no doubt influential. Such a man would never accept the union of his sister with someone like him, someone with a disgraceful heritage who'd lived in the gutter and swilled alcohol until he lost track of the days and the weeks, until his existence was a blur of empty bottles and fuzzy memories.

And Zachariah agreed with Mark.

Knowing what liquor had done to him didn't lessen Zachariah's craving for alcohol. Alone at night when the impulse struck to reach for a bottle, he'd instead grabbed his knife and whittled. At first, he stopped drinking because his conscience demanded he stay alert so he could protect Bekah and James. As a bonus he'd enjoyed seeing the approval on Bekah's face. Once she left, his struggle would seem fruitless, yet he knew he had to win this battle for himself.

As he studied the shapes in the distance, he wondered whether Hank might still be out there. Zachariah swore the man would pay for what he'd done. Since Hank had found the cabin, would the law show up next? Tomorrow Zachariah would take Bekah into Litchfield where she could board a stagecoach to her brother's house in Manchester. Then he'd search for Hank and Grizzly, and with luck he'd clear his name.

Even then, his future looked bleak, but he preferred to focus on the night ahead and not worry about the lonely weeks that stretched before him.

Chilled, he slid on his shirt, buttoning it to his neck. In another month the temperature would plummet. If he wanted to rebuild his house, he'd have to hurry.

He opened the barn door and saw Bekah clad in a white gown. Her damp blonde hair hung clear to her waist. Her freshly scrubbed face was rosy, her lips inviting. Innocence radiated from her trusting gaze, eyes that melted his good intentions in a heartbeat.

"The first time I saw you I thought you were an angel," he said, unable to look away.

Her laughter was music to his ears. "I only wish my brothers were here now to hear you say that."

"I'm glad they're not. I don't want to share you with anyone tonight," he said, stepping closer.

He stopped within a foot of her. Inhaling a ragged breath, he warned himself to stay away.

Not to take what wasn't his.

Not to reach out and stroke her hair of spun gold.

Not to bury his face in her neck and indulge in her sweet scent.

She ran her tongue over her lower lip. "Today when I thought I was going to die, a lot of things flashed through my mind."

For a moment sadness filled her eyes.

He wanted to comfort her with a touch but knew if he laid one finger on her, he wasn't likely to stop. So he stood with one hand wedged in his pants pocket and the other around the rifle, afraid to move for fear he'd take advantage of the angel before him.

"I remembered sitting around the breakfast table with my stepparents and brothers. I remembered laughing and being told not to speak with food in my mouth. Isn't that strange?

There I was about to draw my last breath, and I was thinking of a reprimand back when I was seven."

He moved closer. He felt her breath against his face. She smelled like soap and flowers, a scent more intoxicating than fine whiskey. As he stood there not daring to touch her, she leaned into him.

"I thought of my first kiss from a lad I only remember as Edward. It was a mere brushing of mouths, but to a young girl it was so much more. I didn't sleep for nights after that kiss."

His fingers tightened around the gun barrel. "Whatever happened to him?" he asked, a band of jealousy tightening around his heart.

She touched his chest and ran a finger along the rows of buttons on his shirt. "I don't know, nor do I care. When I feared I'd taken my last breath, my thoughts focused on you, Zachariah."

He heaved a deep sigh, debated whether he should ask the obvious and decided against it. "It's been a long day."

"Aren't you curious to know what I was thinking?"

"You should get some rest."

She leaned her head against his chest. "I was wondering what it would feel like to lie with you all night, to lean into you like this and hear the pulse of your heartbeat beneath my ear. I thought it such a shame that I would die without having lived."

"You've traveled from England to America," he said, hoping to alter the course of this conversation. "I'd say you've done and seen more than most women in New Hampshire will see in a lifetime."

"I've covered a lot of mileage, but until I met you, I'd never really been kissed. Before I lost consciousness, I regretted that I'd never have the opportunity to make love."

Zachariah wiped the sweat from his forehead with the back of his hand. He didn't know how to reply. It struck him that the twinkle in her eyes looked more devilish than celestial.

"So I've decided to live life to its fullest," she said in a sultry voice that worried him. "I'm asking you to kiss me and a whole lot more."

The rifle dropped to the ground. "What in the hell do you think you're doing?"

Looking startled, she planted her hands on her hips. "Isn't it obvious?"

"You don't know what you're asking."

"I most certainly do."

"I doubt that."

"I'm a woman."

"I've noticed," he said with a frustrated sigh.

"So where's the problem, unless you can't . . ."

"Believe me, I'd be more than happy to oblige if you weren't so innocent."

"Since you know little about my past, you can't be sure of my innocence." Her cheeks turned scarlet. "Anyway, I know the mechanics, and I've on occasion diapered male babies."

He looked like a trapped animal. "That hardly qualifies you as experienced."

"True, I may not be ready for employment at the Blooming Garden, but those are my credentials."

"You sound as though you're applying for a job."

She swallowed hard. "You know, I never believed asking you would be this difficult."

He removed his hat and threaded his hand through his hair. "You aren't making this easy for me."

"Once my brothers are around, they'll scare off any man who shows an interest in me. This could be my only chance."

"I doubt that," he said, shaking his head.

"I've heard the gossip among the older ladies. I've decided to satisfy my curiosity. Now that I've been given another opportunity to experience life, I don't intend to miss out on anything."

"Why me?"

"I think you'd be a good teacher. Besides, there's no one else around," she added with a flirtatious smile.

"Are you telling me anyone would do?"

"No."

"For a minute I feared the smoke had addled your brain."

She'd asked herself the same question. "I'm attracted to you. I know you desire me; at least, I think you do."

"Don't ever doubt that," he said, pulling her against him.

The beat of his heart beneath her ear thudded like stampeding hooves. She didn't know where she'd found the nerve to speak boldly, and now that she had, her legs shook so much she could barely stand.

"Ever since we met, you've taunted me with kisses and threats of ravishment." Shyly she looked up, her gaze unwavering. "Now that I've given you permission, it seems you no longer want to."

A tremor rocked his body. He pulled away long enough to reach behind her knees and lift her into his arms. "Are you sure?"

"Yes," she replied, the word muffled because his mouth swooped down on hers.

Her bravery vanished the instant he picked her up. The idea of making love had seemed like a good one until now. She was terrified, yet excited.

He carried her to the ladder that led to the loft. "I'll be up in a minute," he said, in a deep voice. "I want to turn down the lanterns and lock the door."

He pulled her to him and moved his lips over hers, dipping his tongue into her mouth, wrenching a moan from deep in her throat. "You know, it's not too late to change your mind."

"That's hardly a fair statement after a kiss like that," she whispered, her pulse rushing in her ears.

"Bekah, don't expect me to play fair . . . not when the stakes are this high."

After missing several rungs, she somehow managed to climb up the ladder. She sat in the middle of the blanket and wrapped trembling arms around her chest. If Zachariah didn't join her soon, she'd go mad with worry.

Would he expect her to strip naked? Surely, they could accomplish the deed with a level of modesty. She'd heard whispers about the pain involved the first time, and she vowed she wouldn't cry out.

Would he be naked?

Somehow, she was certain he'd shed his clothing, but darkness would hide his maleness from her eyes. She wondered whether he'd expect her to touch him. He'd soon find out she did not intend to do any such thing. She wanted to experience lovemaking, but she wasn't going to act like the town trollop.

Or did he already think poorly of her?

Not only had she requested that he kiss her as he'd predicted, she'd asked him to make love to her. Although she knew what that entailed, the specifics were not clear.

She heard the creak of the ladder, and her heart felt as though it might explode. When he climbed into the loft, she noticed he'd removed his boots and socks. For a moment the enormity of what she'd done came crashing down on her.

She'd asked Zachariah to take her virginity.

"I've given you a little time to reconsider," he said, the planes of his face illuminated by the glow of the lantern.

"Are you hoping I've change my mind?"

"Bekah, I've never wanted another woman as much as I do you."

"I haven't changed my mind," she replied, her steady voice belying her anxiety.

He was beside her in a flash. His mouth claimed hers in a kiss that was gentle yet insistent. "Are you nervous?" he asked, pushing her hair away from her face and tracing her earlobe with his tongue.

She wrapped her trembling arms around his neck. "Perhaps, a little."

"You needn't be nervous. I won't do anything until you're ready."

"I won't even know when I'm ready," she confessed.

"But I will," he replied, pulling away and smiling down at her. "I've dreamed of holding you for so long. Tonight you'll finally be mine."

Then he kissed her long and hard, his tongue dueling with hers until desire chased away her apprehension. He pushed her down on the woolen blanket and stretched out alongside her. Then, leaning over her, he wedged his knee between her legs. Conscious of his fingers undoing one of the buttons at her neckline, she reached up to stop him.

He wove their fingers together. "Just one button so I can kiss your neck." His warm breath skittered along her flesh. The clean smell of him increased her need. As he nibbled the sensitive spot on her throat, his knee inched upward.

"Do you like that?" he murmured.

Barely able to breathe, she nodded.

"Before the night is over, you'll be writhing beneath me, pleading with me to take you," he said in a roughened voice that peppered her arms with gooseflesh.

Readjusting his weight, he leaned on one side and shoved open the loft door.

"I'd hoped it would be dark," she said, her nerves tightening anew.

"I want to see you."

"Oh."

"And I want you to see me."

Her heart skipped a beat.

"When I make love to you, I want you to see the sky ablaze with stars. That way when you're back in England and you look at the evening sky, you'll remember me and this night we spent together."

"Zachariah, even if all the stars should vanish, I will never forget you."

He dipped his head and slanted his lips over hers. Releasing her hand, he traced the contour of her breasts, and flicked his thumbnail over her erect nipple. "Before the sun rises, I'll have touched every inch of you."

"This is not what I'd intended," she said, shivering because of the chilly air or because his fingers skimmed her hip, barely missing that part of her that craved his touch.

"And I aim to kiss every inch of you, too," he promised, swallowing her weak protest with a languid kiss.

He pushed himself to his knees and undid the buttons on his shirt. After yanking out the shirttails, he threw the garment aside.

She stared at his sculptured chest sprinkled with dark curly hair that ended in a whorl at his navel and disappeared beneath his waistband. For a moment her eyes focused on his wide leather belt before stealing a glance—at the bulge in his trousers.

She had the good grace to blush and look away. Out of the corner of her eye, she watched him undo his belt buckle and the buttons on his fly.

"You're curious to see what I look like," he said with a low chuckle.

"No," she replied a little too quickly.

Much to her relief, he left his trousers on. He leaned forward, claimed her mouth, and lifted her onto his lap.

She felt his erection beneath her and a tingling sensation

between her legs.

"You make me so hard, I ache," he said bluntly.

She didn't speak because she couldn't.

"It's your turn to undress," he whispered, skimming a finger along her jaw and kissing her mouth. He molded her breasts until she thought she'd do anything he asked.

"I don't intend to . . ." But his kiss chased away her objections.

"Here, let me help you." Before she could figure out what he had in mind, his insistent fingers toyed with the next ivory button on her nightgown. She felt a cool draft and realized he'd undone all the buttons. Embarrassed she leaned into him, but he pulled away and parted the fabric. Her eyes had adjusted to the dim light, and she could see the planes of his deeply shadowed face. A mixture of adoration and lust carved his features. Unable to move, she sat in the silvery moonlight with her breasts exposed, her nipples peaked from the chilly air and the stirrings in her womb.

"You're everything I imagined and more," he said, bending to claim the turgid peak between his teeth and sucking. Then he reclined and pulled her down on top of him. The wool of his trousers rasped against her bare ankles.

"Today when you thought you'd drawn your last breath, you were thinking of me and what I'm doing to you now," he said, sliding a hand over her hip and cupping her buttock, holding her firmly against his swollen erection.

"Yes," she said, though she hadn't come close to imagining the sensations coursing through her veins.

"When are going to remove your nightgown?"

To silence him, she plunged her tongue into his mouth.

His eyes closed and his hand slid between them to the apex of her thighs. "I have all night," he whispered, his finger toying with the curls beneath her nightgown. "I want to see all of you, feel all of you, and taste all of you. And when I have, I aim to start all over again."

The need to please him replaced her fear that he'd think her too bold. She knelt before him and pulled the fold of material from under her. Before she lost her courage, she grabbed the flounced hem, lifted it over her head, and let it slip from her grasp.

She heard his intake of breath.

He looked at her for a long time, drinking his fill, committing to memory every inch of the woman he loved. Soon she'd be an ocean away, and he'd be here, alone with his memories of the vision before him now.

Slowly, as if afraid to wake from a dream, he lifted his hand and traced the underside of each breast. Taking great care, he continued between them, weighting each in his hand before bending to kiss their peaks. She shuddered under his touch, re-assuring him that he was awake.

He shucked his trousers and pulled her down with him. His pulse roared in his ears. He kissed her until he was dizzy with desire. Until his breath and hers came fast and choppy. When she arched toward him, he brushed his fingers along the insides of her legs, moving upward at a torturously slow pace, finally claiming his prize and dipping one finger into her slippery warmth. For only a second her legs tightened in protest around his hand before relaxing and allowing him entry.

Minutes later, throbbing with need, he parted her legs. He positioned himself over her and entered as gently as he could, but still he felt her stiffen beneath him.

"I'm sorry," he whispered, "It'll get better, you'll see."

He kissed her, tasted her, and loved her with his entire heart and soul. It took all his willpower not to declare his feelings. He saw no reason to complicate their lives with his senseless confes-sion. Instead he smiled down at her before slanting his lips over hers, allowing his body to communicate the emotions locked in his heart.

As the sun climbed over the horizon, Rebekah awoke, wrapped in the warmth of Zachariah's arms. Several stiff pieces of hay poked her backside through the woolen blanket that smelled faintly of horse. She felt the chilly October air against her shoulders and scooted farther under the blankets.

Glancing at the man beside her, she was fascinated with the dark shadowing on his face. She loved his strong jaw and his mustache.

In fact, she loved him.

She wasn't sure exactly when that had happened, but she was finally willing to admit it. She loved him, but she would never commit to such a man.

She'd never forget him.

But loving and living with a person were two different things. She wouldn't allow alcohol to ruin her life.

But she loved him and probably always would.

Never again would she look at another star without remembering Zachariah and their lovemaking. He'd driven her to such heights she'd almost touched the sky. Even now, a lingering glow threatened to erupt into a lustful inferno.

In his sleep he leaned into her and sighed.

Last night he'd done things she had never imagined, and he'd satisfied her curiosity—well, almost.

Resting her arm across his belly, she leaned up on one elbow and kissed him, enjoying the soft brush of his mustache on her mouth. "Good morning, Mr. Thompson."

She traced his navel and marveled at the texture of the curly hair beneath her fingertips. Not coarse, not silky, but somewhere in between.

He blinked an eye open. "You better watch it, Miss Benson,

you're playing with fire. If you don't behave yourself, I'll have to teach you a lesson."

She ran her tongue along his lower lip. "You don't frighten me, Mr. Thompson. Besides, I'm a willing student."

"You're my British pupil," he said with a wink before rolling her onto her back and claiming her mouth. "And you were saying?" he asked a moment later, when she could barely think, much less answer his question.

Wanting to explore the rest of him, she slid her hand downward, wrapping tentative fingers around his length and wringing a groan from his throat.

A euphoric expression claimed his face.

"Why, Miss Benson, you're full of surprises this morning," he said in a strangled tone.

Some time later, covered with a fine sheen of sweat, they collapsed together on the blanket. Zachariah hugged Bekah to his side and toyed with her breast.

"Where will you live now that your cabin's destroyed?"

"I may rebuild, but I'm not sure."

"But this was your home."

"Bekah, it was never a home. It was just a place to hang my hat at night."

"Oh," she replied with a frown.

"Speaking of which," he said, sitting and jamming his hat on his head. "Promise me your hair cutting days are over."

She laughed. "Your haircut isn't that bad."

"Thankfully, it'll grow out."

"I like the way it stands up in stiff little peaks."

"That's precisely what I don't like about it," he replied, tapping his hat more firmly on his head. "Ever since you cut my hair, my hat doesn't fit right, either."

"I like the way you look with or without your hat."

"You're saying that only because you don't want to accept responsibility for the damage."

"I could trim it a little if you'd like . . . to even the ends a bit."

He grabbed her wrists. "Only in your dreams and in my nightmares," he said, hugging her tight. He'd never expected to feel this way about a woman. Warmth surged through his veins and filled his chest.

"It's too bad England is so damn far away." He wished she wasn't leaving today.

"It is a bloody long ride on horseback," she replied, with a laugh he tried to commit to memory.

He filled his lungs with her scent. "How long will you be staying with your brother?"

"I haven't decided. Long enough to get to know my nephews."

Manchester—so close yet so far, he thought, his heart clenching. "What's Mark's house like?"

"I've never seen it, but it sounds grand. The building sits on a five-acre parcel of land, bordered by a brick wall with a gateway that leads to a two-acre garden. The house even has a ballroom on the second floor."

"I'm sure Mark would be shocked to see where you've been living the last few weeks."

"There was nothing wrong with your cabin, Zachariah. It was small and cozy."

"Before your arrival, I'd planned on adding on a ballroom, but never quite got around to it," he added with a smile, kissing the tip of her nose.

She traced the contour of his chest. "And I imagine the brick wall and the large garden were next on your list."

"Definitely."

The kittens bounded toward them. Smokey ran onto Bekah's lap and curled into a ball. Spider leaped onto Zachariah's shoulder, knocking off his hat.

"Were you planning to build a playroom for my kittens?" she asked with a playful grin.

"Before your arrival I didn't know about the kittens, but yes, I suppose such a grand cabin in the middle of nowhere should have at least one playroom for pesky creatures," he said with a kiss, holding on tight and wishing he could build the house of her dreams.

SEVENTEEN

Allowing Bekah a moment's privacy, Zachariah climbed down the ladder and was greeted by Beauregard.

Zachariah dropped to his knees and looked into the dog's clear eyes. Beauregard's tongue lolled to one side, and his tail wagged enthusiastically. "How you doing, old buddy?"

"Is he all right?"

Zachariah glanced up and saw Bekah's head poking over the side of the loft. "He looks fine to me."

"I should change his bandages."

"At this rate, you'll be running out of clothes," he said with a grin. "Not that I'm complaining." Even from this distance, he detected the rosy glow of her cheeks. After the closeness they'd shared, it amazed him that such a simple comment could still make her blush.

"I'll take Beauregard out with me so he can do his business. When you're ready, give a holler."

As the dog hobbled along, Zachariah shut the barn door and sauntered toward the charred remains of his cabin.

He picked up the carved eagle where he'd left it yesterday, brushed ashes from its wings, and walked over the rubble until he reached the stone chimney. Glancing at the poplars alive with bright golden-yellow leaves, he thought of Bekah and how much he'd miss her. In the back of his mind a niggling thought persisted.

What if he could forget his past and give Bekah the kind of

life she deserved?

The idea was too preposterous to consider, but he couldn't shake the thought. When he'd left Maine, he'd vowed never to return. No man should be expected to face his demons, not even for the woman he loved.

All his assets were there, a big house, land on a rocky cliff overlooking the Atlantic, all gained by ill means. All soiled by his mother's occupation, an occupation that had ruined his childhood and ultimately took her life.

As a kid, he was embarrassed to be seen with his mother, and he still remembered the other children's cruel taunts. But when she lay dying, her body crippled and her eyes blind from syphilis, he'd felt empathy for her and something else—his unwavering love.

No, he decided, his fingers tightening around the carving, he would never return to Maine.

Not even for Bekah.

Of course, he could sell his property and rebuild elsewhere.

He cursed.

Life as a drunk had been so much easier. Alcohol had dulled his memories. Now that he had Bekah to think about, he had memories worth remembering.

"Move a muscle, and I'll shoot ya."

Zachariah froze. "Who are you?"

"Name's Hank Hovested. I aim to take ya back to Londonderry to collect the reward."

"You've made a mistake. I'm not the man you're looking for."

"Turn right slow and raise them hands or I might have to take you back slung over my mule," Hank said, with a dry chuckle. "It makes no never mind to me whether I bring ya back dead or alive."

Zachariah turned and eyed the man. He was short, big-bellied, with stocky arms and legs. A large knife hung from his gun belt. There were bloodstains on his pant legs. One torn shirtsleeve exposed deep bite wounds.

Hank spared Beauregard a glance. "Keep that beast away, or I'll kill it."

"Don't you like animals?"

"I ain't got nothin' 'gainst animals, just that one. It done this to me." He lifted a bruised arm.

Beauregard emitted a deep growl.

"Down, boy," Zachariah said in a calming voice, and was surprised when the dog obeyed his command. "No need to harm a defenseless animal."

"He's 'bout as defenseless as the devil himself."

"What brings you to this neck of the woods?" Zachariah asked, leaning against the stone chimney.

"I'm bringing ya in, Zachariah Thompson."

"You have the wrong man."

Balancing his rifle in one hand, Hank withdrew a piece of paper from inside his cowhide vest. "According to this poster, you're 'bout the right height. Ya got the right color eyes and hair, too." He rubbed his whiskered chin. "Kinda hard to tell without the beard covering your face. The poster mentions a reward for information leading to the capture of yer accomplice."

"I don't know what you're talking about."

"Ya can play dumb all ya want, but old Hank's no fool. Matter of fact, I've been thinkin' 'bout the small-built man they say helped ya escape. Wouldn't surprise me none if it was that English gal I met yesterday."

Zachariah's hands fisted. "I don't know who you're talking about. When I arrived this morning, I found the cabin destroyed, but I saw no one around."

Hank indicated the burnt ruins. "Wouldn't be much left of

that li'l gal anyway."

Feigning calmness, Zachariah inched forward. "Let me have a look at that poster. I might be able to tell you where this Zachariah character is. I know damn near everyone in these parts."

"Stay put or I'll shoot."

Zachariah struck a relaxed pose. "Suit yourself. But you're going to look real stupid when you arrive in Londonderry with me and find out you've made a mistake. Meanwhile someone else will end up with the reward money."

Looking unsure, Hank shuffled his foot through the ashes, glanced at Zachariah's face a long time before squinting at the poster.

Zachariah reared back and shot the eagle at his face. The jagged wing struck Hank's eye, causing him to drop the poster, creating enough diversion for Zachariah to leap forward and knock Hank off his feet.

Zachariah wrestled the gun from his hands and then yanked the man upright. "Now what am I supposed to do with you?"

Beauregard lunged forward and tore at Hank's cowhide vest with his large teeth. From deep in his throat came a menacing growl.

"Git that gol-darn son of a bitch away from me!"

"Be careful or you'll hurt his feelings," Zachariah said, grabbing Hank by his collar and smashing a fist into his jaw. "That one's for Bekah." He reared back and struck again. "That one's for my dog, and this one is for my cabin."

"Stop, Mr., like you said, I got the wrong man. You ain't Zachariah Thompson. I see my mistake now. Hell, yer hair and eyes are darker, much, much darker."

"My eyes look black when I'm furious," Zachariah said, allowing his words to sink in. "And I can't decide whether to shoot you first and tie you up. Or tie you up and then shoot. What's that expression? Oh, I remember now. It don't make no never mind to me whether you live or die."

"Look, I made a mistake. I don't even want the reward. If ya let me go, I'll never set foot on this here property again."

"I certainly am not about to fall for that rubbish."

"I would never lie to you, Mr. . . ."

"Zachariah Thompson," he affirmed and saw the terror on Hank's face. "I need to get some rope from inside the barn. There's something in there I don't want you to see, otherwise I'd drag you inside."

"I heard 'bout the treasure. I bet you got gold in there."

"That's it," Zachariah said, with a grin. "I need to hide my gold. Meanwhile, I'm taking your gun, and when I disappear inside that barn, I'm keeping it trained on you. If you move one hair, you'll be eating dirt, and my dog will be eating you."

"I'm not going nowhere."

"Good, now I want you to lie face down on my kitchen floor with your arms and legs spread."

Looking confused, Hank glanced around. "Where's yer kitchen?"

"You're standing in it."

"Are you sure you have everything?" Zachariah asked Bekah, eyeing the swatting paw that stuck out of the basket she'd tied to the saddle.

"Yes." Sitting atop a mare she was decked out in her floral dress hiked above her ankles.

He glanced at her trim leg. "I've never seen such fancy stockings."

"Goodness, the hosiery was drab so I added embroidered daisies. Most ladies would be appalled to see these stockings. It would be best if my creative endeavors remained our small secret."

"I like them. And I wouldn't mind telling the world."

"Well, don't."

He remembered how she'd awakened him, so he winked at her. "With your hair pinned up and your collar buttoned to your chin, you look every inch the proper English lady," he said, with an exaggerated lift of his eyebrow. "No one would guess what a willing pupil you are."

Blushing, she waved a gloved hand at him. "Stop that this instant, you impossible hooligan."

"I'm merely complimenting you."

"Thank you," she said, in the British accent he loved, glancing down and then meeting his gaze. "I had a fine tutor."

His laughter echoed in the crisp autumn air.

Looking worried, she asked, "What did you do to Hank?"

"I tied him up so he wouldn't follow us."

"Did you leave him food and water?"

"Yes, and silk sheets to sleep on."

"You needn't be so sarcastic. I'm simply concerned."

He leaned in his saddle and cupped her elbow. "I know that. But Hank set fire to my cabin. He almost killed you. Given the chance, he'd have killed us both. I can't sympathize with a man like that."

Her troubled eyes met his. "That may be, but I don't believe in being cruel."

"The man deserves anything I do to him," he said matter-of-factly.

"But what will he eat until you return?"

He exhaled a frustrated sigh. "All right, since it'll make you feel better, Mary will be caring for the animals. If she sees fit, she'll feed him, too."

Bekah smiled approvingly.

"When I clear my name, I'll come back with the law. They can do with him what they choose."

"Good, I don't want you to shoot Hank."

"I'll give it some thought."

"I mean it," she said, reaching for his hand. "I hate guns."

"Sometimes guns are necessary."

"Perhaps, but I could never fire at anyone, I just couldn't," she said, undoing the sharp claws from the back of her dress and tucking the kitten's paw back in the basket.

"When it means saving yourself or someone you love, you shoot."

Her chin rose, and she shook her head. "Even then, I doubt I could aim a gun at another person. And if I did aim, I would be bluffing."

"Bekah, you don't have the good sense God gave a goose."

"That certainly didn't sound complimentary."

"You're my silly English goose," he said, with a grin, leaning way over and kissing her mouth. The leather saddle crackled beneath him. "Now let's get going before someone else comes looking for his fortune."

When Zachariah stopped to water the horses, Rebekah hopped down to stretch her legs. "I will not go anywhere until I know what's happened to James," she said, folding her arms in front of her, hoping to change his mind.

"We've already been through this. I want you safely tucked away at your brother's house."

"There you go bossing me again. I'm old enough to do as I wish."

He stepped toward her, tucked his finger under her chin, and gently kissed her. "The last time you did as you wished, you broke me out of jail, ended up an outlaw, you were wounded, and almost died in a fire."

"But I saved your life."

"Yes, and I'm thankful for that, which is why I want to keep you safe."

"I can take care of myself."

"Let me guess, you and your trusty comb are ready for battle." He cocked one eyebrow teasingly.

She broke out laughing and leaned against his chest. As she brushed her hand over his shirt, tears stung her eyes. Would she ever again listen to his heartbeat or rest her head beneath his chin, feel his lips on hers, or make love?

Although she loved Zachariah and wanted to please him, she needed to make her own decisions. She pulled away. "I won't go until I hear that James is all right. I want you to change our course this instant. I will not board a carriage in Litchfield."

His top lip thinned and disappeared beneath his mustache. "Standing there like a stubborn child won't change my mind. You're getting on that carriage even if I have to hogtie you and put you on it by force."

"Well." She wanted to reply in kind, but her mind went blank. "Well," she repeated, turning and walking toward the stream where she bent and dipped her fingers in the icy water.

She heard the crunching of brittle leaves and pine needles beneath his boots. He sat on his haunches beside her, but she refused to look at him. When he wrapped an arm around her shoulder, she kept her gaze focused at nothing in particular.

"I don't want you angry with me."

She might have continued to ignore him had she not needed some vital information. "I'm not," she said, though she was.

"Good." He hugged her to him.

"When you're done forcing me onto the carriage, where do you intend to look for James?"

"I figure I'll ask around at the Blooming Garden and find out whether anyone has seen either James or Grizzly."

"If you don't find them there, what then?"

"I honestly don't know."

"I've been thinking," she said, bestowing her best smile on him.

"That look in your eyes worries me."

"Because of the wanted posters offering a reward for your capture, it isn't safe for you to be seen in . . ." She met his gaze, smiled at him sweetly. "I can't recall the name of the town where the Blooming Garden is located."

"Litchfield."

"While it isn't safe for you to roam around the streets of Litchfield, I could do so without raising suspicion."

He heaved an exasperated sigh, which she'd expected. "And what am I supposed to do while you meander around Litchfield getting yourself into trouble?"

"Hide out, of course."

"You are a silly goose, but you're my silly goose."

If he hadn't added the last phrase, she'd have pushed him off balance.

"I didn't want to worry you, but there's something you should see." He stood, reached inside his saddlebag, and withdrew a folded piece of paper, then dropped back down beside her. "Read the small print below my image."

She glanced at the printing on the poster. "So."

He swore under his breath. "It states my accomplice could be a woman."

"It does no such thing. It simply suggests that the person who helped in the escape could be a woman. That means it could also be a man of small stature or a boy. It could be anyone in New Hampshire under five feet tall."

"Hank didn't strike me as being too smart, and he figured it out."

"Yes, but he thinks I died in the fire."

"And that'll remain the case as long as no one else sees us together."

She studied his image. "It's not a very good likeness. Since you shaved off your beard and cut your hair, few people would recognize you from this poster."

"Then too, if I take off my hat, everyone will be too busy laughing at the porcupine quills on top of my head to notice my face."

"I like your hair."

"But do you like it short like this?"

Instead of answering, she kissed him. "Mmmm."

"You're a conniving woman," he said, kissing her back, stealing the breath from her lungs.

She'd miss him, miss his touch and the way he smelled. Until now, she'd never thought of a man having a scent of his own. She forced herself to concentrate on the matter at hand. "Are Merrimack and Litchfield in that direction?" she asked with a wave of her hand, claiming his mouth again so he'd focus on her instead of the question.

"Humm, you taste so good," he murmured. After a few seconds, he nodded behind them. "Litchfield is about an hour's ride in that direction."

"I don't see a path. Aren't you concerned you might lose your way?"

"As long as I follow this stream, I can't get lost. But don't worry about it because you aren't going that way."

"You're bossier than my brothers."

"If I could, I'd keep you with me."

His declaration warmed her.

"Bekah, if something were to happen to you, I'd never forgive myself. You've already had too many close calls. With James out there shooting off his big mouth about buried treasure, we not only have the law and Grizzly after us, but we also have half the population of New Hampshire looking for the medallion. Like it or not, this afternoon your behind will be on that coach to

Manchester."

It wasn't so much the words as the way he'd issued them. Blunt, forceful, as if speaking to a small child.

She smiled at him innocently and pointed toward a shiny stone a few feet in the water. "Can you reach that rock for me?"

"I suppose I could, but why do you want it?"

"I plan to keep it on my bedroom windowsill."

"But it looks like all the other rocks. Can't you settle for one that's closer?"

"No it's not like all the others. Can't you see the flecks of mica on it? That's the rock I want. When I glance at it, I'll think of you."

He looked pleased. He got down on his knees and reached over the water, one hand on the slippery bank, the other stretching as far as he could.

She shoved him with all her might and ran. Behind her, she heard water splashing and lots of swearing. She leaped onto the mare and glanced over her shoulder.

He stood in twelve inches of water, clasping the rock in a tight fist, shaking himself off and waving his arms. "You conniving, scheming, devious . . ."

"You bossy lout, I'll see you in Litchfield."

EIGHTEEN

Eighty minutes later Zachariah kneed his horse forward. While Bekah's trickery aggravated him, he had to admire her horsemanship.

He could have caught up with Bekah twenty minutes ago, but he preferred to stay in back and enjoy the view. She had terrific form and a great behind. And the way she bent forward slightly and lifted her posterior off the saddle heated his blood.

Her hat had fallen off her head some time ago, and several thick strands of golden hair had come loose, flying in back of her like satin ribbons. She'd hiked her dress to her knees, exposing firm calves that urged the horse to gallop faster.

She glanced over her shoulder and gave a victorious smile.

The woman was impossible.

She never did what she was told.

She never listened to reason.

And she spoke her mind even when common sense dictated otherwise. For years her brothers had dealt with the problem without success. Now the problem was his. Until he put her safely on that carriage in Litchfield.

His clothes had dried in the brisk autumn air. He'd be chilled to the bone were it not for their fast pace and the knowledge warming his blood.

He'd outsmarted Bekah!

By his calculations, they'd arrive in Merrimack ahead of schedule.

Covered with a fine sheen of perspiration, Bekah yanked on the reins and stared at the wooden sign—*Merrimack, New Hampshire.*

She heard the clomping of hooves behind her and felt Zachariah's hand on her shoulder.

She'd fought a good battle, but she'd lost.

Heaving a discouraged sigh, she faced him. "I hope you're pleased with yourself."

His grin widened. "I am."

"You tricked me."

"I did."

She waved toward the sign. "I've never met a bossier, sneakier man in my entire life."

"Look who's talking," he said with a dry laugh. "You're upset because I read your devious mind. I knew you were up to no good when you started asking directions to Merrimack."

"If you're such a terrific mindreader, then how come you didn't anticipate my shoving you into the icy water?"

They back-trailed into the woods, where Bekah changed into a clean dress and tidied her appearance. She combed her hair and twisted it behind her head, holding it in place with pins. "It's your fault I lost my hat," she pointed out, frowning at Zachariah. If she didn't frown at him, she'd cry.

Would he miss her?

He was sitting on a boulder with his hands resting on a bent knee. "I'm willing to take blame for a lot of things, but not this. You're the one who took off as if the devil were at your heels."

"Yes, but you said you allowed me to set the pace, a pace that was way too fast for a refined lady."

"The hot-blooded, stubborn woman on that horse would not have slowed even if I'd ordered her to."

"Maybe not."

"There's no maybe about it. Nothing I'd have done would have altered your direction or your speed, unless I'd confessed you were going to Merrimack."

"I'll never trust you again."

"Bekah, trust goes two ways. Have you forgotten about my swim in the icy stream?"

"I'm sorry about that. But I needed time to escape, and I could think of no other way. Then too, you were issuing orders, refusing to listen to my ideas."

"Your ideas could have gotten you killed. I care too much for you to take chances with your life."

He cared.

His words quickened her heartbeat. She called herself a muttonhead for feeling this excited. It wasn't as though he'd declared his love or told her he couldn't live without her.

It wasn't as though he'd begged her to stay with him or promised he'd never drink again.

And if he had, would she stay?

Of course not.

She knew better.

Was she being honest with herself? For the first time Rebekah understood why her stepmother stayed with her drunken husband, believing he'd eventually change.

With love, everything seemed possible.

He stood and looked at her. One side of his mustache lifted in a half-smile. "Besides, that hat had seen better days."

"That's ridiculous."

He closed the distance between them. "What's ridiculous is that we're wasting the little time we have left arguing."

He crushed her against him and claimed her mouth in a kiss

filled with desperation. She clung to him and grabbed fistfuls of his shirt in her hands. He widened his stance and pulled her roughly against him. She felt his erection pressing against her belly. Dampness gathered between her legs.

She needed him. "Zachariah," she whispered, his name a fervent prayer that he'd never let her go.

He cupped the back of her head with his hand and skimmed his fingers along her neck.

"We have so little time," he said, his voice hoarse, raising gooseflesh on her arms and legs.

He fondled her breasts, and she leaned into him. He undid the buttons on her dress while she tugged frantically at his shirt, yanking it loose. Her fingers traveled over his torso.

This would be their last time together.

Never again would she feel such excitement or the all-consuming love that filled her senses and her heart.

He laid her down on a smooth sun-warmed boulder. "Bekah, I'll never forget you."

She didn't trust herself to speak.

Unlike their unhurried lovemaking beneath the stars, this joining was frenzied. Lips tasted and suckled. Teeth bit. Hands roamed freely. Unwilling to wait a moment longer, she wrapped her legs around his waist. His nostrils flared as he buried himself in her, threw back his head, and groaned. She welcomed the pounding, encouraged him when he grabbed her behind with rough fingers and rammed into her. The friction intensified, and she moved right along with him. His face contorted with passion. She welcomed every thrust until a rippling sensation seized her body and her mind. And she flew with the eagles and circled the sun. Her heart overflowed with love.

He muffled her cry with a kiss. His own shout mingled with

the sounds of the blue jays in a nearby hemlock before he collapsed over her.

Putting off the inevitable until the last possible moment, Zachariah pulled Bekah against him, leaning her head against his shoulder. "I hope I didn't hurt you."

"You didn't."

"I never intended to make love to you here. And I certainly never intended to be so rough." He lowered the brim of his hat over his forehead, kissed the top of her head, and wondered what had possessed him to act like a randy kid.

"Zachariah, I enjoyed being with you. I needed to be with you this way. I'm not complaining."

He wondered whether she really meant what she said. There were two kinds of women, and two ways to treat them. And a man did not take a lady in broad daylight with her skirt hiked around her waist. "A lady should be treated with respect."

She glanced at him and traced his jaw with her fingertip. "You treated me like a woman. I have no regrets."

"I hope not."

"I'll forever be grateful for your tutorage," she said with a teasing smile.

"I only wish there was time for more lessons."

"Me too." She watched a gray squirrel jumping from limb to limb. "Maybe I could stay for a while."

His muscles beneath her head stiffened. "We've been through this. You're leaving in half an hour."

"I don't want you to go into town with me," she said with concern.

"Yeah, right, like I'd trust you to get on that coach by yourself."

"Look," she said, poking his chest. "Someone might recognize you. You said you wanted to keep me safe and that you didn't want anyone to see us together. It only makes sense that I get on that stagecoach by myself. You can watch on the outskirts of town. I'll wave to you when I go by."

"So help me, Bekah, if you pull another of your tricks, I'll tan your behind."

She stood and straightened her skirts. "I don't want to go."

"But you have to."

He kissed her, once, twice, three times.

He brushed his thumb against the tears on her cheek. "Bekah, promise me you'll get on that stagecoach."

"I promise," she said much too quickly, worrying him.

"Promise me again." He held her hand and wove their fingers together.

"Don't worry, I'm going to board the coach. I'll wave to you when I go past." She paused. "I want you to promise me something, too. Say you won't drink again. I don't want you killing yourself with alcohol."

"I've taken my last drink. You have my word."

A deep breath rushed from her lungs. "I'm relieved to hear that. I want only the best for you, Zachariah."

He kissed her one last time, helped her onto the saddle, swatted the horse's rump, and watched her ride away.

Some time later from a distance, Zachariah saw the driver fling Bekah's valise on top of the coach. The man helped her into the coach, handed her the basket, and closed the door. Zachariah lost sight of her because the shades were drawn. He was ready to run across the street and make sure she hadn't escaped out the other door when she slid the shade open.

When he spotted her profile, a great weight lifted from his chest. He'd expected Bekah to pull one of her pranks. If the law, Grizzly, or God only knew who else weren't chasing him, he might have indulged in a few more days together.

He hated to see her go.

Not trusting Bekah one bit, he followed the coach to the outskirts of town, and still expecting some devious act, he tagged along for another mile. He even considered the possibility that she might have gotten off without his noticing. But Bekah leaned forward in plain sight and stared in his direction, assuring him she was safely on her way to her brother's house. He breathed a sigh of relief and lifted a hand to bid her farewell.

He turned his horse back toward Litchfield, already missing the woman who'd become a major part of his life.

Three miles out of town, Bekah heard a rider approaching.

"Pull her over, Frank. One of the passengers wants to get off."

"Whoa," the driver shouted, yanking on the brake and raising a dust cloud.

Holding her basket in one hand, Bekah jumped from the coach and picked up the valise Frank threw to the ground. With a nod, he flicked the reins and continued on his way.

"Sir, I can't thank you enough," she said, securing her bag to the saddle and glancing at the man she'd met at the livery.

"I've wiped her down good and put some feed in a saddlebag for you to take along."

"Do I owe you anything else?"

"You've been more than generous."

"Do you remember what I told you?"

"Yes, ma'am, I saw you get on that coach and as far as I know, you never got off. What do I say if anyone questions this horse's disappearance?"

"Anything but the truth."

Zachariah pulled his collar over his neck and leaned forward in his saddle, eyeing the community of Litchfield in the distance. Though his poster didn't bear much resemblance, he was waiting for sunset before riding into town.

He'd spent the last hour hidden in a grove of trees, feeling sorry for himself, feeling empty inside. For the first time in days, he craved a drink. He realized his battle with booze was far from over, and tonight he wondered whether he had the strength to fight.

The wind blew in from the north, wrapping itself around him like frigid fingers against bare flesh. Soon winter would arrive, and with it, snow and ice. The cold seeped into Zachariah's bones. A shot of whiskey would chase away the chill. A shot of whiskey would help him to forget.

Hunched forward against the cold, he rode into town. Seeing nothing suspicious, he tied his horse to the hitching post and then entered the Blooming Garden.

A smoke-filled haze clouded the air. The smell of whiskey, beer, and cheap perfume penetrated his nostrils as he ambled toward the bar. He thumbed his hat back and studied every man with a beard and full head of hair, noting the description suited half the men inside the saloon.

Rose, the owner of the Blooming Garden, sidled up to him. "Have you seen my girl, Violet?"

"Yes, she was roughed up a bit, but she'll be fine."

"I'm relieved to hear it." Rose wrapped her arms around his chest, kissed the side of his neck, and whispered, "Come upstairs. We need to talk."

Clinging to each other, they walked up the winding staircase. Once her bedroom door shut behind them, Rose pulled away. "Are you mad coming here like this? The sheriff's deputized half a dozen trigger-happy fools. And since that kid showed up here boasting about a treasure map engraved on a gold charm, every idiot from here to kingdom come is out there hoping to snag that charm for himself."

"What do you expect me to do? Hide out for the rest of my life?"

"If you want to get yourself killed, pick another saloon to do it in. Or pay me up front for the cleaning bill. Because I won't be the one scrubbing your blood from the floor and walls of my bar."

"It warms me to know you care," he said with a grin, sitting down on the quilted spread that covered her bed. "When you invited me upstairs, I'd expected a whopping good time."

"It's because I care that I'm booting you out of my bar," she said, with a wave of her arm. "Get as far away from here as you can. Don't come back."

"I can't. I need to try to clear my name."

"You'll get yourself killed."

"Anyway, even if I wanted to run, I couldn't leave without knowing that James, the boy you saw with the gold charm, is all right."

"I saw the kid talking to a big hairy son of a gun they call Grizzly."

"Did James leave with this man?"

"I can't be sure. We were busy that night. I remember seeing the boy sitting at Grizzly's table. I came up here for a while, and when I went back downstairs, both the boy and Grizzly were gone."

"Have you seen Grizzly tonight?"

"Not yet. He doesn't come here every night, but he shows up here often."

"I'm sticking around in case he does," Zachariah said, slapping a gold piece into her hand. "This should cover the cleaning expenses."

An hour later Zachariah sat at the bar with a glass of water in his hands, convinced warm piss would have tasted better and thinking one drink wouldn't hurt.

"I never knew you to be a teetotaler," Joe, the bartender, said.

"I'm not." Zachariah pushed the water glass away. "Give me a shot of your best whiskey."

A moment later Joe set a glass in front of him. Zachariah eyed the amber liquor. No drink had ever looked this inviting. He brought the glass to his nose and inhaled deeply. No drink had ever smelled this good. His mouth watered in anticipation. His muscles clenched with need, and his hand shook. He'd ordered the whiskey to test himself, but now that it sat in front of him, he realized he'd made a mistake. He wasn't strong enough, especially today because he'd watched Bekah ride out of his life.

Her leaving was for the best, but knowing that didn't fill the void inside. He'd somehow go on with his life, but a life without Bekah looked bleak.

He held the glass up to a nearby lantern, swirled the whiskey in the glass, and watched the reflection of the dancing flame.

Just one swallow to ease the tension.

Just one swallow to warm him.

Just one swallow to help him through the night.

"Zack, that's him over there," Rose whispered with a nod across the room.

Grizzly was a fitting name for the giant who filled the doorway: broad shoulders, thick arms and legs like tree trunks, hands like Sunday hams, a long beard that covered his face and dropped over a barrel-shaped chest.

"Joe, gimme a bottle," he said in a voice that matched his size. Grizzly moved toward a table near the bar and sat, his beady eyes studying each man in turn.

Though they'd never met, when Grizzly focused his gaze on Zachariah, his pupils shrank to pinpoints. He sucked his upper lip into his mouth and stared a good long time. Grizzly tucked a chaw of tobacco into his right cheek and grinned. "If you're who I think you are, me and you have lots in common, including a friend named James."

Fear for the boy's safety knotted Zachariah's gut. He covered the distance to the table in two long strides and lowered himself down onto the chair across from Grizzly. He leaned forward and cupped his hand over his mouth to muffle his words. "If you've hurt that boy, you'll be sorry."

Grizzly's gaze never faltered. "Seems to me you should be watching what you say. I have the kid and if you ever want to see him alive again, you'd better show a little respect."

"You wouldn't hurt your own son," Zachariah said.

"He might be my kid, but he's a pain in the butt."

Zachariah remembered his own father and how little he'd cared. His heart went out to James. Unfortunately, they had a lot in common.

Joe delivered a bottle of whiskey and two glasses to the table and then hurried away.

Grizzly poured whiskey into the glasses and slid one toward Zachariah. "As I see it, we both have something the other one wants. There won't be a problem unless you refuse to co-operate."

Grizzly downed the contents of his glass. "Go ahead, drink up. I never did like to drink alone." He was missing the middle finger on his left hand, and when he caught Zachariah glancing, he set his glass down. "My old man cut off my finger to teach me a lesson. It was the last lesson he ever taught."

Zachariah intended to bring the glass to his mouth without drinking. When the whiskey touched his lips, he dipped his tongue into the glass. Unable to stop, he swallowed a large gulp. The whiskey heated a path down his throat, hitting his stomach like a fiery blast.

Feeling like a failure, he turned his attention to Grizzly, who was already on his third drink. "What do you want from me?"

"I want the other half of the medallion. You give it to me, and I give you the kid."

"Doesn't James have the medallion?"

"Look," he said, his fist pounding the table. The glasses clattered from the force. "Don't go playing dumb with me. The kid only had half the medallion."

"Let me think a minute," Zachariah said, hoping to buy some time. Both halves of the medallion had been pinned to Bekah's nightgown. Both halves were missing the next morning. Clearly, James had taken both pieces, but what had he done with them?

"I'm not giving you the medallion unless I know James is all right."

"You don't get it, do you?"

Silence stretched between them. Grizzly refilled Zachariah's glass. "You aren't in a position to set the terms of our little deal. But I am, and I'm not bending one damn bit."

"I hear you, but how do I know James is safe?"

Grizzly issued a dry laugh. "You don't. The boy could already be dead. But he might be alive so you'd best listen up. If you don't hand me that medallion in the next five minutes, I'm walking out of here, and you'll never see the kid again."

"I'm not even sure you have the boy."

"I got proof," Grizzly said, pulling a handkerchief from his pocket. Once he'd made sure no one was looking, he unfolded the white fabric. "This look familiar to you?"

Zachariah saw his half of the medallion hidden within the folds of the handkerchief. A shiver raced down his spine. "I'll give you what you want, but don't hurt the boy."

"So hand it over now."

"I have the medallion, but it's not here. I was afraid someone might try to steal it from me, so I hid it in the woods under some rocks."

"How long will it take you to get it?"

"A few hours, but I don't think I can find it in the dark. I'll need to wait till daybreak."

Grizzly heaved a disgusted sigh. "I was afraid of something like this." He leaned in close, his foul breath striking Zachariah's face. "I've killed before, many times, so don't play games with me or you'll end up like that poor slob in Londonderry. Sometime during the night, I'll tuck a piece of paper between some crates in the alley behind Gay's Tavern with the directions where you can find me and your buddy, James. Follow my directions and come by yourself. You've got until noon tomorrow."

"I need more time," Zachariah said.

"Noon's all you've got, not one minute more."

"What if someone else finds your note?"

"That's your problem. If you're late, I'll shoot the boy."

Zachariah drummed his fingers against the damp wooden table.

"Don't go getting any ideas about following or shooting me in the back. If something happens to me, you'll never find the kid." Grizzly pushed the bottle across the table. "Help yourself. I'll see you tomorrow, twelve o'clock sharp."

NINETEEN

Zachariah tented his fingers in front of his face and blew out slowly. Somehow, he had to find the medallion.

What had James done with it?

If he'd hidden it inside the cabin, it was destroyed along with everything else.

He closed his eyes and tried to focus. Exhausted after a long day on horseback, he yawned. He was about to leave when he heard a ruckus outside.

"Keep your bloody hands to yourself, you dimwitted mutton-head."

Zachariah thought he was hearing things. But the English accent seemed too real to be a hallucination.

He shot to his feet, ran out the door, and almost tripped over a man lying on his back, trying to protect himself from a valise swung at his chest.

Zachariah grabbed the drunk with one hand and restrained Bekah with the other. "What's going on here?"

"This lout made improper advances."

The man scrambled to his feet. "Ain't so, I thought she was one of Miss Rose's girls. All I did was kiss her. Sure didn't mean no harm. You got claims on this gal?"

Zachariah leaned close enough for the drunk to see the fury in his eyes. "Don't ever touch my wife again."

"You got my word, Mister."

Zachariah released the man and watched him dash across the

street and disappear between brick buildings. Then he hugged Bekah to him. He rested his fingers at the base of her neck where he felt her pulse drumming. He'd never expected to hold her again, and here she was. "Bekah, what in hell are you doing here?"

"Kindly lower your tone, or you'll wake up everyone."

"I can't decide whether to throttle you or kiss you," he said, his anger dissolving as he looked at her. "You broke your promise."

She picked up the basket at her feet. From inside came loud meows. "I promised to board the stagecoach, and I did."

"I'm putting you on another coach first thing tomorrow morning."

She gave him a satisfied smile. "I checked earlier, and there isn't one."

"Then I'll rent a carriage and pay someone to take you to your brother's house."

"Haven't you learned anything from this?" she asked, planting her free hand on his arm. "I'm a grown woman with a mind of my own. If you force me to leave before I'm ready, I'll simply pay the driver to let me off outside of town again. I'm not going anywhere until I'm sure James is all right."

Bekah had rented a room on the second floor of Timothy Gay's Tavern. When Zachariah was sure no one was watching, he slipped up the stairs and closed the door behind him. She looked beautiful with her hair cascading down her back, her lips plump and inviting. He wanted to make love to her.

He walked to the bureau and turned the lantern down until they stood in pitch darkness.

"What's going on?" Bekah asked, her voice laced with fear.

"I don't want anyone to see me." He pulled the curtain aside and studied the alley below.

He debated whether to tell Bekah the truth and decided he didn't have a choice. "I need your help. I saw Grizzly this evening, and he has James. He wants me to give him the medallion."

"But . . . I thought James had it."

"So did I."

Bekah joined him at the window. "I don't care about the medallion. I only wish I had it to give to the man."

Zachariah wrapped his arm around her waist. "I don't trust Grizzly. I doubt he'll let James go regardless of what we give him."

"Then you should tell the sheriff."

"If I did that, he'd throw me in jail. I won't be able to help James if I'm locked up."

"The sheriff might not recognize you from the posters."

"If he does, he won't listen to an escaped murderer."

"I could speak to him, too."

"I want you to stay out of this unless it's absolutely necessary."

Bekah rested her head against his chest. "What will you do?"

"Grizzly is supposed to drop off a map with directions. When he does, I'll be waiting for him."

"Allow me to go with you."

"Bekah, this time I'm counting on you to do as I say. Grizzly will show up in the alley down there later tonight. I need you up here watching. If something happens to me and you see Grizzly leaving, you go next door to the jail and tell the sheriff. It'll be James's only chance. Do you promise to stay up here and watch?"

"Yes, I'll do anything to help James."

"Kiss me for luck, and then I have to go," he said, slanting his mouth over hers.

She shoved him away. "Is that whiskey I taste on your lips?"

He considered lying, but Bekah deserved the truth. "Yes."

He saw the disappointment on her face before he turned and left the room.

Zachariah crouched between piles of boxes behind Gay's Tavern where he'd spot anyone entering the alley. After hours of waiting, he'd begun to wonder whether Grizzly would show up.

Zachariah nodded off, but his head jerked forward, and he awakened with a start. From his hiding space he could see the deputy dozing in the next building with his hat over his face and his boots on the desk. Need be, he'd turn himself in and try to get help for James.

Zachariah had tucked a knife in his boot and he'd come armed with his rifle and a handgun. He didn't stand a chance against the giant in a fistfight, and he had too much sense to even try.

Once Grizzly hid the directions behind the tavern, Zachariah would follow him. He'd confront the man outside of town and threaten to shoot unless he cooperated.

Zachariah heard footsteps approaching. He ducked down behind the crates, ready to defend himself if Grizzly should spot him.

"Zachariah, where are you?" came a familiar voice.

He peeked around the box and saw Rose holding a gun in one hand and a piece of paper in the other. "What are you doing here?" he asked in a low tone.

"Grizzly insisted I give you this. I almost told him what he could do with himself, but he said James would die if I didn't bring you this note."

"Thanks, Rose." He unfolded the paper she handed him and was disappointed to see a few scribbled words with instructions where to find the real map. "That sneaky son of a bitch."

"Grizzly knew you'd be here waiting to ambush him. He said

you better not double-cross him again or the boy dies."

Bekah greeted Zachariah at the door. "What happened?"

He tossed his hat onto the bureau. "Grizzly figured I'd be down there waiting, so he sent Rose. Read this."

Bekah turned up the flame on the lantern and glanced at the piece of paper. "Where's Polley's Tavern?"

"It's beyond the Meeting House at the other end of town."

"Maybe you should go there now."

"The note clearly states to wait until dawn. I don't dare do otherwise."

Fatigue lined Zachariah's face. Bekah wanted to ease the tension in his eyes. She wanted to make things right, but she didn't know how. "You look exhausted."

He threaded his hand through his hair. "I'm really beat."

"Lie down and rest. You'll need your strength for your encounter with Grizzly."

"I wish I had the other half of the medallion," he said, sitting on the bed and kicking off his boots. "I'm sure Grizzly will ask to see it long before I can get close to James."

"While you were down in the alley, I had loads of time to think. I may not have the medallion, but I drew the markings in my book."

Zachariah stretched out on top of the covers. "The man wants the gold medallion. He won't be pleased to have me show up waving a slip of paper."

"I'm assuming Grizzly wants the medallion because James told him about the treasure. If I'm right, my drawing should satisfy him."

"It might," Zachariah said, yawning.

Bekah snuggled against his side. "I don't think you have a choice."

He wrapped his arm around her and kissed her. "I always did

like a devious woman."

"That's not what you said when you saw me tonight."

"A man can change his mind," he said with a weary sigh.

She touched the stubble on his jaw. "How will you free James?"

"I won't know until I get there, but before I show Grizzly the paper you drew, I'll insist he let the boy go."

"Maybe, I should go with you to Polley's Tavern and read the directions. I could be hiding behind a tree with the rifle while you talk to Grizzly."

He uttered a dry laugh. "A lot of good that would do. You said yourself you could never fire on a man."

"Perhaps, but I could aim the rifle and sound convincing. I did in the jail when I broke you out."

He rose onto his elbow. "I don't want you involved. Getting yourself killed isn't going to help anyone."

"The note warns not to carry a gun. How are you going to protect yourself?"

He touched the tip of her nose. "I'll have a knife strapped to my ankle, and I'm taking my rifle with me. Once I spot Grizzly, I'll hide the gun behind a tree. If I can free James and somehow get away from Grizzly . . ."

He didn't finish the sentence, and he didn't have to.

A shiver darted down her spine. The odds were not in his favor. Chances were he would not be able to rescue James, and if he did, Zachariah would die trying to escape.

Zachariah fell asleep minutes later. Tears flowed down Rebekah's cheeks. Somehow, she had to help him. As she hugged him, she wished their lives were different. She wished she enjoyed living in the wilderness. She wished Zachariah didn't drink. Most of all, she wished he were her husband. She remembered what he'd said to the drunk.

Don't ever touch my wife again.

Wife—the word conjured images of a fire in the hearth, a man and a woman kissing each other goodnight, babies asleep in the nursery.

She kissed his cheek and whispered, "I will always love you, Zachariah."

The next morning Zachariah walked by Polley's Tavern a few times before entering, making sure he didn't recognize anyone. "A man with a full beard left a message for me. My name's James Tucker," Zachariah said, following the instructions on the note.

"Yes, sir, I have it right here." The innkeeper handed him a sealed envelope.

"Thank you." Zack hurried outside and ripped open the envelope.

Come by yourself, unarmed. Take the path in the woods behind Doc Stimson's place until you see my markers. Follow these until you spot a gray shack. I'll be waiting there with the kid.

Zachariah looked behind him to make sure Bekah wasn't following. He saw a couple walking arm in arm, a mother and child, and an old man with a cane and thick glasses hobbling toward him. Once he was certain that Bekah wasn't up to her usual tricks, he dashed around the back of Dr. Stimson's house. He hurried down the path until sweat poured down his face and his breath came fast and choppy. He set his rifle down and sipped water from his canteen.

Despite his best intentions, he doubted he'd be able to free James. Grizzly had already proved his intelligence by not delivering the map last night. He wasn't likely to agree to anything without seeing the medallion. Once Zachariah offered him the drawing, there was nothing to prevent Grizzly from killing him and taking what he wanted.

About a mile later he spotted six stones that formed an arrow in the middle of the path, pointing left. He changed his course. The trail narrowed, and the underbrush thickened. Fearing he might miss the next marker, he moved cautiously.

Three hundred feet later, he saw four more rocks.

He looked around him. Densely treed, the area provided good cover. Hearing a noise, he lifted his rifle, but saw only gray squirrels scampering in the fallen leaves.

He drank some more water and told himself all would go well. He'd rescue James, capture Grizzly, and clear his name.

He gritted his teeth.

By day's end, he'd be either a free man or a dead man. Refusing to waste time, he climbed over a fallen tree. Thirty minutes later he saw the roofline of a shack in the distance. Crouching, he wove his way between the trees, hoping not to be spotted. The tumbledown cabin sat in a wide clearing, the closest trees a hundred feet away.

As he neared, he saw James tied to a post, bruised but alive.

Zachariah checked his timepiece. Eight o'clock.

Maybe Grizzly was still in town.

Hiding behind the thick trunk of an oak tree, he watched for a while and was disappointed to see Grizzly poke his head out the front door. "Boy, be sure to tell your pa if you see company coming."

"Damn you to hell," James shouted, making Zachariah proud.

When Grizzly went back inside, Zachariah abandoned his rifle behind the tree, ran toward James, and grabbed his knife from his belt, hoping to cut him loose. He motioned for the boy to be quiet, and while fixing his gaze on the cabin door, started to cut through the thick rope, freeing one wrist.

Maniacal laughter roared.

Zachariah's hands stilled.

"Drop the knife, or you're both dead." Shotgun in hand, Grizzly stood about fifty feet to the left of his cabin.

Zachariah dropped the knife where James could reach it.

"You stupid son of a bitch," Grizzly shouted. "Kick that knife over here."

Zachariah did as he was told and waited for an opportunity to grab the other knife under his pant leg.

"Where's the medallion?"

Zachariah started to reach for his pocket.

Grizzly raised his shotgun. "I don't want any tricks, or I'll shoot the kid."

Zack pulled out Bekah's drawing. "I don't have the medallion, but I have the next best thing."

"I'm killing the boy first." Grizzly leveled the gun barrel at James's head.

"This piece of paper shows every marking on the medallion. It'll lead you to the treasure."

"Hand it over here, real slow."

Zachariah stepped forward.

Grizzly snatched the paper from him. "Move back next to the kid."

Zachariah waited for his chance. With the gun pointed at James, he didn't dare reach for his knife.

"This looks like a bunch of scribbles," Grizzly said with a jerk of his head.

"It took a long time for me and James to figure out what the markings meant," Zachariah said, trying to buy time.

"Then where's the treasure?"

"I haven't found it yet, but I know where to look. If the two of us could go for a short ride, I'll show you where it's hidden."

"I'm not listening to any more of your lyin'."

Zachariah tried to remember Bekah and James's conversations. "The wavy lines mean water, in this case, the Merrimack River. The long line stands for the highway between Boston and Manchester. There's a point where the lines intersect. That's where the treasure is. James thought the treasure was buried, but I know of a cave in that area, and I'm sure that's where we'll find it."

"Where's the medallion come from?" Grizzly asked, making it clear he'd never owned the other half.

Zachariah moved closer to James. "The medallion's been in my family for generations. My grandfather told me tales about gold and diamonds."

"If that's so, then why didn't he go get the treasure?"

"Until now, no one has had both halves of the medallion."

Grizzly rubbed his jaw. "Tell me exactly where the treasure is hidden, or I'll kill the kid."

Clothed in a man's black woolen suit and white shirt, Bekah was soaked with perspiration. Back in town, she'd been certain Zachariah had seen through her disguise. But the thick glasses and black wide-brimmed hat had hidden her identity.

She loosened the stiff collar and tried to catch her breath. From behind the tree she saw James, leaning against a post like a whipped dog, his face splotched with cuts and bruises. Zachariah stood, his stance wide, about to pounce at Grizzly, who looked ready to kill.

Certain doom grew closer with every wasted second. Bekah's heart drummed. She clasped her hands and prayed for a solution, then saw Zachariah's rifle leaning against the tree trunk. She grabbed it and aimed. Her hands shook so much she doubted she could pull the trigger.

Maybe she could bluff. She gripped the rifle tighter. "Drop that gun!"

Zachariah jerked around.

Grizzly slammed his weapon between Zachariah's shoulders, hurling him to the ground. "If you don't come out, I'll kill them both."

Enraged, she leaped from behind the tree trunk, squeezed her eyes tight, and fired.

Overhead a limb cracked and slammed to the ground, dropping a few feet away. Someone shrieked and shouted profanities. The force of the blast knocked Rebekah against the tree. She opened her eyes and was shocked to see Grizzly lying on his side, blood gushing from his leg. Having freed himself, James rushed to Zachariah, who was holding a knife at Grizzly's throat.

She dashed toward them with the rifle and watched Zachariah loop a rope around Grizzly's legs and torso.

"Are you going to kill me?" Grizzly asked, tossing Rebekah a mean look.

She sneered. "That depends on whether you confess to the killing in Londonderry."

TWENTY

Once Grizzly was behind bars, Zachariah went next door to Gay's Tavern, where Bekah and James were waiting. He smiled at the clerk at the registration desk and ran up the flight of stairs.

"Grizzly confessed," he said, opening the door.

Bekah rushed to him. "I'm so relieved!"

He swung Bekah into the air. "I can finally walk down the streets of town without looking over my shoulder."

She chuckled. "And even then you couldn't spot someone right under your nose."

"I saw you in that black getup."

"Yes, but you didn't know it was me."

"You make a sorry-looking old man."

"Considering how little time I had to prepare, I thought I looked quite convincing."

"And I wasn't any too pleased to see you show up with my rifle. It's a miracle you didn't get yourself killed."

"I saved your life, Zachariah. I won't allow you to talk to me as if I were a child. And I actually fired the gun!" Her voice rang with pride.

"You had your eyes closed."

"Perhaps, but my marksmanship was right on target."

She looked so pleased he didn't have the heart to tell her Mary had fired the shot that wounded Grizzly. Zachariah had spotted the older woman a few seconds before Bekah showed up with his rifle. "You said you'd never be able to fire at anyone."

"When confronted with necessity, a woman must overcome her fears, so I pulled the trigger. I was shocked at the force of the blast, and I had not expected to hear an echo."

"Sometimes, there is an echo," he said with a grin. *Especially when someone else is firing a second shot.*

"Where did you find the clothing?"

"There's a nice old gentleman in the room next door."

"You're really something," he said, kissing her, feeling lighthearted and so very happy to be holding the woman he loved.

He kissed her until he ached with need, but with James in the room, he'd have to content himself with kisses. "You taste so good."

James stirred and moaned in his sleep.

"I'm worried about him." Bekah sat on the edge of the bed and rested her palm on the boy's forehead.

"He's been through a lot." Zachariah examined the cut on James's cheek. "I wish I could have found him sooner."

"He complained of having a headache and feeling dizzy before he went off."

"We'll have the doctor check him over." Zachariah shook the boy's shoulder.

James jerked awake, looking frightened. "Huh? What's wrong?"

"We wanted to make sure you were all right." Zachariah looked at the child's bloodshot eyes.

"I was fine till you woke me." James paused a moment and grabbed Zachariah's hands. "I should have told the sheriff in Londonderry that I'd seen Grizzly that night in the alley."

"James, I don't want you to worry about that."

Tears rimmed his eyes. "You coulda hanged. But . . . a boy should stick by his pa."

"I know." Zachariah understood the unflinching loyalty of a kid towards his parents—even undeserving parents. He kept his own painful memories at bay.

"I thought if I talked to him, he'd might run off and leave you alone. I told him I'd tag along and help with stuff." The boy blinked away tears. "But . . . he didn't want me around. He wasn't interested in me until he heard 'bout the medallion." James directed his gaze at Zachariah. "Bet you hate me?"

"No, never." He hugged the boy to his chest. He wanted to tell him he loved him like a son. Because he didn't want to give the boy false hope, he kept those thoughts to himself. "And I was damn proud to see how you spoke up to Grizzly."

"So I decided to try to trick him into coming with me to look for the treasure. I had planned to hold a gun on him and force him to confess."

"James, what you did was foolish. You should have told me what you had in mind."

"There wasn't time. You were sending me away. I knew I had to act fast. I'm your friend. A friend doesn't stand by and let another friend take blame for a crime because he's too afraid to speak up."

"I understand. A boy should stand up for his kin. I'd have done the same in your position."

The tension slipped away from James's face.

"I have one question. What did you do with the other half of the medallion?"

James's face split into a wide grin. "I only took your half because I promised Miss Benson I'd never steal again. I figured I was only borrowing yours."

"James, I don't have the medallion," Bekah said, stroking his head.

"Sure you do. I hid it inside the lining of your blue hat."

★ ★ ★ ★ ★

An hour later Rebekah caught Zachariah and James exchanging suspicious glances. "Why do the two of you look so guilty?"

"No reason," James replied, shrugging and hurrying out the door. "Zack, I'll get the horses ready."

Rebekah blocked the doorway. "Are you sure that boy is well enough to be riding?"

"He looks fine to me, but we'll stop by the doc's house and let him have a look."

"Where are you going?"

"I have an errand to run," Zachariah said without explanation.

"That's all you're going to tell me?"

"Yup." He kissed her and moved her out of the way. "Behave yourself while I'm gone. And it'll be your fault if I get arrested for wrestling some poor old man to the ground, thinking it's you," he said with a grin.

A few minutes later she heard a knock. Opening the door, she recognized the man at the desk. "Mr. Thompson said I should bring up a tub. If you'll tell me where to set it, I'll have a member of my staff fill it."

Fifteen minutes later Bekah stretched out in the copper tub filled with bubbles and warm water. The water soothed her aching muscles. She climbed out some time later, wrapped herself in a thick towel, and glanced at her reflection in the mirror.

She looked like the same woman who'd stepped off the ship from England, but she'd changed.

She loved Zachariah and wanted to spend the rest of her life with him. And though she feared his addiction to alcohol, living without him frightened her more.

Without regard for his safety, he'd confronted Grizzly. Zachariah might be a drinking man, but he was also a hero.

Warmth settled in her heart whenever she thought of his bravery.

Zachariah wasn't just a hero; he was her hero.

Zachariah had hoped to come back with good news. Instead he returned empty-handed. He sauntered up the stairs and found Bekah asleep in the chair by the window.

When he shut the door, she stirred and opened her eyes. "Hello," she said, looking soft and inviting.

More than anything he yearned to wake up next to Bekah each morning. Crossing the room, he pulled her to her feet and held her tight. "Mmm, you smell good."

She rested her head on his chest. "Are you ready to tell me where you've been?"

"I was hoping to find your medallion. James and I combed the woods. I'm sorry, Bekah, but we didn't see your hat." He reached in his shirt pocket. "Here's my half of the medallion and your drawing. I know how disappointed you must be."

"Both you and James could have died yesterday. I refuse to grieve for a cold piece of gold."

"I know the medallion meant a great deal to you."

"Only because it came from my parents. But you and James mean much more to me."

He didn't reply to that because he couldn't. Because speaking of love and feelings would only complicate their lives. Besides, he didn't trust himself to fall in love again. *Bekah's not like Elissa*, the tiny voice in his head whispered.

Bekah ran her fingers along his jaw. "When I was a little girl, the medallion was my only link to my parents. In a way they're responsible for our meeting."

He laughed because he couldn't help himself. "You make the damn thing sound magical."

She waved her hand. "If not magic, then surely fate brought

us together."

"I say coincidence." He kissed her soundly. Magic, coincidence, he didn't give a damn as long as she was by his side.

"I've decided to travel to Maine."

Surprised, he looked down at her. "I thought you were going to Manchester."

"First I plan to visit the Abenaki Indians and see whether anyone remembers my parents. It's my last hope of finding out the medallion's history."

Zachariah threw Bekah's valise into the back of the carriage and hopped onto the front seat. Between them rested the basket with the two kittens.

"I hope James is going to be all right," Bekah said, looking concerned.

Zachariah hadn't shared the particulars with Bekah, but Grizzly had slammed the butt of his shotgun into James's head. It was a wonder the boy was still alive. "The doctor is just being cautious. Rose offered for James to stay with her."

"I hope he isn't staying at the Blooming Garden."

"Rose has a small house on the outskirts of town." Zachariah would not have subjected James to that way of life, not even for a few days. He didn't want the boy humiliated, although he suspected James might have enjoyed the raucous atmosphere.

They rode a while in companionable silence.

As they neared the Maine border, Zachariah's stomach clenched. He'd never intended to return, but he was getting closer with each spin of the wagon wheels.

He'd be a sorry excuse for a man if he allowed Bekah to travel unescorted—especially since she'd saved his life; especially since he was looking for any reason to prolong their time together.

Though he loved Bekah, he dreaded facing his past—too

much pain, too many memories, and too many regrets.

After his mother died, he'd boarded up the whorehouse, left it there to rot and fall to ruins into the Atlantic. He'd ridden away without a backward glance.

He'd left a boy and was returning as a man.

His past should no longer hurt him.

Then why did he feel the same inadequacy that had consumed him as a child?

"You're awfully quiet," Bekah said, reaching inside the basket to pat her kittens.

"I was remembering the day my mother died," he replied, his throat closing over the words. "The town bully, the minister's son, said my mother would never go to heaven."

Bekah laid her hand on his arm. "How sad."

"Yes it's sad, but not for that reason. I denied being related to the woman. I've always regretted that. I wished I'd stood up to him and defended her."

He expected to see disgust but instead saw compassion in her eyes. "How old were you?"

"Sixteen," he said, sucking in a deep breath.

"You were just a boy."

"I should have known better."

"You were barely older than James," she said, as if that made any difference.

He found it hard to believe he'd confided in her. "I've never told anyone that."

She wound an arm around his waist. "I'm glad you did."

Surprisingly, Zachariah's confession had lessened his guilt. Maybe Bekah was right. Maybe it was time to forgive himself for the mistakes of his childhood.

"I can hardly sit still," Rebekah said, fidgeting with the collar of her coat. "Just think, my parents probably walked along these same roads. As a little girl, I used to dream about America and the wild savages, but I must confess I'd never pictured such grand houses or white wooden churches with steeples."

Zachariah issued a disgusted noise. "Oh, there are churches all right, with religious fanatics running amok cramming their views down people's throats."

She knew he was referring to his childhood and the shame he'd endured. "I cannot begin to imagine what pain you suffered, but I'm also certain your mother loved you."

He groaned. "You've been raised with your head in the clouds where everything shines brightly. You believe in magic, fate, and for all I know, you have a winged fairy hidden in your valise, waiting to grant your next wish."

"I most certainly do not have my head in the clouds. Unlike you, I prefer to concentrate on the positive rather than the negative. And it's a good thing for you that I do, or the day I strolled into the courtroom, instead of seeing an innocent man, I might have seen the abominable, sarcastic, loathsome man sitting next to me right now. Then I might have been one of the cheering spectators when they looped that rope around your wretched neck." She instantly regretted her outburst and thought he'd be shocked.

His mustache twitched as if he were trying to refrain from laughing. Then he grabbed his chest and howled until he wiped tears from the corners of his eyes.

"What's so funny?"

"I can almost picture you standing by the scaffold, beating the executioner over the head with your valise. You couldn't stand by and watch any man die, especially me," he said, with that damnable grin that she loved.

"Maybe not, but it's a good thing for you I can't get my hands on my valise right now." Then she joined him in a hearty laugh that cleansed the tension between them. "Do you know anything about the Abenaki Indians?"

"They're a generous group of people, working together and sharing what little they have with one another. They got along fine for years without help from the missionaries forcing their way of life on them."

"I feel as though you're attacking me personally," she said. "My parents sacrificed their lives for the Indians."

"I'm sure your parents meant well."

"Of course they did," she rushed in, getting angrier with each passing minute. "My parents helped the Indians to learn how to read and write and to worship God."

He rested his arm around her shoulder. "Bekah, did you ever stop to consider that maybe the Abenaki Indians were happy with their own way of life, worshiping their own gods? Maybe the churches with all their good intentions had no business fixing what wasn't broken."

"If my parents had shared your views, they might still be alive," she said, voicing what she'd buried in her heart. "You once asked—if my parents loved me so much, why didn't they stay home and take care of me and my brothers? As a little girl I'd asked that very question many times."

"Bekah, I never meant to imply your parents didn't love you. They had a job to do, and they did it the best they could."

"I know that. Maybe your mother was doing the best she could, too."

"That's in the past."

"Good, I'm glad we agree. From now on, we're looking only toward the future."

He laughed again. "You're a devious woman, Rebekah Benson."

"I'll take that as a compliment." As she sat on the leather seat, their legs rubbing, their hands touching, the carriage bringing her closer to the Abenaki Indians, her stomach clenched in apprehension.

Bekah gripped Zachariah's arm as they walked past an elderly man clothed in leather leggings and a long-sleeved cowhide jacket with beads around his neck. From his waist hung a short tunic embroidered with flowers and birds. Several round houses, twelve to fourteen feet in diameter, stood nearby. Long bent poles formed the framework of the dwellings, with walls made of straw and bark tightly woven together.

"I wonder if anyone will remember my parents," she said, squeezing Zachariah's arm.

"Don't get your hopes up."

"If no one here recognizes the medallion, I'll have to abandon my search."

"Now that doesn't sound like you. I would expect you to never give up."

"I cannot spend the rest of my life chasing a dream. My head may be in the clouds, but my common sense is well grounded." She was surprised when a brave walked right up to Zachariah and pounded his shoulder.

"Friend, what brings you back?"

Zachariah smiled. "I didn't expect to find you here today. I thought you might be out hunting."

"I returned yesterday from a successful hunt. This camp has been blessed with much, and our bellies will not go empty this winter."

"Thomas, I want you to meet Miss Rebekah Benson."

The tall brave nodded in her direction.

"Thomas was one of my few boyhood friends," Zachariah said with a smile.

"I've kept watch over your house. It still stands high on the cliff above the ocean."

Rebekah was surprised to hear Zachariah had a house.

Zachariah frowned. "Thank you. But that wasn't necessary."

The brave gripped Zachariah's hand. "It's been a long time. I wish for you and your woman to join me and my family for a meal in celebration of your return home."

"We'd be honored," Zachariah said, squeezing Rebekah's hand.

Thomas walked toward a woman with a child in her arms and another by her side. "Ella, my long-lost friend, Zachariah, has come to visit. He and Miss Benson will be eating with us."

Some time later Rebekah sat on a mat beside Zachariah and opposite Thomas, his wife and their two sons, eating corn, squash, and grilled fish from clay bowls. For dessert they had johnnycake with maple syrup.

Afterwards while the children played, the men exchanged stories about their past. Rebekah listened, enjoying the accounts of Zachariah's youth.

Leaning back on his elbows, Zachariah ran a finger along the inside of Rebekah's arm. "Miss Benson's parents were missionaries here about twenty years ago. She wants to speak to someone who might remember them."

"There were many missionaries during that time," Thomas said, lifting a spoon to his mouth.

"I know that," Rebekah said, taking half the medallion and her drawing from her reticule. "Before my mother died, I think she may have hidden part of this medallion inside my doll. I was hoping you might shed some light on its meaning."

She'd expected him to say he'd never seen the medallion, or that the artifact had little or no meaning. She had not expected the shocked glance he exchanged with Ella, or the way he rushed from his dwelling as though chased by the devil.

TWENTY-ONE

A short while later Rebekah was ushered into another dwelling where an elderly woman with long gray braids sat before a fire, her hands clasped on her lap. "We've been expecting you," the old woman said.

Rebekah felt Zachariah's fingers tightening around her arm. "How can that be? I didn't even know I was coming here until yesterday."

"As a little girl my mother told me stories about a fair-haired brave and his sister an ocean apart, and how a magical golden disc would draw them together. Finally your two souls will be united."

"The medallion is magic." Rebekah slid an I-told-you-so glance toward Zachariah, who shrugged.

The old woman continued, "The golden disc was cut in half, one part hidden inside the belly of a doll, the other hurled over a cliff where it would be found and passed from hand to hand until its arrival here today. My mother, a shaman, possessed great powers. According to her this charm would join two people from many miles away."

Rebekah ran her fingers lovingly over the medallion. "Are you saying this medallion is responsible for bringing Zachariah and me together?"

"I can't be sure, but it is possible that the medallion united you with more than one person."

Rebekah chewed her lower lip. "Is there someone else I'm

supposed to meet?"

"Yes. When your mother died in childbirth, her baby survived."

Rebekah stood silent as she tried to digest the elder's words.

The old woman rested her hand on Rebekah's shoulder. "You have a brother named John."

Rebekah covered her mouth with her hands. "John," she repeated after a moment, trying out the name for the first time.

"Do you want me to leave you alone?" Zachariah asked.

Rebekah grabbed his arm. "I need you with me." She'd come to rely on him and needed his support and strength. "All these years I didn't know I had another brother. I can hardly wait to tell the others. I wonder what he'll look like." She threw back her head and laughed nervously. "I bet he'll be bossy. That seems to be an inborn trait among the men in my family. But he'll be a younger brother, so I don't know what to expect. I hope he likes me." She meshed fingers together. "Of course he'll like me, I'm his sister." She frowned. "How should I greet him? Should I just hold his hand, hug him, or kiss him and hug him? Oh, never mind, the instant I see him I'll fling myself into his arms." She glanced anxiously at Zachariah. "I can't believe I'm carrying on this way. Look at my hands, they're shaking."

Zachariah wiped a tear from her cheek. "Try to calm down. I'm sure all will be fine once he gets here."

"Yes, I'm certain you're right. After all, I have a winged fairy in my valise. And just think, I now own half of a magical medallion."

Zachariah squeezed her shoulder. "There's no magic here. Your mother died giving birth to a boy. Coincidence brought you together."

She waved away his statement. "Believe whatever you wish, but I'm convinced the medallion has special powers."

He rolled his eyes, and she shoved him playfully.

She heard the rustle of the canvas flap over the entryway and saw a blond, blue-eyed brave enter the dwelling. Rebekah could barely breathe. Her pulse pounded in her ears. Instead of running to her brother, she froze.

"John," she finally said, her voice barely a whisper. He stood like a statue, his back stiff, and his arms by his side. "When our mother died, I didn't know you'd survived. None of us did. Otherwise, we'd have come for you much sooner. You have two brothers—William's in England, Mark lives in America," she continued with a shaky laugh that erupted on its own.

"My mother is alive," he said in a strong voice. "My brothers and sisters are here, too. Until today, I did not know I had a white sister. You've come many miles, but I cannot accept your family without denying the people who raised me."

Rebekah felt the blood draining from her face. "You're my brother. Nothing can change that."

"Your coming here was a mistake. I'm part of this Abenaki tribe. Go back where you came from and forget about me."

Zachariah helped Bekah into the carriage. His heart went out to her. "I'm sorry things didn't work out."

She dashed a tear from her eye. "It seems my winged fairy has let me down." She bit her lower lip and forced a smile.

"Maybe not," he said, lifting her chin. "You came here looking for answers."

"John didn't exactly welcome me with opened arms."

"In time, he might." He kissed her forehead gently. "Bekah, maybe you need to be with your family in Manchester."

She reached out and stroked his face. "There are still questions that need answers."

"Like what?" he asked, wondering what she meant.

"You must realize that I love you. Why are you sending me away?"

"Bekah, you deserve better."

"That may be, but it's you that I want."

"It wouldn't work out."

"Why?"

He remained silent.

"I think I know where to look for the answers you aren't willing to give me. I want you to take me to your house."

"That's out of the question," he blurted.

But he couldn't deny her, and so some time later they rode up the curving drive. The rays of the setting sun cast long shadows on the brick structure overlooking the ocean. In front, a sign swung from rusty hinges—The Bayside Inn.

"Zachariah, it's lovely. I even like the name."

"Don't let the name fool you."

As he sat beside Bekah, he looked at the bank of windows facing the Atlantic, opaque with sunlight, hiding the past and its ugliness.

A chill swept over him.

"Well, I like it. Besides, only a fool would blame a building for people's mistakes."

"Are you calling me a fool?"

"I didn't specify anyone in particular. But if you think my statement applies to you, so be it."

Against his better judgment, he opened the door and stepped into the foyer with Bekah by his side.

He waited for her to comment on the thick crimson velvet drapes, the paintings of naked women. A familiar feeling of shame consumed him.

"If I lived here, I could visit John from time to time. After a while I'm sure he'd accept me as his sister. This would make a wonderful home to raise a family, a large family," she added with a smile.

"Don't you see what I see?" he asked.

"I see lovely stained-glass windows and large rooms. Perhaps we could do away with some of the paintings."

He strolled into the living room and braced his hands on the mantel of the granite fireplace. "Are you asking me to marry you?"

"I would never do such a thing unless you loved me, of course."

This was his chance to tell her how he felt, but standing here looking around him, he could barely think, much less plan his future. Hoping to drop the subject, he sauntered toward the piano, removed the cloth drape, and ran his thumb along the keys.

"Zachariah, look at me," she said, coming up behind him. "Do you love me, even a little?"

"My feelings don't matter. It would be wrong of me to keep you here. You deserve more than I can offer."

"You're a generous man and a brave man."

"Don't forget a drinking man," he added and watched fear cloud her eyes.

"Zachariah, if you love me, say so. If not I need to hear that, too."

"Of course I love you." He pulled her against him and kissed her, clung to her like a drowning man. He wanted to stay like that forever.

"Zachariah, my stepfather had a drinking problem, but he fought a brave battle. When he was sober, he was loving, patient, and the best father a girl could have. Just promise me you won't ever again drink alcohol, and I'll believe you. I'll stand by you, just as you stood by me today."

He glanced away, wanted so much to agree and get on with his life, but he couldn't lie. "I can't make that promise because

I don't know."

"Then at least promise you'll try to stop drinking. I'll settle for that."

He buried his face in her neck. "Right now I'd promise you anything to take you upstairs and make love to you."

She wrapped her arms around his neck, and pulling his face down, she kissed him. "Love me with all your heart, Zachariah, and I'll stay with you always."

He carried her up the winding staircase, down the hall into what had been his mother's private chamber, a room that held some good memories, some bad. When he laid Bekah down on the wide bed, he knelt beside her and started to undo the buttons at her neck. "I was sixteen when I left this house, and I hated every board and brick as if it were a breathing, living thing."

She caressed the side of his face. "How do you feel about it now?"

"It's nothing more than a building."

Her fingers toyed with his earlobe. "Don't you have any good memories of your mother?"

"Yes, I remember her bandaging a bruised knee and rocking me when I was sick. She'd never wanted to be saddled with a child, but I think she did her best."

She kissed him, held him to her, and as they clung to one another, he started to think what life would be like with Bekah by his side.

They made love twice, and then they talked for hours. Long after she fell asleep, Zachariah lay with one arm behind his head, the other around Bekah.

Clouds skittered across the sky, chasing the moonlight from the room. A roll of thunder echoed in the distance. The lace curtains fluttered in the cool breeze from the slightly opened window. As Bekah snuggled closer to him, he knew what he had to do.

He no longer worried that she'd betray him the way Elissa had. Bekah was a woman he'd trust with his life. For that matter, he owed his life to her. Yet he needed to send her away until he was certain he could control his drinking. And that might never happen. The urge to imbibe struck him several times a day. So far, he hadn't reached for a bottle, but how long could he avoid temptation?

With a heavy heart, he slipped from the bed, kissed Bekah one last time. He went downstairs and opened the mahogany cabinet where the liquor was stored, opened a bottle and filled a glass to the rim.

Rebekah was surprised to wake up and find Zachariah gone, the scent of him and their lovemaking still in the air. Thunder rattled the windowpanes, and lightning zigzagged across the early morning sky. The gloomy weather could not dim her bright mood.

Zachariah loved her.

As she climbed out of bed, she felt as though she were floating with happiness. Her toes barely touched the floor as she wended her way along the hall and down the twisting staircase.

The house was truly beautiful. In time they'd fill it with laugher, lots of children, and many happy memories. She entered the expansive living room and glanced out the window where waves churned and angry clouds gathered.

Yet, her spirits soared. A woman in love, she decided, did not need an umbrella to keep the rain away. She was humming to herself when she spotted Zachariah asleep in a chair. She was ready to run to him when she spotted the empty bottle in his lap and a glass tipped over on the table. As she moved closer, the pungent odor of whiskey met her nostrils.

Heartbroken, she stared down at him, furious that he would betray her. She wanted to beat her fists against his chest. She wanted to run her fingernails down his face. She wanted him to cry out in pain because she hurt more than she thought possible, and she wanted to hurt him, too. But more than anything, she wanted him to hold her and swear he'd never drink again.

Only a pathetic woman would settle for a life of uncertainty. Angered with herself, she reared back and slapped her palm across Zachariah's face.

His head jerked to one side, but he still didn't wake up.

"Damn you, Zachariah Thompson, you've made your choice. I will not live like this."

TWENTY-TWO

Four weeks later

Zachariah grabbed an armful of bottles, carried them outside, and threw them against the rocks. As the whiskey splashed and trickled onto the jagged ledge, a deep sense of satisfaction filled him. He finally felt in control of his life.

"Look what I found behind some boxes in my bedroom," James said. "I'm gonna hang it over my bed."

Zachariah eyed the portrait of a scantily clad woman. "That picture is better suited for the fire we're having tonight."

"Shucks, that ain't fair. I'm near grown."

"I don't want you waking up and seeing a woman's large breasts first thing every morning."

"Why not? I bet you saw all this stuff when you was my age."

"Go inside and get the rest of the bottles, then throw that painting in the heap with the others." Zachariah glanced at the growing pile of erotic statues and artwork, red velvet drapes, garish furnishings, and everything else that belonged in a brothel.

When James returned a moment later with the remaining liquor, Zachariah nodded toward the rubbish. "Where's the painting?"

"Shucks," he said, stamping his foot. "I'm almost a man."

Zachariah laughed at the childish behavior. "All right, keep the wretched thing, but hang it where I won't have to look at it."

"Gee, thanks." James shuffled his foot. "I don't see why we can't go visit Miss Benson."

Zachariah hurled another bottle and watched it shatter. Flames leaped around the shards of glass. "Bekah has her own life. Beside, it's better this way."

"Better for who? I could tell she was smitten with you. I bet she misses us, too."

Zachariah heaved an exasperated sigh.

"Besides, you love her. I can tell by looking at you."

"It isn't fair for me to ask Bekah to return when all I can offer is a life of uncertainty." He glanced at the jagged cliffs in the distance. "If I was sure I'd never drink again, I'd run to her brother's house and beg her to take me back." He ached with the need to see her. His hands clenched as he remembered their time together. He could almost see her face, almost smell her. He'd give everything he owned just to kiss her again.

"That's the dumbest thing I ever did hear."

Zachariah scowled at the boy. "What do you know, you're just a kid."

"Maybe so, but at least I'm smart enough to know nothing in life is a sure thing. A kid is supposed to live a long time, but I coulda died when Grizzly hit me. A smart man would grab whatever happiness he can because there's no tellin' what the future holds. Seems to me, a smart man would choose the woman he loves over a bottle of booze."

"Don't you think I know that?"

James nodded toward the rocks wet with whiskey. "I think you're headin' in the right direction. Only problem is, you're moving so goldarn slow, I'm afraid it'll be too late when you finally get around to seeing things my way."

Two weeks later Zachariah hurried up the walkway of the impressive brick manor. He was too nervous to notice much of anything but the pounding of his heart.

A servant answered the door.

"Is Miss Benson here?"

"Come in."

Relieved, he stepped inside.

A woman entered the foyer a moment later. "I'm Mrs. Benson. Can I help you?"

"Zachariah Thompson," he said, extending his hand. "I'm here to see Rebekah."

The woman frowned. "I'm sorry, but she left a while ago. If the coach departed on time, I expect you're too late."

He didn't remember thanking the woman or going back down the steps, but he found himself running down the hill. Even before he reached the main road to Boston, he saw a coach fading in the distance.

His shoulders drooped.

The hollow ache settled in his chest. As he turned, he spotted a woman wearing a hideous white hat with large blossoms. Several long feathers speared the hatband and fanned out. By her side was a familiar battered leather valise and a basket.

Fearing he might be mistaken, he moved behind her and caught a glimpse of her face. "Bekah?"

She turned. Tears misted her eyes. "I've been calling myself a muttonhead for not boarding that coach."

He reached for her hands. "You'll never know how happy I am to see you."

"I haven't changed my mind about your drinking."

"There's not a drop of liquor left in my house."

"You can easily buy more."

"I know you'll leave if I drink again. That's enough incentive to keep me sober. James is living with me now," he added, hoping she'd smile. "I've made a lot of changes."

She stared at him as if deciding what to believe.

"I want you to marry me. I've designed a bed especially for us, the oak headboard carved with the image of the medallion, its two pieces forever joined. I want it to represent the two of us growing old together."

A smile touched her lips. "I want to believe you, but when I saw you passed out that last time . . ."

"You saw what I wanted you to see." He rubbed his cheek. "I can still feel the sting of your palm."

"You were awake?"

"And sober," he added. "I sent you away because I wasn't being fair to you. I was afraid I'd drink again."

"And now you're not?"

"Oh, I'm still afraid, but a smart fellow I know made me see that I couldn't let you go. I love you, Bekah. Marry me."

She wrapped her arms around his neck.

Her kiss was all the answer he needed.

Plump snowflakes floated on a chilly winter breeze as Zachariah and Rebekah stood on the steps of the church where they'd exchanged their vows.

Zachariah wrapped his arm around her waist. "I bet your ears are freezing."

Her earlobes tingled from the cold. "I'm fine," she lied. "This was the prettiest hat I could find for the most important day of my life."

Zachariah grinned, looking handsome in his woolen suit and white shirt. "But a pigeon perched on some weeds hardly fits the occasion."

"I'll have you know this is a sparrow on carnations."

"A sickly looking sparrow if you ask me."

She would have elbowed his ribs had he not looked at her, his eyes filled with emotion. "I love you, Mrs. Thompson."

"And I love you, Mr. Thompson," she replied, "even though

you know absolutely nothing about women's fashions."

He tipped his head against the side of her face, his warm breath thawing her ear. "I'll be disappointed if you aren't wearing fancy stockings for me to roll down later tonight."

She slapped his arm. "Hush, you incorrigible hooligan."

As he held her close, Rebekah heard the sound of hooves. She looked up and saw her brother John, approaching on horseback. Looking out of place, he waited a distance from the other guests.

Zachariah nudged her. "Bekah, go to him. See what he has to say."

She hurried toward John.

He dismounted. "I've come to offer my congratulations."

Her heart lurched at the sight of him dressed like an Indian. She wanted him to be her little brother, but she doubted that would ever happen. "I'm surprised to see you here."

"My mother says only a weak old woman would run in fear from her past. I am an Abenaki brave and I run from nothing, not even from my white sister."

"You, too, are white," she pointed out.

He pressed his hand over his heart. "Inside I am Abenaki."

"Will you be staying for the celebration?"

"No." He glanced at the people milling around. His gaze riveted on Mark.

"That's Mark, one of your older brothers. Do you want me to introduce him?"

"Not yet. First I have to accept that I have a sister," he said with the briefest of smiles. "There'll be plenty of time later to become acquainted."

"Yes," she said, certain they'd eventually become friends.

He swung onto his horse. "Take care, little sister." His voice had the same bossy ring as her other brothers.

"I'm not your little sister, I'm older than you are."

"But you are smaller. To me, you are a little sister."

She knew then he'd inherited the Benson stubborn streak. "We'll discuss this some other time," she said and wondered if he'd heard as he rode away.

James ran up to her, carrying a large box. "Are you ready for my surprise?"

Zachariah offered her his hand.

"Do you know what's inside?" She hoped Zachariah would drop a hint.

"James has been carrying on about this for a few weeks. I tried to bribe it out of him, but he wouldn't give me a clue."

James set the box in the back of the carriage. "Open it, Miss Benson . . . er, I mean, Mrs. Thompson."

Rebekah lifted the lid. Inside was the hat she'd lost, faded, ripped, and missing most of its flowers.

"The medallion is still in the lining, right where I hid it," James said excitedly.

She lifted the hat from the box and turned it upside down. She saw a small slit in the lining and when she pushed her fingers inside the opening, she found her medallion.

Digging in her reticule, she pulled out the medallion's other half and slid the two pieces together. "Finally everything is as it should be," she said with tears in her eyes, flanked by James on one side, Zachariah on the other.

Later that night Rebekah woke Zachariah from a sound sleep. He covered her mouth with his. "Woman, I cannot keep up with you."

"I'm not waking you for that reason."

He kissed a path down her throat.

She tugged on his arm. "Get dressed."

"No bridegroom wants to hear that."

She giggled. "I want you to come outside with me."

He climbed out of bed and slipped on his trousers. "It's freezing out there. You better have a good reason for getting me up in the middle of the night."

She pointed out their bedroom window. "With the full moon lighting our way, we should have no trouble following the path that leads to the ocean."

"The path is even easier to find in the daylight," he said, cramming cold feet into cold shoes. "Taking a moonlight stroll in zero-degree weather is not my idea of fun."

A few minutes later, dressed in warm clothing, they hurried along the rocky path. Rebekah heard the roar of the ocean long before she saw it. "The beauty of the setting steals my breath."

"I suspect it's the nippy air doing the stealing," he said, holding her tight.

She lifted the pieces of the medallion for him to see. "I'm certain this medallion is magic."

"You can't prove it."

"Were it not for this medallion, I would never have met John. I would never have met either James or you."

"I'll admit there've been many coincidences."

"Although we may never know the results, there is a way to prove whether this medallion has magical powers."

She glanced at the two halves in her palm and watched silvery moonlight bouncing against the shiny surface. Before she could change her mind, she hurled both pieces into the Atlantic.

Zachariah looked confused. "Why did you do that?"

"I have everything I could possibly want. I'm freeing the medallion to work its magic on somebody else."

Zachariah pulled Bekah against him and kissed her. High on the cliff above the ocean they stood, swaying slightly, the cold breeze nipping at their ears, their love for each other keeping them warm.

Meanwhile, one half of the medallion clung to the jagged edge of the cliff. The other half sank deep into the churning icy water of the Atlantic and started its long journey. . . .

ABOUT THE AUTHOR

Diane Amos lives in a small town north of Portland, Maine, with her real-life hero, who after thirty-plus years of marriage, can still put a smile on her face. They have four grown children, four grandchildren, a finicky Siamese named Sabrina and an energetic miniature Dachshund named Molly. Diane is an established Maine artist. Her paintings are in private collections across the United States. She is a Golden Heart finalist and winner of the Maggie Award for Excellence. Diane loves to hear from her readers. To contact Diane or learn more about her books, check out her Web site, www.dianeamos.com